"We must spread the word of God. This is our calling," said Torris. "Perhaps we should bring our message to one of the truly alien races—creatures utterly different from us. What of that, Captain? Is there a chance of it?"

Enskeline leaned far back, scratched his topknot and went on thoughtfully: "If I put you down on Rakhshee, you'd see creatures different enough to satisfy anyone. But no one's certain whether they're intelligent or not, that's the problem. Nobody ever came back from Rakhshee sane enough to tell."

Torris boldly said, "I'll try. Take me there, Captain!"

THE MANSIONS OF SPACE

JOHN MORRESSY

ACE SCIENCE FICTION BOOKS
NEW YORK

THE MANSIONS OF SPACE

An Ace Science Fiction Book / published by arrangement with
the author

PRINTING HISTORY
Ace Original / July 1983

ISBN: 0-441-51886-9

Ace Science Fiction Books are published by Charter Communications, Inc.
200 Madison Avenue, New York, New York 10016.
PRINTED IN THE UNITED STATES OF AMERICA

For Barbara

"Across the margent of the world I fled,
And troubled the gold gateways of the stars. . . ."
—Francis Thompson

I.

Peter's Rock: The Rimjack

In the clear golden light of third Graceday morning in the trisept of Second Pentecost, the *Rimjack* landed on Peter's Rock. She settled in slow majesty onto the venerable landing ring, within view of the monastery walls. High atop those walls, in the morningside gallery, Abbot Rudlor and his prior stood watching, transfixed with joy and wonder.

"The ship! The ship has returned!" the prior cried. "Praise God!"

"Praise and thanksgiving!" Abbot Rudlor said fervently, dropping to his knees on the cold green stone.

The prior followed his pious example. Both men knelt in silence, heads bowed for a brief time, and then Abbot Rudlor, gripping the parapet, pulled himself stiffly erect. "Praise and thanks to His name," he repeated, his voice hushed, and reached up to wipe his eyes with the rough red sleeve of his robe. He laughed aloud, a wordless, childlike outburst of delight, and extended a hand to assist the prior to his feet. "Come. We must welcome our brothers and sisters in godly fashion," he said, and hurried to the sacristy.

"And we must receive the Holy Shroud in a fitting manner," said the prior.

"Yes. Oh, yes," Rudlor agreed.

As he passed under the rounded arch and into the shadowed passage, a doubt crossed Rudlor's mind. He murmured a brief prayer and turned his thoughts to the robing for the procession, but the doubt persisted. The ship on the ring was too small to hold those hundreds of schismatics. Its shape, too, seemed wrong.

Rudlor shook his head and closed his eyes as if to block out

1

the troubling thought. The depictions of the original ship were vague in his fading memory. He had not even glanced at them since his days as novice master, so long ago. This had to be their ship. The alternative was simply beyond imagining.

The landing ring was set in the rocky floor of the valley, below the terraced hillside fields and the sheer walls of the monastery, so the ship's descent was visible to all on that side of the mountain. The quarriers and timberers who worked on the far side and those who tilled the outermost fields, though they could see nothing, had heard the high whine of the drivecoils and their quick subsidence into the lower registers. Now, in the restored stillness, they began to flow over the crest to seek the source of the unfamiliar sound. Singly or in little groups they came, and ahead of them, converging on the ring, they saw their neighbors streaming down the valley sides.

Before the shrilling of the drivecoils had died, a crowd was gathered in the clearing around the ring. It grew steadily as newcomers arrived from the town, the monastery, and the fields, woods, and quarries.

The mood was festive. The young—even the novices, who were traditionally a somber, studious lot—ducked and squirmed through the crowd while their novice master, oblivious to their behavior, chatted with a little cluster of farmers and townsmen. Two scriptors, pale and bent, joked with the burly smith. Townspeople bore baskets of fruit and cakes. The cellarer's assistants, having set up benches, were fetching buckets of cold water, and the rumor quickly spread that meat and fresh bread were being brought down from the monastery. Those who were not talking with their neighbors or working were staring eagerly at the ports of the ship, pointing, waving, or shouting a welcome. There was no fear, no hesitation, only a great joy. The prodigals had returned at last.

Within the *Rimjack*, Jod Enskeline was puzzled. He had landed on inhabited worlds before, but never to such a reception as this.

"They be human, Captain. Undoubt for it," his bridgeman said without raising his eyes from the scanner screen.

"I don't need a scanner to tell me that, Zacher," Enskeline said irritably.

"No, sir."

"This ring was made by Earthers for an Earth-built ship."

"Yes, sir."

"All I have to do is look out any port and I can see that they're human."

"All one kind, too, Captain. Scanning no one who unbe white, me."

"You're right, Zacher. That could mean they've been here for a long time."

"Maybe long time and no be seeing anybody but themselves. Here to now, they be doing all friendly, Captain. Scans to me, they offer welcome."

Enskeline frowned and grunted sourly under his breath. "I'm not impressed by welcomes anymore, Zacher. I still remember those harmless-looking little haystacks on Orychma."

He scratched his chin, tugged at his topknot, and studied the crowd surrounding his ship. They seemed overjoyed at the mere presence of the *Rimjack* on their world, and after what he and his crew had gone through on this run—all of it for nothing, so far—the thought of a stay among humans was all but irresistible. These were humans, real humans, people who shared his blood and his ancestry and his Earthly heritage. Plenty of women in that waiting crowd, too, cheering and waving, eager to greet the starfarers. More women than men on this world, judging from the crowd out there, and that could make for a pleasant stay. He ached for the touch of a human woman, the sound of a human voice other than Zacher's.

However great his eagerness, Jod Enskeline was an experienced starfarer. He knew the survival value of prudence. First contact was a touchy business, even between members of the same species. The only thing a man could do was think carefully, plan ahead, anticipate every problem and danger—and then count on a thousand surprises and hope none of them would be fatal.

As he gazed out the port, wondering what lay before him on this pleasant-seeming world, Enskeline saw the crowd part. At the same instant, Zacher cried, "Top-sounder be coming, Captain! Scans to me, be bringing heavy muscle."

"I see them. Close up on the scanner, and let's have a good look," Enskeline said, turning from the port.

Bending over the main screen, he watched the procession

of robed figures moving directly toward the ship through a host that drew back respectfully to permit their passage. Here was the top-sounder indeed, to judge from the show of deference. The foremost man was dressed in a red robe, with a long sleeveless vestment of pale green over it. The outer garment was carefully embroidered and richly decorated; it flashed brightly in the morning sun. Enskeline tightened focus, and smiled cozily to himself. Such craftsmanship and lavish display offered promise of a profitable visit.

The leader was an old man, white-haired and parchment-faced, thin under those bulky trappings. Behind him, in robes of varied colors, walked a score of husky, well-fed younger men. Some carried standards, other swung little pots from which arose curls of smoke. There was no sign of hostility. All the crowd were singing in a slow deep chant that sounded pleasantly in Enskeline's ears.

"Things they be carrying, Captain—be weapons?" Zacher asked.

Enskeline strained to remember something he had seen on a distant world long ago, and abruptly replied, "No, not weapons. I've seen them before, but never used outside, like this. They're religious symbols."

"Unknowing all that, me," Zacher said, shaking his head. "Run it closer, Captain."

"They're some kind of Christians," the captain said. "See that long pole with the crosspiece near the top? That's the Christian symbol."

"Here to now unmeeting Christians, me. They killing or unkilling people? Hand-swing smoke-risers scan could be dangerous," Zacher said uneasily.

"You mean those little pots? They're not weapons. They're some kind of ceremonial gadget. As I recall, these people believe that it's wrong to kill."

"They be unkilling all total?" Zacher said, turning to his captain. Zacher's eyes, ringed in a fantastic multicolored design, were wide in astonishment.

"I suppose they make an exception now and then—I'd be surprised if they didn't—but I believe they teach their followers not to kill."

"Then how they be living to nowever? People everywhere be free-killing to pleasure for unbelieving, Captain."

"If you're wondering how they managed to survive, I'd guess that they found isolated worlds like this one, and hid on them. And were lucky enough to have no visitors," Enskeline said.

Zacher shook his head slowly, disapproving of what he saw on the scanner. "They be unlearning to careful, Captain. See them milling and waving hands at *Rimjack*? And unseeing any weapons, me!"

"We're probably the first ship to land here since . . . maybe since they came here themselves. They're aching to see us and talk to us."

"Be going out, you?"

"I have to. You'd better come along, too. We'll go as soon as the readings are complete. I think we'll be able to manage this world without special gear."

"Be going out, others?"

"No. Not yet. I don't see anyone but humans out there, and if they haven't seen their first alien, it may be wise to sound them out before we make any introductions. Faranaxx and Scragbones can stay aboard for the time being, and out of sight."

"Yes, sir. Be bringing weapons, us?"

"Not much point. The ones we have couldn't do more than annoy a crowd this size. Anyway, we want to be friends with these people. Good friends. I think maybe they're going to make us rich, Zacher."

The main port of the *Rimjack* lowered silently and clicked into place to form a level platform about three meters from the ground. A prolonged, jubilant cry went up from the crowd, and all surged closer, looking with eager, expectant eyes at the dark opening in the ship.

Abbot Rudlor, in the foremost rank of the multitude, raised his open hands in a gesture of peaceful welcome. As he did so, a pair of figures stepped from the ship to the platform and returned his gesture.

The crowd cried out; then there came a sudden hush, as of surprise or disappointment. But in a moment the shout of welcome arose redoubled, and this time it endured.

The abbot, regarding the two figures, understood the reaction of his people. His initial doubt had been well-founded. These were not the lost brothers and sisters returning to rejoin the one true flock. The Holy Shroud was not aboard this ship, and that was cause for sadness. But the coming of strangers was a great wonder. It might mean fruition of the dream of generations. That was cause enough to rejoice, and the abbot raised his voice with the rest. Their prayers had been answered, but in a totally unexpected way—perhaps in a far greater way than any of them had ever dreamed.

A stepped ramp scissored downward slowly, and the crowd moved to make way for its descent. When it touched ground, the abbot took his place at the foot and extended his open arms in welcome.

The starfarers came down slowly, with dignity, looking from side to side to acknowledge the greeting of the assembled crowd. They were an impressive pair. Both were tall, the foremost a broad man, the other slender of frame, younger, and well-muscled. Their clothing dazzled the rough-clad onlookers and overshadowed even the splendor of the abbot's attire. Crimson cloaks flung back over their shoulders revealed plain uniforms of immaculate white, tight-fitting, aglow with their own soft inwoven luminescence. Their boots and crested helmets were of a glossy silvery substance that looked like supple metal, reflecting the morning light.

Upon reaching the open space at the foot of the ramp, the newcomers smiled genially at the faces encircling them, and then removed their helmets and raised them high in salute. Those nearest were astonished to see that the slender starfarer was completely hairless except for thick black brows, and his face and shaven skull were covered with an intricate and brightly colored design. His heavy set companion wore his pale hair in a topknot that uncoiled to fall loosely between his shoulder blades.

The onlookers murmured, pointing excitedly and jostling one another for a clear view of these odd creatures. No one on Peter's Rock had ever seen a tattoo, and men and women alike wore their hair in a simple bowl-shaped cut. All the men above a certain age had thick, untrimmed beards, and the common dress for all who were not in clerical robes was a loose, knee-length tunic or a long poncho. The men from the stars gleamed like exotic jewels among the drab throng.

Taking a single pace forward, the abbot raised his hands high. Silence fell upon those nearest him and spread quickly to the outskirts of the crowd. "In the name of Mother Church and her faithful children, be welcome to Peter's Rock," he said. "May your stay with us be happy and peaceful, and may it bring grace upon you and all who speak with you."

The portly starfarer listened attentively, nodding eagerly when the abbot paused, his expression showing comprehension. In a thick accent, with halting words, he returned the abbot's greeting. "We make you . . . our thanks . . . from long wandering now to rest. We come . . . in peace . . . with friendship our offering," he said earnestly.

The abbot and the prior stepped forward to embrace the two starfarers. "I am Abbot Rudlor, of the Monastery of the Holy Sepulcher. And this is Rever Mullman, my prior."

"My name is Jod Enskeline, master of the driveship *Rimjack*. This is my bridgeman, Zacher."

"And where do you come from? What is your world? Your civilization? Are you from Earth?" Rudlor asked eagerly.

Enskeline jerked his thumb in the direction of the ship. "That's my world. I'm a free trader." When the abbot shook his head, uncomprehending, and the prior responded with a polite but vague smile, Enskeline said, "I'll explain later."

"You are not from Earth, then?"

"No."

"Are *you*?" the abbot said, turning to Zacher.

"Not from Earth, me. Be born and growing on Better Luck, in Lilienthal, me. Going starside at standing-forth time," the bridgeman said.

The abbot nodded thoughtfully. He had understood enough to know that the answer was negative. "Not from Earth. But your appearance . . . and you speak Church English sufficiently well for our communication. It is a mystery."

"Church English? I'm speaking starfarer's pidgin. The trading language," Enskeline said.

"Do you know nothing of Church English?"

"Nothing at all."

"And you were not sent? You came voluntarily to Peter's Rock?"

The abbot's term was unfamiliar. Enskeline replied, "I come here . . . to this world . . . at my choice and no man's order. I am a free trader. Is that what you ask?"

"It is. But come, take bread with us and accept shelter

under our roof. We have many things to discuss and much to share."

"If it's talk you want, I'm willing," Enskeline said, taking his place at the abbot's side. "And I'd enjoy a good meal, too."

The husky younger men in the abbot's entourage had moved out to form a tight circle around the abbot, the prior, and the two starfarers. With this escort, the little group proceeded up the winding mountain trail to the monastery while the crowd, all thought of feasting forgotten now, flowed around them like a slow wave moving up the mountainside.

The old starfarers' complaint, that all downside roads are uphill and against the wind, proved to be an exaggeration in this case. The gentle breeze was at their backs. The way was steep, but the gravity was not excessive. Once they regained their planetary equilibrium, Enskeline and Zacher found the upward progress easy. They walked slowly, conversing with the abbot and prior as they climbed. Amid the noise and press of the crowd, limited by their imperfect knowledge of each other's languages, starfarers and monastics communicated little, and their conversation was soon reduced to simple phrases and gestures.

Enskeline preferred observing a new world to hearing about it, even from a native, but surrounded as he was, he could observe little except the building complex that appeared to be their goal. Nodding now and then and smiling in response to the smiles of others, he concentrated his attention on the buildings at the mountaintop.

He estimated the entire complex to extend about two kilometers from end to end; he could not judge its depth. It rested on the mountain crest with a lightness and delicacy that contrasted sharply with the raw strength of the great knuckles of green stone that jutted from the base of the lofty white wall running from end to end of the complex. The stone vanished under soft fingers of red-gold vegetation lower down the slope. From this distance, the wall appeared smooth and seamless along its bottom length. Above, near the top, it was pierced with rows of arches and several elaborate round designs of fine tracery, like great many-colored blossoms incised in the stone. The tops of two long buildings could be seen beyond the wall, and one high round tower. Above all else stood a high structure with an angled roof that soared to a peak. From that peak, dominating all else on Peter's Rock, rose a cross.

Enskeline and Zacher found their hosts to be considerate, generous, and above all, patient. Though they were obviously bursting with questions, Rudlor, Mullman, and the other monks asked none except those directly concerned with the needs and wishes of the starfarers.

The food served at the meal of welcome was plain but abundant, and the conversation in the long sun-washed refectory was animated. Enskeline did much more listening than speaking, and more eating than either. He asked from time to time about the meanings of particular words, but said hardly anything else. Zacher talked freely to everyone within earshot, but little except mutual confusion seemed to come of his loquacity.

When they rose at last from their long meal, the abbot himself conducted his guests to their quarters, two adjoining rooms opening onto a private gallery on the morning side of the monastery, where they might see their ship at will. Enskeline found his room sparsely furnished, but the table and chair by the open window were exquisitely carved in a handsome substance of deep red, striped with heavy graining in green and gold. The bed was bigger than any Enskeline had seen in a long time, and though firm, it looked comfortable.

By the bed, on a small table of that same bright-grained material, placed there as casually as one would lay a dish, a knife, or a tally-rack, lay three priceless objects. Enskeline saw them, swallowed audibly, and forced his eyes away.

"You must consider yourselves at liberty to come and go as you please," the abbot said. "You will not be disturbed. You may take meals with us in the refectory or here, if you choose, at any hours that suit you. When you are inclined to speak with us again, I will be happy to receive you in my chambers. In the meantime, if you have wishes or requirements, you need only ring." Rudlor pointed to a small silver bell that stood beside the books on the table.

"Abbot . . . those books," Enskeline said.

"Yes? Oh, forgive me. Please forgive me my thoughtless-ness. We of Peter's Rock are accustomed to dealing only with those of our own faith, and we forget. . . . I will remove them."

"No, leave them, please," said Enskeline, laying his hand upon the stack.

"Oh? Are you interested in learning about our faith?"

"Yes. Yes, I'm very interested, Abbot. Leave them."

"How wonderful that our new mission bears fruit so quickly! I will have other books sent here if you like—books perhaps more suited to one who is a stranger to the faith."

"Other . . . *more* books?"

"It will spare you the long walk to the library."

The term was one that Enskeline had heard before, but never had he heard it fall from a man's lips so carelessly. "A library . . . is a place where books . . . many books . . . are hidden. Is that not so, Abbot?" he asked.

Rudlor smiled. "Not *hidden*, Enskeline. We would say *gathered*, or *collected*. We keep most of the monastery's books in the library, arranged for the convenience of those who wish to use them."

"Many books?"

"Ours is a small library. We have perhaps . . . oh, perhaps twenty thousand, or even twenty-five. But no more. Rever Commian, our precentor, can tell you the exact figure if you are interested in knowing."

Enskeline swallowed once more, not as loudly as before, and nodded. He did not trust himself to speak. The abbot added, "You and your associate may use the library freely, of course, if you so desire."

"Freely? Whenever we like?"

"Certainly. It lies on the third level below, next to the chapel. Anyone will gladly show you the way."

Left alone, Enskeline sprawled on the big bed, his boots dangling over the side, gazing up into the high shadows of the ceiling. He laced his hands over his ample stomach. He was numb with delight.

Zacher burst through the doorway that joined their rooms, and Enskeline raised himself on his elbows. The bridgeman was doing a little dance of sheer exuberance, beyond words to express his feelings. Beneath the whirl of colors tattooed on his skin, his face was flushed. He held two books in one hand

and one in the other, and waved them aloft like a man displaying trophies.

"Captain Enskeline! Be leaving books to lie everywhere unguarded, they!" he said excitedly.

"I know. I have three myself," Enskeline replied, nodding in the direction of the little table.

"Be thinking, Captain," Zacher said, lowering his voice to a confidential tone. "Be grabbing these books and slip-legging to *Rimjack,* us, and be off. . . ."

"Forget it."

"These be *six* books, Captain! Be worth enough to buy *Rimjack* time over time double again!"

"I said forget it, Zacher. You talk like a dumb pirate."

The bridgeman said sullenly, "They unbe giving them to us, be thinking, me."

"Maybe not. But they'll trade."

"How be trading for books, us? Taking all trade goods on *Rimjack* together, be throwing in the ship, too, be unworth to these."

"But they don't know that. And they won't if we keep quiet about it." Seeing comprehension dawn on the young man's polychrome features, Enskeline went on, "Do you know how many books there are on Peter's Rock, Zacher? Maybe twenty-five thousand. I think we can get as many of them as we want, if we just do this right."

"Twenty-five thousand books. . . ." Zacher repeated weakly.

"That's what the abbot said. They're all in a big room, where we can go whenever we like. I told you, didn't I, Zacher? I had a feeling these people were going to make us rich."

II.

Peter's Rock: The Covenant

Enskeline had learned to adapt quickly to new worlds and new conditions; it took him scarcely any time at all to adjust to life on Peter's Rock. Of all the worlds he had visited, this came closest to the hypothetical Earth-normal. Gravity was slightly less, and the atmosphere was oxygen-rich, but the exhilarating effect of these conditions was balanced by a longer planetary day. An afternoon rest was a custom observed by all.

The monks had based their time measurement on the Old Earth day, expanding it to thirty-two hourly units. Every seventh day was Lordsday, devoted to special worship. Three of these seven-day periods constituted a trisept, and eighteen trisepts—more accurately, seventeen trisepts and one quadsept, Greater Advent, comprised of four seven-day periods—made up their year.

The names of these units had some significance in the monks' religion, as did the names they had given to the days. Enskeline committed them to memory with little difficulty, though without much understanding. It was simple work for a man who had traded on Bila-Brem, where every daily unit had four names and the appropriate name in each context depended on whether one were calculating by solar, major lunar, minor lunar, or sidereal reckoning. To add to the complication, the names had three different forms. A man who had learned to handle the Bila-Brem system could handle any.

The only complication to the day on Peter's Rock was the observation of canonical hours. At regular intervals a bell rang to summon monks, or laymen, or both, to one of the chapels or to the great church where, Enskeline assumed, they took part in some kind of worship ceremony. Since he was not obliged to participate, he did not. There was too much else to do, and he had little interest in worship.

He adjusted easily to the food. The monastics observed a simple diet, filling and doubtless nutritious. It tested out safe, but was flat-tasting and monotonous. Their wine, however, was excellent. It was made from a grayish-brown, fist-sized fruit covered with flabby protuberances and most unpleasant to look upon, but it had a crisp tang that made the bland food delicious, and a pleasantly tart, long-lasting aftertaste. Since Peter's Rock appeared to offer no other beverage but its astringent-tasting water, Enskeline considered himself fortunate to find the wine so palatable. He made a mental note, though, to raise the question of a trade in spices and seasonings when the time was propitious.

Before speaking more with the abbot, Enskeline thoroughly explored the monastery and the surrounding area. He was required to do a great deal of climbing, an activity not customary among starfaring men, but the low gravity made it endurable. He learned his way around all nine levels of the monastery complex, then investigated the outbuildings, took a cursory tour of the fields and vineyards, and strolled about the larger settlements. Everywhere he went, he was recognized and greeted with respectful curiosity that never overstepped the bounds of politeness. If he spoke to anyone, he drew an eager response, but no one forced conversation upon him. By the third morning of his stay, he was familiar with the layout and ready to get down to business.

The abbot's chambers were surprisingly small and cluttered. Rudlor rose to greet his visitor; as he ushered Enskeline to a chair, the bell tolled sixteen times, marking midday.

"I'm sorry if I come at an awkward time," the starfarer said. "I'm not sure yet when your worship times fall."

"Not at all, my dear Enskeline. I've been hoping you would choose to speak with me."

"Isn't this a time of ceremony? Whenever the bell rings, people seem to go up to the church."

"Ah, I see. No, the Divine Office is not obligatory for all on Peter's Rock. But many observe the hours voluntarily, to help keep the tradition alive. That, after all, is our primary duty. Hence the name of our monastery," the abbot said. When Enskeline showed no sign of comprehension, Rudlor asked, "Does the name 'Monastery of the Holy Sepulcher' have no significance to you?"

"It means this place."

"Nothing more? Do you know nothing of the Holy Sepulcher?"

"Nothing."

The abbot seemed deflated by this response. He asked, "Have you seen no other Christians in your voyaging?"

"I've met people who called themselves by that name and used the symbols you use, but they were not much like you. They didn't live like this, or worship as much as you do."

"Not all Christians are monastics. There were very few on Earth when our ship left, and now we may be the only ones. We believed that on a new and unknown world some fixed and tested structure was essential to our survival, so we adopted the monastic system. It served well on Earth in troubled times."

"It seems to have worked for you, too. You've survived long—considering time dilation."

"I know nothing of time dilation."

"It doesn't make much difference if you stay in one place. It only affects travelers."

The abbot nodded. "I hope you will explain it to me. But first, I would like to know about these Christians you met. Did they ever speak of the Holy Shroud? Do you remember those words?"

"They never spoke them to me."

The abbot nodded again. "What were their beliefs?"

"I didn't ask. That's not my business."

"Did you see no rituals or ceremonies? Did they say nothing of their creed, or their laws and observances?" the abbot asked with plaintive eagerness.

"They said very little on the subject, and I could tell nothing from the way they behaved. One man did tell me that a Christian doesn't take another person's life or property . . . but then I met other people who said that they often do. Anyway, those are not unusual beliefs. Most Rudstromites oppose killing. Even Mechanists, as a general rule . . . although they're always ready to eliminate a dysfunctional component. On the other hand, there're the Thanists. And the dramaturges of Av."

"Are these all peoples you have encountered in your travels?"

"Yes. Far from this sector, fortunately."

The abbot shook his head in wonderment. "The children of Earth have spread far indeed."

Enskeline hesitated, then nodded silently as a sudden cautionary thought came to him: if the abbot did not suspect the existence of alien intelligent life in the galaxy, it might be wise not to correct his misconception at this point. Instead, Enskeline steered the conversation to safer ground.

"Abbot, what exactly is the significance of the monastery's name?" he asked.

"Forgive me my wandering, Enskeline. The sepulcher is the place where the body of Christ reposed between His death and His Resurrection."

"Christ. . . . He's the founder of your religion?"

"He is," said the abbot.

"And . . . he died? Did you say he died?"

"He died on the cross for the sake of all mankind, and rose from the dead on the third day after. We of the monastery hope, like Him, to rise again and bring the message of redemption to all the galaxy."

"I think I understand. The monastery is a kind of resting place."

"Our mission is twofold," the abbot explained. "First, we are to keep the faith alive and intact. Secondly, when the moment comes, we are to rise and go forth to preach the Gospel to all the worlds of man."

"That's quite a task you've set for yourselves."

"God will provide. He has guided us to this beautiful, nurturing world and kept us safe here for centuries of Earthly time. He has brought us through struggle and uncertainty, and given us the strength to endure great sorrows . . . terrible losses."

"What were they, Abbot?"

"A schism that divided us; a plague that slew hundreds; the loss of our ship and of the most precious object on Peter's Rock."

His last words were of the sort to quicken Enskeline's interest. The trader asked, "What object, Abbot?"

"Our relic. It was the last surviving portion of the Holy Shroud."

"I'm sorry, but I don't understand. I've never heard of a 'relic.' "

"Ah, of course you would not know." Rudlor paused, as if gathering his thoughts for a proper response, then said, "A relic is a sacred object—something closely associated with a holy man or woman. It was customary, during monastic times on Earth, for a monastery to possess some relic pertinent to its patron or to its mission. When the Order of the Holy Sepulcher was founded, by the Pope himself, the most sacred relic in Christendom was given into our charge. We received the last remaining portion of the shroud that wrapped Christ's body when He lay in the sepulcher."

"I see. Yes, that would surely be precious to you."

"To us—to any Christian—it is priceless. Literally priceless, Enskeline."

The trader nodded, concealing his disappointment behind a show of interest. A scrap of cloth that had touched the corpse of a holy man, or even a man-god, or whatever this Christ was supposed to be, might be priceless to this community of hermits on their isolated world, but it meant nothing to Enskeline or to anyone he was likely to encounter. The only Christians he had ever met were too poor to pay him a decent price for anything; anyone else simply would not care. But the abbot's next words roused his interest anew.

"Others would see only the value of the reliquary. It is valuable, too, in the material sense," Rudlor said.

"The 'reliquary'?"

"The case for the relic is called a reliquary. It is made of precious metals and covered with gems. Much of the wealth remaining in the Vatican treasury in those times went into the reliquary. When it was completed, the artisans declared that it was the most beautiful object ever fashioned by the hand of man—as was only fitting when one considers what it was to hold."

Enskeline was very still. Here was a treasure indeed, something more precious even than the books of the monastery library. "And what became of the relic and the reliquary?" he asked.

"When the Galacticians—the schismatics—left Peter's Rock, they took not only our ship but our relic, too." Rudlor sighed and murmured softly, "And may God forgive them."

"Did any of them know how to handle a driveship?"

"The ship had stood empty for many years."

"Does anyone know where they hoped to go?"

Rudlor gazed past him with unfocused eyes and slowly shook his head. He sighed once more, deeply, then he was silent for a time.

Enskeline's mind was whirling. A stolen driveship manned by fanatics who had been groundlings for generations was doomed. There was no question about that. Even now, it might be headed out of the galaxy, a silent ship full of dust and bones. But perhaps, on one of the nearby worlds, lay a pile of wreckage worth more than he had ever dreamed of possessing in his life. He began running through a mental inventory of this sector, but the abbot's voice interrupted.

Rudlor smiled at his guest. "Forgive my idle talk. Will you take dinner with me? There is so much I have to tell you, and so much I wish to learn." When Enskeline accepted the invitation, the abbot reached for his bell, saying, "The morning terrace will be in shade now—a pleasant place to enjoy dinner and a leisurely talk."

In the course of that long afternoon, the abbot talked almost without pause, giving Enskeline a detailed account of the history of Peter's Rock and the Monastery of the Holy Sepulcher. In the presence of this first visitor to his world, a stranger to his faith, the abbot could scarcely be silent. Yet even as he spoke, he ached to learn of the great galaxy from one who had walked on other worlds. All the zeal of his calling, all the joy he took in the struggle and triumph of the order, barely checked his dizzying curiosity to know what lay beyond. But he knew that much depended on the help of this stranger, and he believed that Enskeline could not deny him help once he knew the truth.

On Earth, by the early years of the twenty-first century, the orthodox faiths had fallen on evil times. Old long-discredited beliefs were revived and soon flourished. Strange new ones also sprang up—the Delvers, the mysterious Uno Mundo movement, the frenzied Eden People—while the traditional churches were threatened from all sides.

Then, for a time, Western Christianity seemed on the verge of a new age. Reforms led to reunification, after six centuries of separation, into a single church under a single leader. But the political powers of the time were not pleased. No state would accept the existence of a moral force exterior to, and exempt from, its own power. And so the persecutions began, subtly at first, but growing ever more blatant and severe.

The greatest outrage came at the hands of the tyrant Bordon Moran, who ordered the execution, for treason, of all participants in the Council of Ottawa, known ever after as the Council of Martyrs. And even Moran's fall did not bring an end to the persecutions. Other tyrants arose, and other tyrannies, and plague and famine followed, and men ceased to believe in a loving God, or an afterlife, or anything but the brute fact of each day's struggle.

When the discovery of the drivecoil principle opened the stars to men, the reigning pontiff saw deliverance. In strictest secrecy, he gathered a small group of believers, laity and clergy, and sent them forth to find a sanctuary in space where they might persevere in the faith and hold out against the encroaching darkness until the summons came to preach the gospel once again.

The pilgrims found a hospitable world and named it Peter's Rock. There they settled, and worked, and rapidly increased in number. Life was simple and peaceful for two centuries; then, in the third century of settlement, a question that had long been buried flared into impassioned debate. Once raised, the issue grew like a weed, spreading its tendrils in a web of subtle ramifications that caused doubt in the minds of the most steadfast believers. In a short time, Peter's Rock was threatened with schism.

The question was this: would the summons to arise be a physical summons from Earth, or a purely spiritual revelation to the faithful on Peter's Rock? And that question gave rise to others. Were the pilgrims to return to Earth, or to spread the Gospel among the settled worlds? Were they to accept whatever changes might have taken place during their absence from Earth and adapt their teachings accordingly, or keep intact the faith they had brought to Peter's Rock and guarded there? And what was to be done if their missionaries encountered nonhuman intelligence?

Little factions began to form and angrily break apart, only to rejoin in new configurations. Before long, there were three major parties, each at odds with the others. After several violent clashes, the smaller groups withdrew from the settlement to form their own communities. The abbot pleaded with them in vain; they were irreconcilable.

One group settled in a valley on a distant part of the planet. The other removed only two days' rapid walk from the monastery, but avoided all contact—until the deep night of a rare double eclipse. Then they swarmed aboard the drivership that stood unguarded on its ring and left Peter's Rock behind. With them went the relic of the Holy Shroud.

Two generations later, an emaciated woman, her body aflame with running sores, a dead child in her arms, came to the outposts of the monastery fields and there collapsed. Before she died, she rasped a fragmentary tale of a wasting disease that appeared from nowhere to ravage the valley settlement. She was the last survivor.

And so the belief of the monastery prevailed and became the sole faith of Peter's Rock. The Galacticians, who believed that the universe contained other forms of life than human, and that God's will was that His message be brought to these aliens by His chosen servants, had fled. The Ubiquitarians of the valley, who held that God was everywhere in His universe and had no need of men to convey His message, and that the anticipation of a summons to leave this world was presumptuous and vain, were all dead. The ruling abbot set the minds of his followers at peace by proclaiming three pious beliefs: that the summons would come from another world settled by humans; that the missionaries would go to that world to begin preaching the Gospel they had preserved; and that any intelligent being must exist in the image of the Creator, and would therefore resemble humans in action and appearance.

"For centuries we have lived and labored in those beliefs," Abbot Rudlor said when he had finished his account, "and now you are come, and your coming may cause great disturbance among the faithful."

"I didn't come to cause trouble, Abbot. I just want to trade."

"I know you mean us no ill. And you may yet be the agent of great good. But you come from no other world, and you do not seek the word of God for your homeworld. Your very presence disproves the pious beliefs we have held for so long."

Enskeline felt that the time had come to reveal the whole truth. "I think I disprove the last one most of all," he said. "There's a pair of aliens aboard the *Rimjack*. They're pretty close to human, close enough to be good crewmen, but they're not humans like us. They don't look like us, and they don't think like us, either."

Abbot Rudlor's jaw dropped. He gaped at Enskeline for a silent, awed moment before saying softly, "Alien beings . . . aboard your ship . . . ?"

"Two of them, Abbot. No need to worry. They're harmless, and they'll stay put until they hear from me. Faranaxx is too dumb to act on his own, and Scragbones is so bound up in that Lixian code of honor—"

"Alien beings . . . on Peter's Rock! Will you take me to them, Enskeline?"

"Any time you say. I realize that my arrival—"

"Now? Please, Enskeline!"

"Let's go, Abbot," the trader said, rising.

On the bridge of the *Rimjack,* less than an hour later, Abbot Rudlor stood face to face with two beings unlike any in his experience, or his imagination. He was excited, overjoyed, awed at this proof of the Creater's bounty, and he felt no fear at all. These creatures could not be mistaken for Earth humans, it was true; their proportions had never been seen on Earth, nor their coloration, nor their size. And yet they both had human symmetry and the power of reason.

"What is your world of Lixis like?" Rudlor asked the barrel-chested, lean-limbed creature who stood half again the height of all those around him. "How do you live? What are your beliefs?"

"We believe in honor," came a booming voice like the roar of falling waters.

"Is that why you live—for honor? Is honor what you worship? Do you have worship on your world?"

The Lixian paused. Whether he was struggling to decipher unfamiliar words and concepts or to frame an answer that would reveal no precious private truths, the others could not tell. At last he replied, "We live to rejoin the infinite. Honor is the way. I say no more."

"You can speak openly, Scragbones," Enskeline assured him. "The abbot is interested in the beliefs of all races. He intends no dishonor."

"I believe you. But I say no more."

Abbot Rudlor nodded graciously and turned to the other alien, a Quespodon from the world Dumabb-Paraxx. He was shorter than the two humans and the Lixian. The top of his hairless skull reached only to the abbot's chin. But he was more massive than any creature the abbot had ever seen: a trunk like a block of stone, arms and legs like columns, a small rounded head set on a stubby neck between massive shoulders. His pale skin was mottled with patches of blue and purple, like great bruises. Standing silent and unblinking, the Quespodon radiated dormant strength, like some biding force of nature.

To the abbot's question he answered, "We do not worship."

"Have you no god? No power higher than yourselves?" Rudlor pressed.

"We have an Over-being. No god for Quespodons."

"Has the Over-being a name?"

"He is Keoffo," said the Quespodon uneasily.

"You can trust the abbot, Faranaxx. He seeks knowledge, nothing more," Enskeline said.

The Quespodon remained unconvinced. Frowning, he said to the abbot, "Why do you ask about Keoffo? Have you no fear of him?"

"Why should I fear your Over-being, Faranaxx?"

"Keoffo is the Disrupter. The Trickster. He torments us for his amusement. Better not to speak his name," said the Quespodon.

The abbot was silent and thoughtful as he and Enskeline trudged up the path to the monastery by the clear light of the moons. At last he said in a low, reflective voice, " 'Other sheep I have, who are not of this fold. . . .' "

"What was that, Abbot?"

"His words, centuries ago. And now at last we know their meaning. Other worlds, other races . . . enduring in darkness and ignorance . . . waiting for His word."

"Oh. Yes," the trader said. The abbot's words meant nothing to him.

"How many, Enskeline? You've been out there, crossed those great gulfs—how many alien races will we meet? How many human settlements are scattered among the stars?"

"I don't think anyone really knows. No one's even sure how many ships made it from Earth. But most of the ships I know have been used to settle three or four planets. It seems that every few generations some people get restless all over again and want to move on. As your Galacticians did."

"They left because of a belief, not a hunger for adventure," the abbot corrected him.

"I know. But maybe there was just a touch of hunger in it. I've never been able to understand how people can stay planetbound for generation after generation. I guess it takes all kinds. . . ."

They came to a level place in the upward path. Inside a woven shelter was a broad, high-backed bench facing out over the valley. At the abbot's suggestion, the two men sat down to rest. Settling into the cool, yielding material of the bench, Enskeline stretched his legs and gazed out at the *Rimjack*. Her silver surface was turned to a pink-and-gold harlequin's vestment under the bracketing glow of the moons. Eyes of small night creatures glittered in winks of green light inside the vegetation all around the ship.

Now that the sun was down, the driftwebs had risen, floating lightly up from their stalks, while sticky tendrils dangled from all sides of their pale blossoms to trap the low-flying night insects and draw them up to be digested. An hour before sunrise the driftwebs would begin to sink again, their color would brighten, and all day they would emblazon the field with color. Only their incongruous scent, the faint sweet reek of carrion, marred their beauty. The trader looked on, sighed, and crossed his ankles before him.

"What is it like out there?" the abbot asked after a long silence.

"It's good. Not all worlds are as pretty as Peter's Rock—

some of the prettiest are not at all friendly—but if a man keeps his wits and takes no foolish chances, space can be a good place. One lucky trip, and he can be richer than a thousand emperors. It's happened to people I know. And even if you're never that lucky, you're free. You go where you like, leave when you want to. You can see everything that's out there, if you live long enough."

"Have you ever returned to Earth, or wished to return?"

"No one returns to Earth. Our ancestors risked everything to leave that planet. There's nothing to return for. There's a whole galaxy out there, and beyond it more galaxies than we can imagine. Why go back?"

"Have you encountered many alien races?"

"About a dozen, I guess. Understand, Abbot, I'm not an explorer; I'm a trader. I don't go looking for surprises. If I hear of a humanoid race—one I can communicate with—I might visit their world to see if we can do business. But I tend to be cautious."

"So, it was pure chance that brought you to our world," the abbot said.

"That's right. Nobody's been to this sector, as far as I know. It's considered uninhabited. I just took a chance and hoped I'd be lucky. This time I was."

"Incredible," the abbot murmured, and shook his head.

"There's an odd thing about aliens," Enskeline said. "Every race I've met, and every one I've ever heard of, is less developed than we humans. A few are downright primitive. Odd, isn't it? Oh, here and there they have a trick or two that we don't know—motion painting; soft glass—but overall, they're anywhere from a few centuries to a couple millennia pre-exodus in their technology. The odds were that some would be far ahead, but no one's met any like that yet." The trader was silent for a time, then he laughed quietly and said, "Maybe the smart ones heard us coming and ran. That's how some people explain the First Travelers, you know."

The abbot, preoccupied with his own thoughts, was immune to the trader's laughter. "A universe filled with life . . . souls we can reach, and understand. . . . This is the most momentous . . . the most significant . . ." His voice trailed into silence as the meaning of this night's encounter reverberated in his mind, leaving him bereft of words.

"Once you've worked with them and traded with them, they get to seem as human as Earthers. They do surprise you now and then, though," Enskeline said. He laughed again, more deeply, and began an intricate account of a trading journey to the lowlands of Toxxo with a wildly assorted crew, but the abbot broke in on him sharply.

"We must go out there," he said, confronting the trader with bright, eager eyes.

"You probably will, one day."

"Not one day. Now."

Enskeline stared hard into the abbot's shadowed face. "Now? On the *Rimjack*?"

"Yes. Only a few, at first. Not I, certainly," the abbot said, raising his hands in a placating gesture. "But we must begin."

"Abbot, your boys would be eaten up. They're not ready for space."

"You can prepare them," the abbot said placidly.

"Me?"

"You have traveled far. You know what a man must know."

"One thing I know, Abbot, is that the galaxy is not sitting patiently out there, waiting for a shipload of preachers to come and tell it how to behave. They'd meet opposition. Their lives might be in serious danger, simply because of what they'd say."

"We trust in God to protect us. You need only teach them how to travel safely."

"I'm no teacher. Especially not of—" Enskeline halted awkwardly. Before he could go on, the abbot laid a hand on his forearm and said "Not all in the monastery are old and frail, or young and overfed. The priest-voyagers will learn your lessons quickly. Trust my judgment."

"No, you trust mine. I know about time dilation and what it can do to a man's mind to find that on one slow-acceleration trip he might outlive three generations of his descendants and come back looking and feeling no more than a few years older."

The abbot reflected on these words for a few moments, then replied, "The priest-voyager is customarily a celibate ministry. There need be no problem of descendants."

"Parents, then. Friends. Old companions. Whole communities, aged and dead and forgotten. Maybe the whole civilization of Peter's Rock gone, and nothing left here but ruins. Will that make no difference to them?"

"They know the way can be hard."

"They sound hard themselves."

"Not hard, Enskeline. Dedicated. The priest voyagers have trained for generations to prepare themselves for this opportunity."

Enskeline gave a sour grunt. "I've seen dedicated men before; I'm happier the less I see of them. Anyway, all the dedication on Peter's Rock can't bring some people through the drivespeed conversion without their guts getting tied in knots. And it won't make them immune to lung leeches, and boneworms and the fifty kinds of blood-rot that a man—"

"How many of our books would you ask in return for carrying only twelve priest-voyagers?" the abbot interrupted.

"I can't take twelve passengers. The *Rimjack* isn't made to hold that many."

"How many can you take?"

"Maybe six, if I convert cargo space."

"Take six, then. We will pay their way with books from the monastery library."

After a long pause, Enskeline said, "Well, let me think, Abbot."

"I know that our books are valuable to you. I could not help but notice your expression when you saw them, and Prior Mullman told me your friend reacted as you did."

"It's true I'm interested in your books, Abbot . . . but purely as an antiquarian. You can hardly expect a cargo of books to cover the passage of six men."

Enskeline saw a faint smile appear on the abbot's face and broaden. He heard the sound of private laughter. "Now you speak as a trader, Enskeline," the abbot said.

"That's what I am."

"Then, let us trade. If our books are worthless to you, perhaps we can find other goods."

"I didn't say they were worthless, Abbot. They might have a certain value, if I can get them to the right world."

"Excellent, excellent. Then you will help us train six

priest-voyagers for the other worlds, and transport them, and we will pay you with books. Good, Enskeline. I am glad.''

"I'll have to speak with my bridgeman and crew before I give you any definite answer. They have a right to know.''

"As you wish,'' said the abbot.

They rose then and resumed their slow walk to the monastery. As they drew nearer to it, the sound of low chanting came to them, accompanied by a deep throbbing music that seemed to resonate from far within the mountain. Noticing Enskeline's expression, the abbot explained.

"This evening they sing the Litany of the Crossing. I think even one who does not share our belief would find it beautiful. Would you like to attend?''

"I would. I've never heard music like this.''

They ascended to the main chapel, entering through a small side door. The ceiling arched high overhead, curving into shadowed darkness. The rose window glittered in the wall overlooking the valley, reflecting the light of many lamps. Sweet sound filled the vast space, sound in every range, from a child's piping treble to the deepest bass. Under all was a deep drone that carried the simple melody which clustered voices sang antiphonally.

"From the darkness between the worlds . . .'' sang the deep voices, and the treble responded, ". . . oh Lord, deliver us.''

The notes hung in the air, fading into silence. Then in the stillness came the booming of more voices, "From madness and violence . . .'' and the response, ". . . oh Lord, deliver us.''

Again silence, then a plea for delivery from mutiny and insurrection, from the wrath of the persecutor, from eternal flight. And always the sweet assurance came back, ". . . oh Lord, deliver us.''

A longer pause, and then the music resumed, but in a different mood and a new form. Now the high voices sang the first phrase, and the deep voices repeated the appeal. It was a more personal plea, at once abject and filled with hope:

"God the Helmsman, . . .'' they began, ". . . have mercy on us.

"God the Starmaker, . . . have mercy on us.

"God of air and water, . . . have mercy on us.

"God the Lifemaker, . . . have mercy on us.

"God who directs all things, . . . have mercy on us."

On and on went the appeals, and then the music changed yet again, a shift that transformed the mood from fearful hope to one of joy and certainty. The response now was a triumphant and love-filled "Praise to Thee!" as the sweet voices sang, "Lord of the life systems, . . ." and "Lord of the guidance systems, . . ." and "Lord of the charts, . . ." and "Lord of the coils, . . ." and "Lord of the crystals, . . ." with mounting intensity, until the final ringing "Lord of the universe, . . . praise to Thee!" that rippled through the interior of the chapel, ever dwindling yet never faded, as if it would go on forever, could one only listen closely enough.

Enskeline, who believed in scarcely anything beyond the *Rimjack* and often enough abandoned faith in her as well, was moved by the experience. He did not believe as the monastics did; he doubted that he ever could, or would wish to, but their song was beautiful. As they left the chapel, he turned to the abbot and said, "I think the crew will agree."

The crew agreed. The training program began. If there was any dilution of piety resulting from his arrival, Enskeline saw no evidence of it. Everyone seemed willing to accept the new realities and get the good work under way as soon as possible.

At first Enskeline worked alone with the thirty young men chosen, but after they had mastered starfarer's pidgin, he turned much of the training over to Zacher and even called upon Scragbones and Faranaxx for the benefit of their experience on worlds unfamiliar to him.

Reluctant at first, Zacher quickly came to enjoy the work. His patois caused some initial confusion among the students, but they were patient and attentive, and soon came to understand him most of the time. The aliens were cooperative, but their information was frequently cryptic. Questioning them about an unclear word or phrase led, most of the time, only to further mystification.

In the case of Faranaxx, the confusion was simply a matter of his own mental limitations. He was strong, trustworthy, and brave, but he was a Quespodon. A question that could not be answered by pointing to a present object or reciting a few familiar words was enough to baffle him.

Scragbones, on the other hand, showed evidence of a mind as subtle and penetrating as a priest-scholar's but displayed little will to employ it and used a baffling system of expression in which certain concepts could not be articulated. Among other Lixians he would speak the Inner Formal tongue to those unrelated to him, the Inner Informal to blood-kin. For matters of honor or reputation and certain abstract concepts, he was obliged to use High Lixian, the Tongue of Honor. But since he was now speaking with otherworlders, he used the Outer Tongue exclusively, and this was a purely functional speech shorn of most abstractions and value terms.

As a consequence of these inbred linguistic strictures, Scragbones—the very name was a translation from the Outer Tongue—could pursue a topic just so far and no farther in a language accessible to the humans of Peter's Rock. Thus, his instruction and that of Faranaxx often only took their audience from ignorance into utter befuddlement.

Despite pleas from his charges when this occurred, Zacher did not intervene. He knew from experience that much of a starfarer's life—particularly those portions of it spent dealing with aliens—was a matter of coping with misunderstanding, confusion, and uncertainty. The sooner the priest-voyagers learned to make decisions and act on the basis of fragmentary and incomprehensible data, the sooner they would be ready for space. Zacher encouraged them as much as he could, but he did not pamper them.

While his crewmen worked with the aspiring starfarers, Jod Enskeline spent his days in the monastery library. The first thing he looked for, and quickly found, was a picture of the reliquary. It was even more splendid than he had hoped: a golden case a meter long and about half a meter deep, with a high rounded top, every bit of its surface covered with a glittering mosaic of inlaid gems of great size and flawless perfection. Nothing like it existed on the known worlds. Enskeline made a careful copy of the picture, then turned his attention to the books.

He set about a methodical survey of the monastery's holdings. He knew that any book printed on Old Earth was a precious rarity, but in his voyaging he had heard of certain volumes that were of exceptional worth, and it was these he sought among the rows of shelves. Though he had had little motivation and less opportunity to practice reading, Enskeline was literate. He was also persistent and very determined; his skill improved greatly during his stay on Peter's Rock.

All worked on at their appointed and chosen duties, and the trisept of Second Pentecost slipped quickly by. Third Pentecost came and went, and Recollection, and then, on the second Almsday of Fourth Pentecost, the four starfarers realized they had taught the young men of the monastery all that they could. Early the next morning, a cool and rainy Penanceday, Enskeline informed the abbot that their preparatory work was done. On the following Spiritsday, in the abbot's chambers, the starfarers met with the abbot and Prior Mullman to learn the names of the six who would go to the stars.

After the selection had been made, the two aliens returned to the *Rimjack* to begin preparing the ship for its long run to the next system. Mullman left to arrange the ceremony of departure. The abbot, Zacher, and Enskeline remained behind.

"We will miss you," the abbot said. "Your visit has been short, but it will always be recalled as a momentous event in the history of the monastery. Your coming has enabled us to complete our mission."

"I'm glad we found Peter's Rock. It's been a good stay," Enskeline said.

"A pity you and our voyagers could not be here for the celebration of Year's End. But we must all be about our proper business."

"So we must, Abbot," said Enskeline. He started to rise, but at Zacher's blurted words he dropped back into his seat.

"Be wanting to stay on Peter's Rock, me," the bridgeman said. After a moment's silence, he went on, "Be thinking they need someone here with seeing and remembering from out there. Scans to me someone should stay on, and the best, me."

"Stay planetside? Do you mean you want to give up your berth on the *Rimjack* and be a groundling?" Enskeline asked, unbelieving.

"Yes, sir. Be asking your permission so, Captain."

"And how am I supposed to get the *Rimjack* up without a bridgeman?"

"Scragbones be good bridgeman, Captain. And two good

men from settlement downside shadowward be asking to sign aboard, be that you permitting.''

It was the abbot's turn to be startled. ''Villagers seeking to leave Peter's Rock? But why?''

Enskeline smiled reluctantly. ''I told you a starfarer's life was a good one. Maybe they figured that out, and now they want to try it.''

''But that's absurd, Enskeline. They know nothing . . . nothing of the dangers, the trials . . .''

''Be close around, these two and others, when I be giving word to priest-voyagers. Scans to me, making good starfarers, be given chance, Captain.''

Enskeline nodded, sighed, and rose from his seat, saying, ''Stay on here if you like, Zacher. It's your life.''

''Thanks, Captain.''

''Do I understand that you wish to stay on at the monastery and continue instructing future priest-voyagers?'' the abbot then asked.

''Yes, Abbot.''

''I can't deny that an experienced space traveler would be most helpful in preparing our missionaries for their work. But it will be a far different life from the one you've known, young man. Peter's Rock is an isolated world. The next ship may be a long time in coming. Our ways are simple and austere.''

''They be good ways, Abbot. Be thinking, me, here to now never found people like you, to say a thing and act same thing,'' Zacher said. ''Be hoping to learn more, me.''

''Then we welcome you,'' said the abbot, rising and extending his arms. ''Stay and learn, and be one of us.''

The succeeding days were busy ones, filled with comings and goings between the monastery and the settlements, days loud with song and public prayer, bright with processions and benedictions, solemn with ceremony. On Hopeday, the last day of Fourth Pentecost, after the chosen priest-voyagers had offered a final concelebrated Mass of dedication and joined in a great feast, every inhabitant of Peter's Rock followed them down the long path to the landing ring. There, before their friends and companions, the six priest-voyagers and the two townsmen joined the three starfarers aboard the *Rimjack*.

The ports of the ship clanged shut. The crowd moved back to safer ground. Celebrants in their gold-mounted robes and high crowns, ministrants in solemn black, scholars in red, and voyagers in brown mingled with plainly clad villagers to look on in silence.

A high whine came from the *Rimjack.* Motionless for an instant, the silver ship began to lift slowly, then ever faster, and in the duration of a held breath it dwindled and blurred with distance and vanished into the fellowship of the stars.

III. _____

Sassacheele: The First Mission

The new crewmen, Waghorne and Isbinder, proved thoroughly spaceworthy. The priest-voyagers did not fare quite so well. Three of them took the drivespeed conversion with only mild queasiness, but two others were wretchedly ill; and one, a lean and dour youth named Sterman, lay supine for three full watches after liftoff, waiting for the death he was certain must follow upon such misery.

But Sterman eventually rallied, took some food, and found hope in Enskeline's assurance that the first liftoff was always the worst and that it would never again be as bad. By the time they were ten watches out from Peter's Rock, Sterman and the rest of the missionaries were making their way about the narrow confines of the *Rimjack* with the ease and grace of old spacehands. They studied everything they saw, and the more they saw, the more curious they grew.

Their preparation had been thorough and conscientious; but this, they soon realized, was reality and not training. Questions that had been theoretical on Peter's Rock were now matters on which their survival might depend. The answers they had previously accepted with trusting complaisance they now subjected to close scrutiny.

Though he grumbled at their questioning, Enskeline was actually glad for it. Drivespeed travel could be a lonely, boring business. With nearly two hundred watches between them and their next planetfall, he was happy for any diversion. He answered their questions as best he could. He willingly spent the better part of a watch relating some strange adventure on a remote world. Some of his stories were so mind-stretching that his passengers suspected a joke. But the sight of Faranaxx or Scragbones reminded them that other worlds than theirs must indeed exist in this galaxy, and so they listened and believed.

Late one watch, when Enskeline had been reminiscing about the trading venture into Farr's System that first brought him into contact with the small, furry race of Quiplids, Sterman asked a question that had long been on his mind. "Has it never struck you as odd that all the aliens resemble us, Captain Enskeline? Even the Quiplids. . . . They may reach only to a man's knee, but they have two arms, two legs, symmetrical features—just like us."

"The Quiplids do resemble us in some respects," Enskeline said.

"You'd think somewhere, some creatures completely different from us would exist—creatures utterly nonhuman."

"They do," said Enskeline matter-of-factly.

Sterman and his companions on the watch, Torris and Cotteral, looked at Enskeline with sudden attention.

"They . . . do?" Sterman repeated incredulously. "Are they . . . really very different? Un-human?"

"Some of them."

"You never mentioned . . ." said Cotteral, and then fell silent, shaking his head slowly.

"I didn't see much point in mentioning them. I never bother with the really strange ones. Hardly anyone does. It's a lot of trouble, and there's no real profit in it."

"Has anyone ever tried?" Torris asked.

"Oh, certainly. They still do, sometimes. They usually regret it." Enskeline frowned, gazed down on the mess table, and said, "I once lost two men because I took a chance that a bunch of harmless-looking little creatures were as harmless as they looked. They weren't. I learned a lesson from that."

"Where did this happen, Captain?" Cotteral asked.

"Never mind."

"I'm only curious. I don't want to go there."

"Don't be curious, Rever. Just stick to your work. You'll have all the trouble a man could wish for just doing your preaching."

"Do you really believe we'll meet resistance?"

Enskeline looked steadily at Cotteral, then glanced at the

others. After a pause he sharply demanded, "How many
fingers does your god have?"

"Fingers?" Cotteral repeated, puzzled.

"Fingers. These," Enskeline said, thrusting his hand before Cotteral's nose and waggling the fingers. "How many?"

"God is a spiritual being. Spirits don't have fingers."

"Abbot Rudlor told me your god turned himself into a man
and died. So tell me, how many fingers did he have when he
was a man?"

"Five. Just like us."

"Well, you tell that to a Karrapad, and he'll tell you that
your god is maimed. Normal human beings have seven fingers.
Every Karrapad knows that." As the three young men exchanged uncertain glances, Enskeline asked, "Does your god
have tentacles?"

"No," said Sterman with obvious distaste.

"Then no Thresk will want to hear about him. If you're a
Thresk, you look on anyone without shoulder tentacles as . . .
as sighted people look on a blind man. What color is your
god?" Enskeline went on relentlessly. The three priests-voyagers
were silent. "I saw the pictures in your chapel," said Enskeline.
"What will you say when a blue man asks you that question,
or a mottled man like Faranaxx?" He looked from one to the
other. When they offered no reply, he went on, "You've all
been sitting on Peter's Rock for centuries, preparing yourselves,
waiting for the day when you'd go forth and bring the old
faith to people just like yourselves. But there aren't that many
out here like you, and the ones that are have their own
beliefs. They might not care to listen to yours. If you spread
your message at all, you may find yourselves bringing a new
religion to alien races."

"Perhaps we should seek out a human settlement, Old
Earth descendants like us," Cotteral said hesitantly.

Enskeline shrugged. "You could do that. I don't know
what Abbot Rudlor had in mind when he picked you, but I
suppose you could do it."

"Did the abbot tell you anything more than he told us,
Captain?"

"The abbot gave me no sealed orders for you. I run the
Rimjack, you do the preaching. I have no interest in what you
tell people, as long as it doesn't interfere with my trading.

What I mean is that the abbot seemed to believe that your god is everybody's god. If that's what you really believe, it looks to me as though you can't be choosy about where you go or who you preach to," said Enskeline, quickly adding, "You ought to be careful, but you can't be choosy."

"But some of those races will never be able to understand us," Torris pointed out.

"Probably not. Some humans won't, either."

"If we started out by preaching to the ones most like us," Cotteral said hopefully, "the ones that differ from us only in some slight way—like the number of fingers, as you pointed out—they'll listen to us, won't they?"

"There's no such thing as a slight difference. You've still got a lot to learn about contact. I don't know how it was back on Earth, but out here people notice the differences and it affects the way they think."

"You seem to travel safely from world to world. There may be some danger, as you said, but it doesn't sound as though you encounter hostility and suspicion everywhere you go," Torris objected.

"My secret of survival is that I'm careful. Believe me, if I had detected a clear sign of danger, I would have lifted off Peter's Rock without opening my port. Besides, I'm a trader, Torris. I bring people things they want, and I try—as well as I can—to go where I know I'll be welcome. But you're coming to people with something they never asked for, and you're challenging things they've believed for generations. That's bad enough, but add to that the fact that you're offworlders, aliens, and then you've got trouble."

"But we must spread the word of God. This is our calling. If it places us in danger, then we accept the danger," said Torris.

"I don't doubt your courage, Rever. I'm not trying to warn you against the danger as much as I'm warning you against failure."

In the silence that followed Enskeline's words, Sterman said, "Perhaps we should bring our message to one of the truly alien races—creatures so utterly different from us that all differences would be swept aside if we could find a single point of similarity."

"What of that, Captain? Is there a chance of it?" Cotteral asked.

"All the chance you want. That opens a lot of territory to you. In this sector, you could try the Lopsiders. Or maybe the Shriekers." Enskeline paused, as if searching his memory, then said, "There's a race on one of Zicatur's moons, things that look like a round bush covered with buds. They're ambulatory, and very agile, and they seem to be able to read human minds. . . . At least, they can figure out someone's intentions toward them. If you think of harming them, they scoot off too fast to catch, but if you think of powdered sweetroot—that's a great delicacy among them—they crowd around you and give off a pleasant smell. But it's all one way. Nobody's ever been able to read anything back from them. So, you'd never know whether they heard you or understood." Enskeline leaned far back, scratched the base of his topknot, and went on thoughtfully, "If I put you down on Rakhshee, you'd see creatures different enough to satisfy anyone. But no one's certain whether they're intelligent or not, that's the problem. Nobody ever came back from Rakhshee sane enough to tell."

Torris boldly said, "I'll try. Take me there, Captain."

"And I'll go with him," said Sterman.

"You will not. Rakhshee's a quarantined world. No man in his right mind goes within light-years of a q-world if he can avoid it."

"Then take us to the other world you spoke of," Sterman said. "The moon of Zicatur, where the bush-creatures live."

"Too far," said Enskeline flatly. "Besides, I made a promise to your abbot, and I keep my word. That's one thing about a free trader—he keeps his word. I told Abbot Rudlor I wouldn't send any of you to certain death, and I won't, even if you want to go."

"The bush-creatures didn't sound dangerous."

"Nobody who comes in direct contact with them, or breathes their fragrance, lives much more than . . ." Enskeline paused to calculate the time and translate it into a familiar term, then said, "not quite a trisept. And there's no known protection. It isn't a bad death, from what I've heard. But dead is dead, and you're not going near them."

"We want to be about our work, Captain," said Torris firmly. "We don't want to be protected."

Enskeline looked at their earnest expressions and nodded gravely. He thought for a moment, then said, "If you want to experiment on something really alien, you may be able to start at our first planetfall. I'm stopping on Sassacheele. There's a small human settlement there, and I've heard that they need something I've got. But they're said to have very strong views on religion. They don't tolerate anyone who disagrees with them. Foreign preachers are particularly unwelcome. I didn't intend to let any of you off the *Rimjack* except to stretch your legs."

"But now you'll let us bring our word to these settlers, won't you, Captain?" Sterman said happily.

"Don't run ahead of me, Rever. No, I will not let you say a word to the humans. All you need from them is directions, and I'll get them for you. You'll want to go to the western highlands. There's an intelligent race out there. Wishbones—that's what they're called."

"Aliens?"

"Yes. I've never seen one myself, but I've heard them described. They use tools and have a system of communication. That seems to be about as far as their civilization goes. Nobody's ever worked out their language, as far as I know, but they've never been known to show any hostility toward humans. They're not especially friendly, understand, but they're not openly hostile."

"What are they like?" Cotteral asked.

"I can only tell you what I've heard. They're symmetrical bipeds, a little taller than us, but not as tall as Scragbones. Nobody ever said so, but I'd guess they're pretty husky. Sassacheele's gravity is 1.12 standard. So, they'd probably be strong, too."

"They don't sound so terribly different from humans, Captain."

"They are, Cotteral. They have no heads."

"No heads?" Sterman repeated in a small voice.

"No heads at all. Just a hump of muscle between the shoulders. They have all their sensory apparatus in their chests. Presumably, that's where their brain is located. As good an arrangement as any, I suppose."

"Yes," Torris said faintly, and Cotteral nodded.

"Well, now you have something to think about, you and the others," Enskeline said, rising and smiling broadly at them to indicate that the session was over. "I hadn't planned to drop any of you until Roharr, but if two of you want to try preaching to the Wishbones, I can look into the possibility once I'm on Sassacheele."

"Thank you, Captain!" they cried in unison.

"I make no promises. Remember that. I must be satisfied that the settlers have no objection and that the Wishbones really are tolerant of humans. I gave Abbot Rudlor my word."

"We understand, Captain," Sterman said.

"And just in case a pair of you are going to be making contact sooner than I expected, I want to go over a few things with all of you. Tell the others we'll meet here in three watches." The priest-voyagers glanced about the tiny ship's mess, looking pained, and Enskeline added, "This is the biggest space in the *Rimjack*. Revers. We'll be crowded, but I don't much feel like saying everything twice."

All were present at the appointed time. Their mentors on Peter's Rock had prepared them spiritually; Zacher, Scragbones, and Faranaxx had trained them in the routines of drivespeed travel; Enskeline had told them in logical, orderly fashion of the human worlds and their ways; now Enskeline wanted to pass on to them the whole jumbled store of his own hard-earned experience. He knew that the truly important lessons could not be taught, even by the greatest teacher, but had to be learned, often at the price of suffering. Still, he could not let these dedicated young men go off to encounter alien races without offering such help as he could glean from his own travels. He was pleased to find that they listened attentively.

He was able to begin on a positive note. The liturgical English so carefully preserved through the centuries on Peter's Rock was close enough to starfarers' pidgin to enable them to get along on any world settled by Old Earth colonists and with traders and travelers of most other races. That was a considerable boon, but no guarantee of easy communication. Enskeline had learned that there was no such thing as a pure dialect. After centuries of isolation on a new world, even the most conservative speakers evolved their ancestral tongue into something new—though they never seemed to realize, or admit, that they had done so.

He recalled Zacher, whom they all knew. Zacher's patois left Enskeline frequently mystified by its odd constructions and expressions; yet Zacher took pride in his belief that his homeworld had preserved intact the speech of Southwestern America in its purest twenty-first-century form. Perhaps it had, though Enskeline had his doubts, and Dallamer, the youngest of the priest-voyagers and an expert on Old Earth history, could not settle the point.

Alien races, with their own particular speech mechanisms and linguistic patterns, presented a different problem. With them, one could only hope.

Granted some kind of communication, though, other possibilities for disaster were numerous. A world might have had previous visitors. If a roving outlaw ship had struck, or slavers had raided, the waiting crowd around the landing ring might be eager to tear into bloody tatters anyone who emerged. At best, they would fear and suspect any offworlders, and keep a close watch on them. That was a bad atmosphere in which to do business, and probably a worse one in which to preach.

Even among people who welcomed offworlders with genuine hospitality, local customs were always a pitfall for visitors. Gestures, facial expressions, manner of dress and grooming, inflections, eating and drinking patterns, all might signify something unintended. And this was true not only among aliens. Enskeline had seen a man executed where he stood merely for turning his hands in a certain manner while speaking with a woman of rank, and another made into a demigod for no other reason than that he had one eye missing and his beard was black. He had traded junk for treasure; more than once he had exchanged priceless valuables for trash merely to buy his way safely off a planet that had suddenly and inexplicably turned hostile. Twice he had been forced to leave shipmates behind to save his own skin. He was not proud of these memories, but he knew that a man had to make such choices from time to time if he expected to survive as a free trader. He counted himself lucky that he had been forced into doing nothing worse.

Even if all else went well, there was still the physical

adjustment to make: to a new gravity, to a day and climate unlike any other, to food and water that might tie an offworlder's guts into knots until his system grew accustomed to them. Sickness awaited, infections and diseases for which the body had no immunity. And whatever the pain, however great the exhaustion or debilitating the weakness, the work had to go on.

To say these things, and to support them with accounts of his past voyages, took Enskeline longer than he had anticipated. After he had met with the priest-voyagers five times, he had Faranaxx join one of their sessions; the next time, Scragbones was present. The aliens said little unless questioned directly; but Faranaxx's undisguised suspicion and Scragbones's impenetrable insulation against all values but his own were lessons in themselves.

There were occasions when Enskeline despaired of ever awakening a true sense of the alien among his charges. They seemed able to go just so far beyond the customs and attitudes of their homeworld, and no further. During one of their sessions, Enskeline became exasperated by this attitude.

"You have your own clear ideas of what's right and what's wrong," he broke in. "They worked for you on Earth, and they worked on Peter's Rock, so you think the whole galaxy is just waiting for you to bring your laws and prohibitions to every world. You think you just have to read them off and everyone will start living by your rules the next morning."

"We do not expect our work among other races to be so easy," said Fielden.

"You still don't comprehend how *other* some of these other intelligent races are," Enskeline retorted. "For example . . . a woman on Peter's Rock told me that you have laws against men and women taking their pleasure with one another. Even if they're both perfectly willing, you say such a thing is wrong."

"We believe that love between a man and a woman is a good thing. But its proper place is within a marriage."

"Why?"

"We have always believed that the true end of sexuality is the creation of new life, not merely pleasure."

Enskeline had anticipated this response. He looked at the young men in turn, smiled, and said, "Let me tell you about a race I once traded with. They call themselves K'hiliot, and they're reasonably humanoid in appearance, once you get used to the way the parts are arranged. Their sexual functions are pretty close to human, and for them sexuality is a social act. It's the K'hiliot way of showing gratitude, friendship, admiration—their equivalent of smiling at someone, or giving a little present. They place no restrictions on it. Any K'hiliot can enjoy sex with any other, as much as they both want."

Dallamer said, "But such behavior is genetic suicide! It would destroy any race that practiced it."

"There's something else about the K'hiliot. Their reproduction is nonsexual," Enskeline said, smiling pleasantly.

"But how . . . if they're humanoid?"

Enskeline shrugged. "I don't understand how, Rever. It's complicated, I know that much. Fairly painful, too, and for the parent it's almost always fatal."

"Which parent?" asked Fielden.

"There's only one. A K'hiliot reproduces by impregnating herself—or himself, if you like—through a series of encounters with four designated individuals. I don't know much about the process, but I know it's nonsexual and nobody enjoys it very much. They do not reproduce by choice. If a K'hiliot is ordered by its Throde-master to breed, he's not pleased at the prospect. It amounts to a command to sacrifice oneself for the race. There's a certain distinction involved in being chosen, but most K'hiliot would prefer to pass it up."

The missionaries were silent for a time, then Dallamer said, "So you believe that the K'hiliot would find our precepts incomprehensible."

"No. I think they'd find them subversive: evil," Enskeline said with obvious pleasure. "And not just your teachings about love, either. You have a rule against killing—"

"Surely all civilized races condemn the taking of life," said Cotteral.

"The Hendrary don't. Their culture is based on the ritual execution of the male parent by his oldest child."

"Is that really so, Captain?" Dallamer asked after a shocked silence.

"It's absolutely true, Rever. For a child to refuse to kill its male parent at the prescribed time is the greatest disgrace, the worst . . . sin, you'd call it, that their race can conceive."

They were still for a time, absorbing Enskeline's words. At last Dallamer said, "We have hard work before us."

Enskeline threw up his hands and stalked out of the compartment, leaving Faranaxx in charge. Two watches later he was back, working with the missionaries as earnestly as ever.

The voyage was a long one, but the busy watches passed quickly. By the time the *Rimjack* entered orbit around Sassacheele, the men from Peter's Rock had learned all that could be learned, short of actual contact.

They made three full orbits before Enskeline located the landing ring, and he did so only because he had come prepared with precise directions. The ring—without which a landing on the rocky terrain of Sassacheele would be too risky—was concealed in an upland valley, where the shadows of the surrounding crags kept it from view. The possibility of chancing upon it during a casual overflight was remote, and its positioning lent credence to the stories Enskeline had heard of the settlers' wish for isolation.

If isolation was indeed their goal, the colonists had chosen an ideal world. Sassacheele was about two-thirds water, with a single major land mass that snaked around it in an almost continuous belt, a scattering of small island chains, and three large islands. At its widest parts, the continent rose to a bare, rock-strewn plateau, with a lake here and there, but little sign of vegetation. The coastal lowlands and the slopes of the uplands were a lush green. Nowhere, except for the obscured landing ring, was a trace of human habitation to be seen. No lights shone on the darkside surface. No buildings rose, no towers, domes, or any other hint of human dwellings. No roads or trails led inland, no quays or harbors lined the shore, no craft could be seen upon the waters.

"Is this planet really inhabited, Captain? Are we too high to see the signs of human life?" Dallamer asked.

"It's inhabited. And we're low enough to pick up anything humans might construct."

"It looks empty. Is it possible they're all dead?"

"It's possible," Enskeline said, unperturbed. "That's happened more than once. But I didn't expect to see any signs. These people don't like visitors. They'll put up with an occasional free trader, but that's all."

"How will you find them?"

"I found the landing ring, didn't I? Stop bothering me, Dallamer. I have work to do. We're coming down on the next orbit."

Enskeline brought the *Rimjack* down to a smooth lock-in on the landing ring. When he gave the clearance for exit, the six priest-voyagers tumbled out eagerly. After more than ten triscepts in space, they were able at last to put one foot in front of another and not see a bulkhead three paces before their noses. Even Sterman, who had found the conversion down almost as painful as the initial step up to drivespeed, staggered feebly down the ramp to walk on open ground under an open blue sky.

When they had exercised themselves to near exhaustion and were sprawled on the stony ground, enjoying the long-forgotten feel of stretched muscles and a breeze on their faces (though the air bore scents unknown on Peter's Rock) Enskeline announced that he was leaving for the settlement. He extracted their solemn promise that they would not follow or wander off.

"Will you be away long, Captain?" asked Quarrier, a thickset youth with pale hair.

"A few days. Don't look so unhappy—the days here are shorter than you're accustomed to."

"And will you know—?" Sterman began.

"I'll be able to tell you whether you'll be allowed to go off to the Wishbones," Enskeline broke in. "Just don't get any ideas of starting out on your own."

"We've given our word," Sterman said.

"Remember that you have. As far as I know, there's nothing loose on Sassacheele big enough to hurt you. You can sleep outside, if you like. Have a look around, but never get out of sight of the ship, understand?" They nodded, and Enskeline went on, "Scragbones is in charge while I'm gone. You do as he says, and do it fast, and do it right. If you don't like taking orders from an alien . . . well, you should have thought of that back on Peter's Rock. Am I understood?"

"Yes, Captain," they said, with one voice.

Enskeline reentered the *Rimjack*. He emerged a short time later dressed in black from head to foot, a dark gray cloak over his shoulders. Under his arm was an elaborate helmet.

No sooner had Enskeline touched the ground than the ramp shuddered under the weight of Faranaxx, carrying out a large box. The Quespodon, too, wore a gray cloak closely drawn around him. With no more farewell than a careless wave of his hand, Enskeline set off, Faranaxx clumping along in his wake.

The settlement was built on a cliff overlooking a sheltered cove. The inland portion of the perimeter was girdled by a ditch and a wall. Enskeline's first impression was of a fortress or an embattled outpost deep in hostile territory; but as he looked more closely he saw no trace of attack or repulse, only neglect. The ditch was full of stinking litter, and the wall was in poor repair. It could not have kept out an army of children.

The gate was made of the cargo port of a second-stage driveship, mounted in a rusted framework of metal beams from the decking supports. It hung ajar, half off its makeshift hinges. Enskeline was not surprised to learn that the name of the settlement was Here-We-Stay.

The starfarers were closely questioned by the gate guard, who carried a weapon of Old Earth origin. It was a simple projectile rifle, coated with rust, the bolt missing. As a weapon, it could be useful only as a club; yet the guard carried it proudly.

They were admitted, grudgingly, only after Enskeline displayed his major trade item: a Skeggjatt field medical unit, complete with refining equipment for replenishing its full stock of medications. Enskeline and Faranaxx were taken to the head people of the settlement; while there was no show of hostility on anyone's part, there was a definite lack of hospitality. They passed at least a score of people as they walked down the dirty streets and lanes of smooth gray stone, past long low buildings of the same stone; only two people gave them so much as a glance.

Enskeline found this lack of interest puzzling. Sassacheele was an out-of-the-way world and received few visitors. Perhaps once every four or five planetary years a trader came by, but that was all. He had expected that an offworlder would cause a bit of stir; so far, he had been treated as if offworld visitors were as common as dust.

The ruling heads of Here-We-Stay were small improvement over their subjects. Enskeline was kept waiting in a bare room for an uncomfortably long time, then brought into the presence of two women and a man. All three were dressed in worn, filthy garments and smelled rank. Their dirty, blotchy faces were flat, thick-featured, and dull-eyed. Their expressions suggested a great reluctance to speak to him. All three seemed irritated by his arrival.

After a long time in space, Enskeline had been eagerly anticipating his first sight of a woman. But these two were so repellent to his eyes that he now wondered what sort of companionship he might have to settle for on Sassacheele.

"Who are you, and what do you want on our world?" the younger woman demanded. Her face and hands were covered with a rash, her arms furrowed and blood-caked where she had scratched with her dirty nails.

"I'm Jod Enskeline, free trader. I've come in hopes of doing mutually profitable business."

"Last trader come here made trouble," the man said in the same flat, nasal voice as the woman.

"I don't want trouble, I want trade."

The older woman said accusingly, "That one with you, what's wrong with him? What happened to him, got him all bruised up like that?"

"There's nothing wrong with him. He's a Quespodon. They all look like that."

The young woman quickly asked, "You saying he's not human like us? He's an alien?"

"He's a good crewman. I trust him with my ship."

"But he's not human. He's not, is he?" she persisted.

"No, he's not."

"Least he got a head like a human. He's not like the things on this planet," said the other woman. "You ever seen a Wishbone, trader?"

"No, I haven't," said Enskeline.

"They got no heads. No heads at all. And they're stupid," the woman said.

At this, the three of them fell to mutual complaining about the natives of Sassacheele, and seemed to forget Enskeline's presence completely. He looked on in silence, his spirits sinking. It was all too clear what had happened on this world.

He felt as if he had come upon a society ruled by children. The wrangling among the leaders went on for a time; then abruptly the young woman addressed Enskeline.

"What you looking for here? What you want with us?"

"I want to trade. I told you that."

"Why should we trade with him?" the man asked, but the woman ignored him and demanded. "Show us what you got to trade. Come on, show us."

Enskeline took the field medical kit he was carrying, opened it, and began to explain in the simplest terms the great good it might do for the residents of Here-We-Stay. It was a slow, frustrating process. By the time he reached an agreement with the three, the short day had ended and he was very hungry and thirsty. His head was throbbing with a dull ache. The settlers were surly and resentful, filled with a suspicion that they could not hide; and though Enskeline had many questions to ask, he felt he could not endure their presence any longer without food and rest. When he asked about lodgings, they stared at him blankly.

"No room in my house," the older woman said.

"Not mine, neither. No room for an outsider," said the other woman, raking at the raw flesh of her forearm.

"Is there a place in the settlement where I can buy food and get a place to stay for the night?" Enskeline asked.

"We don't know about them places. Guards will tell you, maybe, but we don't know them things," the man said. The women added their denials to his.

"I'll ask the guard, then. Can I speak with you again tomorrow? I have more things to show you, and some questions to ask, if you don't mind."

"What questions?" the man asked, glancing suspiciously at the others.

"About other visitors. People who came here long ago. It's a long story, and it would be better to talk about it tomorrow."

"Why?" the younger woman asked.

"Because I'm hungry and thirsty and tired and have a bad headache," Enskeline snapped, at the end of his patience.

The woman looked blankly at him, then nodded, and said, "Oh. That's all right, then."

Enskeline left while the three watched him in silence. A guard was slumped outside the door, and Enskeline asked him about accommodations. The guard, with a knowing grin, agreed to take the starfarers to a place he knew down by Farwall, where a man could get food, drink, and whatever kind of company he wanted.

The days of waiting were not unpleasant, though the impatience of the priest-voyagers to hear Enskeline's news made it impossible for them to enjoy their first planetfall to the full. By the standard of Peter's Rock, the day was only eighteen hours long; the sun seemed barely to have risen before it was sunset again. And the nights on this moonless world, where the black sky was bedecked with points of light as thickly sown as the white Word-of-Grace that bloomed in the abbot's garden every year from Lent Major to the last days of Trinity, were like no nights ever known under the bright twin moons of Peter's Rock. Space had been a radically new experience for them; this first encounter with another world was dazzling. They were awed by the evidence of God's benevolent power.

They gradually accustomed themselves to the shorter day. The higher gravity of Sassacheele left them weary and ready for sleep when the sun had raced to its early setting; and they awoke with good appetites. Scragbones kept them busy, but allowed ample time for them to explore the immediate environs of the landing ring, which proved to be bare, rocky, and rather dull. However unexciting their surroundings might be as landscape, though, they were a welcome relief from the claustrophobic confines of the *Rimjack*.

Near sundown of the fourth day after planetfall, Enskeline returned. His eyes were puffy and slightly bloodshot. He appeared displeased with the results of his excursion. Faranaxx trudged behind him, a chest balanced on his massive shoulder. Crew and passengers gathered to greet him, but Enskeline waved them off.

"Is all well, Captain?" Scragbones asked.

"Not what I'd hoped," Enskeline replied, pausing for a long yawn. "I'll tell you about it after I've had some sleep."

"Captain . . . our mission . . ." said Sterman anxiously.

Enskeline looked at him blankly for a moment, then said, "You can preach to the Wishbones if you like. Nobody here cares what you do with them. These people are too stupid to care about anything." He yawned again and said grumpily,

"I want a good, long, undisturbed sleep. Undisturbed—I mean that. Am I understood?"

All nodded assent. Enskeline climbed wearily up the ramp. Faranaxx, grinning like a gargoyle, took a glance around and followed him into the ship.

Enskeline rose at midday. After he had eaten, he assembled crew and voyagers alike to announce that he was returning to the settlement and that Waghorne and Isbinder were to accompany him. Scragbones and Faranaxx were to prepare the *Rimjack* for the voyage to Roharr.

Turning to the expectant priest-voyagers, he said, "You can choose among yourselves who stays. When I come back, the *Rimjack* is lifting off."

"But we need information, Captain! We don't know—" Sterman objected.

Enskeline broke in, "I'll bring back all the help you need. Now, start getting ready. Scragbones is in charge when I'm gone, same as before."

The wait this time was shorter, but considerably more anxious. Enskeline's much-awaited return was spectacular. Walking at his side, behind the two crewmen, was a tall, headless creature. It wore a brightly patterned cloth around its lower body and a similar cloth draped over its shoulders. On its chest was what at first appeared to be a large multicolored amulet that glowed faintly as it caught the late sunlight. As it drew near, though, the starfarers could see that the object was no amulet but an oval lenticular organ, like a disk of horn, set into the creature's broad chest.

"You're lucky," Enskeline said to the staring missionaries. "This fellow's important among the Wishbones. He's agreed to take you to their part of Sassacheele. It's a long way off. You'd never make it without a guide."

"Does he speak our language?" Cotteral asked.

"He doesn't speak at all. None of them do. But he's worked out a communication system with one of the settlers, and their pidgin is close enough to your own speech to serve. You can learn it on your way to Wishbone territory. Who's staying?"

Sterman and Cotteral stepped forward from the group. Enskeline looked from one to the other and said, "Is it by your own free choice? No one forced you, did they?"

"It's my free choice," said Cotteral, and Sterman added, "I want to stay on Sassacheele. No one is forcing me."

"All right, then. Here, take these," Enskeline said, presenting two boxlike objects, each with an opening into which a hand could fit comfortably. The front of the box was a translucent plate. On its side was a triple row of buttons in various colors. The boxes were encrusted with dirt and grime. They appeared very old and neglected.

"What are these, Captain?" Sterman asked.

"Communicators. The early settlers developed them. Most of the people in Here-We-Stay are too dumb to use them, but they still work."

"Too dumb? Why don't they—? I don't understand, Captain."

"Inbreeding and isolation. I've seen it happen elsewhere. A few more generations and these colonists will die out. There's nothing you can do about it. If you tried, they're so suspicious they wouldn't accept your help. They'd probably blame all their troubles on you. Forget them."

"But they're fellow humans!"

"Work with the Wishbones. That's what we agreed on."

"We will, Captain," said Cotteral. "How do these things work?"

"Wishbones can't speak, and as far as anyone knows, they can't hear either. They communicate through that shining spot on the chest. It's sensitive to color gradations. Tap that blue button—the top one in the nearest row—about a dozen times very quickly. Go on, do it."

The two priest-voyagers followed Enskeline's directions, sending a flickering blue light from the lanternlike devices in their hands. When they finished, the Wishbone responded; the pale plate in his chest shone a brilliant blue, pulsating rapidly and fading to a pale orange afterglow that lingered as if in anticipation of a new exchange.

"You've just greeted each other. Now press the first three buttons in the middle row in succession. Not too fast," Enskeline directed. In response to this signal, the Wishbone emitted a succession of flashes in yellow, red, and indigo, fading to blue, then glowing a deep red.

"Now you're introduced. You gave the signal to say you're humans, and he told you he's a Wishbone—or whatever he calls himself in his own language."

"Are we really communicating with him, Captain?" Sterman asked.

"An old-timer at the settlement told me it works. Of course, you're at a pretty basic level. It will be a long time before you can work out a language that you can preach in, Rever."

"We'll have plenty of time now, Captain."

'You surely will. You'll be on Sassacheele with these creatures for the rest of your lives. You're making a pretty big decision, you two."

"We made it freely, Captain," said Cotteral.

"I heard you say so. I still wonder if you know what you're choosing. This is a big world, and the Wishbones are a primitive people. They won't hurt you, but the time may come when you'll give anything for the sight of another human face and the sound of a human voice. The settlement people won't take you in. They're a touchy lot. Maybe there won't even be any of them left. Have you thought what it will be like when one of you dies and the other is left alone in a world of aliens?"

"We've considered all those things, Captain," said Cotteral.

"And you have no doubts? No second thoughts?"

Sterman and Cotteral exchanged a glance. Sterman said, "This is the work we've prepared for all our lives. We consider ourselves blessed to have this opportunity."

"All right, then. Good," Enskeline said, trying to cover up with a brusque manner his show of concern. "I've done what I agreed to do. I took you where you could preach your message. Sassachele isn't much of a world, but you're safe here, and you've got the Wishbones. If things really get bad—I mean absolutely desperate, life-or-death—you can try the settlement. But not before. You've got what you wanted, and I've kept my bargain with Abbot Rudlor. Just remember that, all of you. Now, let's have one last good meal and enjoy ourselves. The *Rimjack* lifts off tomorrow."

Faranaxx arranged rocks into a rough circle and ignited three small fireblocks. Waghorne and Isbinder unwrapped a haunch of very dark, strong-smelling meat they had brought back from the settlement, drove sturdy skewers into both ends, and set it on the top ledge of the rocky ring. The others looked on queasily until Enskeline assured them that the meat became sweet and almost odorless in the cooking and was not only edible but a great delicacy among the humans of Sassacheele.

Wishbone, as they had taken to calling the alien, joined their feast but did not partake of the meat or the odd-looking but delicious vegetables that Enskeline provided. The alien ate small pellets which he withdrew from a pouch concealed in his garment, inserting them delicately into a small orifice just under his communicator organ. The hand with which he ate was a clublike stalk that opened into three identical fingers which fit closely together when the hand was at rest. Around his wrist the creature had a ring of slender tentacles of various lengths. He used three of these to grasp his food pellets. From time to time, faint colors flickered in the plate on his chest, but he did not turn to any of the humans.

"Is he trying to communicate with us, Captain?" Cotteral asked when this had happened several times.

"I don't know. Maybe he's just talking to himself. Or thinking out loud. For all I know he could be belching."

"I'm going to try to respond."

"Just repeat his signals until you know more of the language. You might accidentally come upon an insult and ruin everything."

As Cotteral rose, Torris asked, "Why do they call them Wishbones, Captain?"

"They don't have a spine like ours, just two big bones curving up to form the chest walls. The arms are hung off the ends, and the legs fit into a socket in the base. It's a very simple skeleton. First time someone saw it, he thought it looked like a wishbone."

"They must be very rigid . . . awkward in their movements."

"Not at all. Except for the main bones, they're mostly cartilage and muscle. Very tough and very flexible." Enskeline paused for a moment, then laughed softly. "Those hands are more flexible than anything else I've ever seen. They've got a game—or an art form, an exercise, whatever it is—that's fascinating. I watched three of them at it when I was at the settlement. They take two containers and set them by each player. Then they dump a pile of coarse sand in front of them, black and red grains all mixed together with the white. The one who picks out the most black and red grains in the allotted time wins. You should see those tentacles move when they get to it!'' He shook his head, laughed once again, and said, ''Don't let them talk you into a game, whatever you do.''

''Can they see that well?'' someone asked.

''Pretty well, apparently. They've got a ring of small eyes around that communicator, and a larger one in each shoulder. Hard to notice them unless you're close up. The only problem they have is a blind spot. Don't get too close to this one, or he may feel threatened.''

''Would he hurt us?'' Torris asked.

Enskeline looked over toward the *Rimjack*. Wishbone and Cotteral had walked off, and now the alien's silhouette loomed over the priest-voyager's dark outline. An occasional flicker of light passed back and forth between them. The alien's torso was like a great goblet of solid muscle and bone, his long arms like two dangling maces. ''He might not mean to, but I wouldn't do anything to upset something that big,'' Enskeline said. He rose, murmuring, ''I think I'll tell that to Cotteral.''

As Enskeline approached, Cotteral turned to him and said excitedly, ''Captain, I think I've found the signal that asks for identification! We can start to build a vocabulary now.''

''That's mighty fast progress.''

''Well, Wishbone pointed to the ship and flashed green-yellow-green, then flickering violet. I didn't respond, and he did it again, but I still didn't know what to do. So he pointed to me, and then he gave the green-yellow-green-violet signal. After a pause, he gave the same signal I gave to say that we're human. He was asking me a question and showing me how to ask him one!'' the young missionary said triumphantly.

''That's good. You'll be speaking to them sooner than you expected.''

''At this rate, yes. I'm so excited. . . . Captain, you've done a wonderful thing for us and for these people,'' Cotteral said, turning to him with shining eyes, moved to tears by his joy. ''You're truly an instrument of God.''

''That's something I've never been called before. Listen, Cotteral, I came over to tell you something. This creature has a blind spot—''

''We noticed that, Captain. It's just under a meter straight before his blinker. We try to avoid it. But thank you for the warning. Thank you for all you've done.''

"I'm a free trader, Rever Cotteral. All I've done is keep my word by dropping two men on a bleak world where the natives talk in flashing lights and the only other humans are a pack of hopeless morons. If that's the work your god wants done, I'm glad I'm a Mechanist.''

Sterman's voice came softly from the shadow of the *Rimjack*. "Don't belittle yourself, Captain. You're a good man.''

"I'm a good trader. Sometimes it's hard to be both.''

"You didn't have to tell us about the Wishbones, but you did. And when we opted to work with them, you could have dropped us here and left us to fend for ourselves. You didn't do that.''

"I did what a decent man does, Rever, and no more. That doesn't make me an instrument of your god. After all, I might want to trade here someday.''

"Whatever you say, Captain. But we'll never cease praying for you,'' said Cotteral warmly.

"Thanks all the same. Pray for your friends—and your selves.''

As Enskeline turned to rejoin the others, Sterman said, "Captain, about the humans on Sassacheele—what are they like, really? What can we expect of them?''

"I don't think they'll seek you out, but you must avoid them. They were a pack of fanatics to begin with. They've degenerated. They're stupid and sickly now, but they may still have that fanatic impulse.''

"Aren't you being harsh on them? They seem to have treated you well.''

"We had business with each other. They don't treat the Wishbones well, and I don't think they'd treat you and Cotteral well, either.''

"What makes you say that, Captain?''

Enskeline hesitated. Frowning, he said, "I was able to go through a lot of old records, from liftoff right to the time they just gave up recording anything. I can tell you what they started out believing, and it's pretty bad. I don't think they believe much of anything any more, but if you were to start talking about your god, it might just get them remembering.

Once that happened, there's no telling what they might do. They might even kill you.''

"But why?''

"Have you ever heard of Bermerites? They may have sprung up after your ship left Earth.''

"I guess they did. The name is unfamiliar.''

"Bermer was a man from a country called Europe, back on Old Earth. One day—so he said, anyway, and a lot of people believed him—he had a vision. A true revelation, 'straight from God.' God told him that all human life was going to destroy itself. All of it, everywhere in the universe, except for the people who accepted the word from Bermer. Nobody else had a chance, but Bermer's loyal followers would be preserved. And when everyone else was gone . . .'' Enskeline paused, took a deep breath, and went on, ''. . . a great fleet of heavenly chariots would come down to carry off the true believers to a new universe so they could begin all over.''

Sterman sighed and was still for a moment. Then he said, "It's a strange creed. . . . Still, if they tried to lead a good life . . .''

"Twice each day, everyone in the settlement falls on his face and prays for 'The Great Purification.' I don't think anyone knows what it means any more. They just jabber a lot of meaningless words. But 'The Great Purification' was Bermer's name for the end of all human life—except theirs.''
Enskeline gripped Sterman's arm and said, "If you and Cotteral ever have to go there for help, they'll probably let you die. Other people's lives don't mean anything to them. Back in the early days of the settlement, if a trader brought news of war or plague, they'd hold a celebration! Do you want to stay on a world with people like that?''

"I think we must, Captain,'' Sterman said.

"Once the *Rimjack* lifts off, it's gone for good. Do you realize that, Rever? You're on Sassacheele for the rest of your lives, you and Cotteral.''

"You've pointed it all out before. We know, Captain. We've made our choice.''

"Then, good luck to you. I hope you never change your minds.''

The *Rimjack* lifted off the next day. Enskeline was the last to board. As the ramp lifted and the port closed, he saw the two missionaries, one on either side of Wishbone, a hand raised in farewell. The blinker on Wishbone's chest was blazing forth a wild display of shifting colors, and his clublike hand was lifted in imitation of the humans. They were too far away for Enskeline to see the expressions on the missionaries' faces, but he had no doubt that they were alight with joy. Turning to the controls, he muttered, "They're crazy. The two of them are crazy."

Scragbones, seated opposite him, said in his booming voice, "They seek honor in a strange way, but the seeking is good."

Enskeline grunted, but said nothing more. He was looking down at the dwindling seas of Sassacheele, wondering if the schismatics' ship and the relic lay buried beneath them. On this, the logical stopping place for a shipload of fugitives unaccustomed to starfaring, there was no record of their landing. They might be under that great planetwide ocean. They might have crashed in some remote valley and been covered by centuries of vegetation, or buried somewhere by Wishbones.

Or they might have gone on to Roharr, where the *Rimjack* was now headed.

IV.

Peter's Rock: The *Garrashaw*

Trisepts and seasons came and went. Generations passed away. The visit of the *Rimjack* faded to a misty memory of childhood tales in the clouded minds of elders. And then the *Garrashaw* came to Peter's Rock.

She was a great white ship, smooth-surfaced and clean of line. Despite her bulk, she had a vaulting grace that seemed to draw her upward even as she locked solidly into the landing ring before the marveling eyes of monks and townsfolk.

This time there was no wait and no time for a crowd to gather. As soon as the whine of her drivecoils had died, the *Garrashaw* clanged and spat forth a landing ramp. Down the ramp, with martial tread, came two men and a woman, their faces as somber as the black uniforms they wore and the black cases they carried. Without hesitation, they set out in a tight little wedge, the tall man with the close-cut, gray-flecked hair in front, the woman and the younger man two paces behind him on either side, marching in step up the wide cobbled road to the monastery under the bright sun of the first Almsday of Trinity.

Abbot Gossard, his mantle of office thrown hastily over his rough brown robe, came forth to greet them on the upper terrace. He smiled and extended his hands in welcome as they approached. The starfarers stopped before him. Their manner was respectful but reserved.

"You are most welcome to Peter's Rock and the hospitality of our monastery. I am Abbot Gossard," said the monk.

The leader of the three said, "I am Commander Cormasson, Primary of this mission. My ship is the Sternverein driveship *Garrashaw*. These are my assistants, Secondary Zuern and

First Officer Kallry,'' he added, nodding to indicate the woman and the young man. He spoke Church English perfectly in a flat, clipped accent.

"You are welcome, all. And do you bring . . .?'' The abbot faltered, then he blurted, "Have you word of our voyagers?"

"My last information was that two are on Sassacheele among aliens. Two more are working on Roharr. The rest went on to an unknown destination,'' Cormasson answered.

"Still working . . . still alive . . .?'' Gossard shook his head, bewildered. "They left Peter's Rock before the oldest man now living was born.''

"Time runs differently for travelers, Abbot Gossard. Perhaps trader Enskeline and his crew chose not to mention that to your predecessor.''

Abbot Gossard recovered quickly. "There was mention of the time dilation phenomenon, though not of its extent. To think that some of our voyagers still live, Commander! Tell me, is their message heard?''

"Those on Roharr are said to have met with some success. They have built a place of worship, and people come to them. Roharr is a world populated chiefly by humans.''

"What of those on . . . on the other world you spoke of?''

"On Sassacheele the original human colony is dying out. It may already be extinct. Your voyagers have settled with a race of aliens, creatures that cannot speak or hear as humans do. It seems unlikely that their efforts will have any result.''

Gossard smiled. "God sometimes achieves His ends in ways that seem unlikely to men.''

"I would not place my hope in the creatures of Sassacheele.''

Cormasson's cold reply checked the abbot, but only for a moment. He brightened and went on, "Yet our voyagers live, and their work proceeds. It is . . . it is almost a miracle.''

"There is nothing miraculous about a scientific fact, Abbot Gossard.''

"Perhaps not, Commander. But do you bring word of our first ship, and of our schismatic brothers and sisters? If they should be found—they and our relic—that would indeed be a miracle.''

"I know nothing of this, Abbot; only of the trader Enskeline and your voyager priests.''

Glancing about, Gossard noticed the monks and townsfolk gathering around them, and others far below converging on the ship. Extending a hand toward the broad stairway that led to the refectory level, he said, "Come, refresh yourselves and partake with us of the midday meal. After that, we will talk."

Cormasson drew a small object from his tunic, palmed it, and spoke into it. He used a rapid speech pattern that Gossard could not follow, although the few words he caught were intelligible. As Cormasson returned the instrument to his tunic, the gangway of the *Garrashaw* was flung upward to fold back upon itself and lock into the side of the ship with a sound that reached the little group on the terrace, seconds later, as a faint ring of metal on metal.

"Your crew are welcome to our world, Commander," the abbot said. "There is food and lodging here at the monastery for all."

"In time, perhaps. Not now. They have much to do."

"As you wish, Commander," said the abbot, turning and leading the way to the guest chambers.

The midday meals of Trinity were long and leisurely, for reasons climatic as much as liturgical. This was the warm season, when days were longest and hottest, and a meal eaten slowly and followed by a rest made the heat more bearable. It was also the climax of the Paschal time in the ecclesiastical year, a period of rejoicing and fulfillment, when special prayers and blessings were recited before and after meals and at intervals in the dining.

The three starfarers were patient participants in the meal and intent observers of the attendant rituals. Though they gave no outward sign, they were busy in the performance of their duties, and had been since the moment Peter's Rock had first appeared on the ship's instruments.

Cormasson, Zuern, and Kallry, together with the small team of advisers and the security force still aboard the *Garrashaw*, constituted a Special Contact Team. Their mission was essentially a standard Third Contact: to establish trade relations, offer advice and assistance on planetary security, and induce the ruling body of the planet to join forces with the Sternverein. But they had other mandates as well. They were to map the planet completely, and they were to undertake the sociohistorical analysis customarily done by a Second Contact Team. Most important of all was the time margin: the first phase of the mission to Peter's Rock was to be completed within one Galactic Standard Year—about thirteen trisepts by planetary reckoning. By the onset of the next trisept of Epiphany, the *Garrashaw* was to be off the planet.

Kallry, the security chief of the mission, was appalled by the planet's lack of defenses. These people seemed to him like children, innocent and unsuspecting. Unless they had developed measures that Kallry's trained eyes, backed by the *Garrashaw's* instruments, could not detect—an unlikely possibility—they were defenseless on a planet ripe for plunder. The populace was a healthy breed. The women were comely, the men strong, the children quick and alert. Many of both sexes displayed valuable skills. An armed slaver crew could ravish this world of all but the oldest and weakest, and face no organized resistance. And slavers were not the only danger, or even the chief danger. Kallry had not yet seen the monastery's library, but he heard rumor of it. In the proper market, such a quantity of printed Old Earth books was beyond price. They could buy a man his own planet, a lifetime of indulgence, an army and a driveship fleet to protect him, and still leave him with more wealth than he could squander in ten lifetimes. The galaxy was filled with men and humanoids who would wipe out every living creature in a planetary system for such a prize. Only luck had kept Peter's Rock hidden from them for so long. Now, with unthinking starfarers babbling of their homeworld's wealth and vulnerability at every planetfall and the word spreading to every world with a landing ring, such good luck was nearing an end. This planet needed the help of a Sternverein defense specialist, and Kallry ached to begin his work.

Zuern, the mission Secondary, did not feel Kallry's sense of urgency. Instead, she experienced the exhilaration of confronting the greatest opportunity of her career. Here on Peter's Rock was a segment of Old Earth society of the Late Exodus Era, preserved intact and isolated for centuries. Acculturation emphasized conservatism regarding all facets of Old Earth tradition. Even their language checked out nearly ninety percent congruent with known twenty-first-century forms. To Zuern, Peter's Rock was a window on a fascinating past.

Mission Primary Cormasson had the most demanding task of all, because it was the most delicate. It was for him to persuade these dwellers in the comfort of a dead past to move, with one decisive leap, into the galactic community. He could offer great inducements: travel and trade on most of the known worlds; the power of the Sternverein to protect them; the knowledge of scores of races; the opportunity to share in the mastery of the stars. In return he asked only their loyalty and cooperation.

Cormasson had been about his work for a long time, and he knew it well. On worlds like this one, his offer was generally accepted with eager gratitude. Occasionally he encountered divided opinion and was forced to manipulate local politics to bring about a change in attitude; a good, thoroughgoing Secondary was invaluable at such times. Rarely, reluctantly, he was forced to employ his strongest means of persuasion: the company of security troopers who waited aboard the *Garrashaw,* ready to move at his command. He disliked this last measure; it generated tensions that endured on some worlds to the third generation. But on the two occasions when it had been clearly necessary, he had done it without hesitation or regret. It was for the good of all. People could not be permitted to deny their destiny under the delusion of freedom.

Several evenings later, alone in his chambers, Abbot Gossard listened in amazement to the account that flowed smoothly, in the dialect of Peter's Rock, from the soundscriber on his table. The priest-voyagers who had gone out from this world so long ago had accomplished great things. They had paid a high price, but they had begun the mission for which the monastery was founded. Now, at last, Gossard knew that for a certainty.

The narrative ended. The soundscriber shut down, and Gossard sat before it for a time, deep in contemplation. So absorbed was he that he did not notice Cormasson's entrance until the man in black stood before him.

"Forgive me, Commander," he said with a start. "I was much taken with the message of this wonderful instrument."

Cormasson smiled at him. The man's smile was unexpected, for his lean, hard-featured face did not appear to be made for such expressions. "The soundscriber is a useful tool, is it not,

Abbot?'' he said. ''On many worlds it has replaced the printed word completely.''

''I can understand why,'' said Gossard, rising and gesturing to the gallery beyond, where comfortable benches stood in shadow, placed to take the cool night breeze. They seated themselves, and Gossard went on, ''We have heard of such things, of course. Some of our books contain elaborate diagrams for building them, but we lack the technology. Perhaps some day . . . but so much was left behind, on Earth. It will take long.''

''Much was lost, but much has been saved—and rediscovered.''

''Indeed?''

''Yes, Abbot. And Peter's Rock might contribute greatly.''

''We hope to make a great contribution to the people of the galaxy, but it will not be material. That is far from our mission, Commander.''

Cormasson looked at the abbot and again smiled that ill-suited smile. ''The Sternverein knows of your mission, and favors it. We wish to help. The *Garrashaw* can carry many of your voyagers and take them farther, and in greater safety, than any trader's ship. And the *Garrashaw* is only one ship of a great fleet.''

''What do you ask in return? We have little to give. Why should the Sternverein take an interest in our work? The soundscriber said yours was a trading organization. What have we to trade?''

''It's not entirely a matter of trade, Abbot.''

''What, then?''

''The Sternverein began as a merchants' alliance, but it has grown to be much more. On some worlds the Sternverein is the only government, the only repository of knowledge, the only power of healing that backward people know. The monks of Peter's Rock are better prepared for such work than the traders and troopers of the Sternverein. By helping you fulfill your mission, we also help ourselves.''

Gossard weighed these words, then said, ''This scans to me as reasonable. But do you ask nothing in return?''

''We have certain requests. We would make soundscriber and visual copies of the books in the monastery library. This will require the assistance of many of your scholars.''

"I agree to that gladly, Commander."

"We wish also to establish a small base on Peter's Rock. The men will maintain the landing ring and assist in the defense of the planet in case of an attack."

"Attack?" Gossard smiled and shook his head. "In all the centuries, only two ships have visited us, and both brought friends."

"The next may bring enemies."

"What enemies could we have? Who knows of our existence?"

"We learned of you from those who had heard the tales of priest-voyagers. Doubtless, others have also heard. As for enemies . . ." Cormasson paused. His hand brushed the butt of the long-barreled ripgun holstered across his chest and lingered for a moment; then he let the hand fall and said, "There are some who would cheerfully kill every living creature on this planet for the contents of the monastery library. Books are rare among the civilized worlds, Abbot. Those who want them don't care how they get them. And there are slavers who would carry off every healthy adult on one of their lag-ships; free traders who might come in friendship, yet bring with them a plague to wipe out all life on Peter's Rock; or dishonest ones, to cheat you of your rarest treasures."

"The trader Enskeline treated Abbot Rudlor fairly, Commander."

"He cheated him and the monastery. The books given to Enskeline were worth ten times the passage of six men."

"Enskeline enabled us to set out on our true mission. Any abbot would have given him all he asked."

Cormasson laughed gruffly. "You're a poor bargainer, to tell me that."

"I am no bargainer at all, Commander. I simply speak the truth. You have come to us in good faith, and you deserve the truth."

"I've come in better faith than any free trader, that's certain."

"It scans to me you dislike all free traders," the abbot observed.

"They make our work hard. The free traders cheat and deceive people, and then when our ships arrive to offer honest trade, they're met with suspicion. Sometimes they even face open hostility. Most free traders are little better than pirates— alien crews, the dregs of alien races.''

"You are severe, Commander," Gossard said, his voice pained. "The aliens of Enskeline's crew were most helpful in preparing our voyagers."

"Then your voyagers were lucky. We know something of Enskeline's crew. The Lixian was a fugitive from his homeworld, and the Quespodon . . . typical of his kind, a dumb brute."

"The bridgeman, Zacher, stayed with us. He became a respected towndweller and a valued instructor of priest-voyagers. Some of his descendants still live below.''

"Zacher got out of the life before it ruined him. Believe me, Abbot, I know free traders better than you do.''

Abbot Gossard sighed. "You make the worlds beyond, and the space in between, sound like harsh places.''

"They are," Cormasson said. Both men were silent for a time, then Cormasson went on, "Your priest-voyagers may help to make things better, though. We want to offer them the chance to do so, and to protect them and you here on Peter's Rock until you're able to protect yourselves. Accept us and work with us, Abbot. The galaxy needs what you can give.''

"We will work with the Sternverein," Gossard said. "Our mission allows us no choice.''

On the way to his chamber, Cormasson stopped to confer with his Secondary. He found Zuern busy at the consoles of four triple-soundscribers, collating scraps of cultural notation into a single account. They spent an hour planning future operations on Peter's Rock; Cormasson left her with the task of evaluating personnel profiles while he proceeded to visit Kallry.

Despite the hour, the first officer was awake, working at a table covered with diagrams. When Cormasson told his news, Kallry's pale eyes lit up eagerly. He brushed his materials aside and sketched out a defensive plan for the monastery.

"I can have it done quickly, Commander. This place is in a perfect position for defense. After I'm finished, I could hold off an army with a dozen troopers," he said.

"This looks good," Cormasson said as he studied the plan.

"The best part is that nothing need be visible. If anyone attacks, they'll be trapped before they even know there's opposition."

Cormasson nodded. "That's just what we want. The abbot can see your plans whenever he likes, but he's to know only of the passive defenses."

"Yes, sir."

"Gossard is a decent man, but he's totally unaware of the kind of scum that are sure to be drawn here. He's uncomfortable at the prospect of a defense force, so I want it played down. We'll leave a small detachment here as advisers and landing-ring crew. He's to know no more than that."

Cormasson took the long way back to his quarters, traversing the upper galleries and pausing twice to look down on the moon-mottled hills and fields below. He felt satisfied with this night's work and with the progress of this entire mission. The hardest part of his work had been accomplished as smoothly and swiftly as anyone could wish. Peter's Rock was drawing toward the Sternverein orbit now and would soon be there to stay. He walked to his chamber, whistling a lively Dilkean timing-tune under his breath, and slept well until daylight.

Left alone, Abbot Gossard paced the gallery for the space of an hour, weighing his conversation with Cormasson and his final decision. It seemed to him that he had done the right thing. These men and women in black would help bring the word of God to worlds that had struggled long without it. This was the capstone of the long preparatory work. The little *Rimjack* had been a beginning; now this great white ship, and others like it, would bear messengers of salvation to the farthest reaches of the galaxy. In conscience, he could have chosen no other course of action, or even delayed for a single day in accepting the Sternverein's offer. He had done his duty to God and humankind.

Quietly, unseen, he made his way to the chapel, where he passed the night in prayer. When, at dawn, he stiffly and painfully unbent his knees, he was confirmed in his decision. And yet, unaccountably, a tiny grain of doubt remained in his mind.

The next five trisepts were busy ones. On the day after the agreement between Cormasson and Gossard, men and women in black descended from the *Garrashaw* and began to work among the people of Peter's Rock. The ship itself rose the next day to begin orbital mapping.

Kallry seemed to be everywhere in the town and the monastery, and at all hours. No sooner had he marked out a ditch to be dug around the town than he was groping in the dank lower levels of the monastery, tapping walls and floor and placing mysterious markings here and there, then rushing to the long upward road to direct excavation, and next to the terraces to lay out new irrigation canals. Then it was back to town again, this time to supervise the tearing down of a row of sheds.

Cormasson visited the abbot and monastery officials daily, but his calls were brief and businesslike. Most of his time was spent with Secondary Zuern, examining, singly and in small groups, members of the security force. An important selection process was under way.

As Third Pentecost drew to an end, Cormasson made his last inspections and drew up his final report. The report was terse and confident; he was pleased by all he saw. Kallry had built defenses that would allow a small force to hold the town and the monastery against attackers ten times their number. The mission Tertiary, psycholinguist Aksaar, had completed the soundscribing and copying of every book on the planet, and arranged secure transit for the twenty-two books Gossard had presented to the Commander. Zuern had selected from among the troopers those whose heredity and homeworld environment best suited them for easy integration with the inhabitants of this world. In accordance with the male-female ratio on Peter's Rock, twenty-four men and seven women were picked.

The *Garrashaw* rose from Peter's Rock on the second Spiritsday of Recollection. Left behind on the planet were thirty-one men and women of the Sternverein. Ostensibly, their duties were to maintain the landing ring and to train the future missionaries who would depart with the *Garrashaw* when it returned. Their real mission was to defend Peter's Rock.

Cormasson watched the green-and-white world diminish to a ball, then to a speck, and then drop from sight as the *Garrashaw* heeled over to enter a long orbit at a velocity well below lightspeed. They would be out for two hundred and thirty watches, ship's time, during which seven years would pass on Peter's Rock. By Cormasson's best estimate, that would be just enough time for everything to fall into place.

Cormasson felt a rare contentment. He had brought off the opening moves swiftly and well, and his subordinates had performed their duties to perfection. The next move in the endless game was up to the vermin of the galaxy. They would take the bait; he had no doubt of that. It was only a matter of patience and readiness.

Meanwhile, there was much to be done before his return to Peter's Rock, and no time to waste. He decided to begin by checking into a matter Zuern had called to his attention. He signalled for the Secondary to report to the ship's record center, then left at once to join her.

She was waiting when he entered. Two soundscribers stood ready before her. He motioned for her to be seated and dropped into the chair beside hers.

"I'll hear these later," he said, indicating the soundscribers. "Right now, I'd like your own summary of your findings."

"Do you recall our first meeting with Gossard? He inquired about his voyagers, and then he asked about an earlier ship and a relic."

"I recall that."

"Three times during our stay I tried to learn more about the first ship and the relic. He was very evasive each time and changed the subject as quickly as he could," Zuern went on.

"I questioned him about it myself once, and he behaved in much the same way. I understood all this to be a shameful episode in the monastery's history. His reluctance to discuss it seemed natural. Do you suggest another possibility?"

"I do, Commander," Zuern said confidently. "Let me give you my summary. In the third century of settlement, a doctrinal dispute split the monastery and the townspeople into three factions. Eventually, two of these dissident factions settled elsewhere on Peter's Rock, and there was no further contact between the groups. Then, after a period of quiet, one faction returned to the monastery, stole the ship and the monastery's most precious treasure, and left the planet forever."

"That's not an unusual pattern of events, Zuern. I've heard of similar incidents on a score of worlds—and so have you, I'm sure."

"True, Commander, but there's a difference here. The

treasure they stole was not valuable in the material sense alone. It's an artifact of immense value, to be sure—I have faxes of it here—but it's of inestimably greater value as a symbol. In the eyes of the monastics, the symbolic spiritual value far outweighs the material."

"Go on, Zuern."

"These people call themselves Christians. They believe that their faith was brought to Earth by a man called Christ, who they believe was also a god. Now, this Christ was put to death at one point in his Earthly life, and buried. According to their creed, he later was returned to life in some miraculous fashion. The monastics believe that their relic is a piece of the cloth that wrapped their god's body in the tomb. As a sign of respect and veneration, they've encased it in precious metal and adorned it with jewels; but to them, the value is in the piece of cloth."

Cormasson nodded thoughtfully and was silent for a time. Then he asked, "Is there any evidence that Enskeline knows about the relic?"

"None, Commander."

"Still . . . the way Gossard greeted us suggested that he was expecting news of it."

"I agree," Zuern said emphatically.

"So, it may be that Enskeline, or the missionaries, or perhaps everyone on board the *Rimjack,* is seeking that relic."

"But for very different reasons."

"Yes. Oh, yes," Cormasson said with a dry laugh. "The trader wants the container, and the holy men want the contents. Perhaps Enskeline has struck a deal with them already."

"He might even have agreed to bring the relic back to Peter's Rock. I'm sure the monastics would give him everything they possess for it."

"That would be very dangerous," Cormasson said thoughtfully. "For centuries those monks have remained steadfast to an ideal. Even when this relic of theirs was stolen from them, they did not abandon their mission. Such loyalty is admirable . . . but with their relic returned to them, their dedication might turn to fanaticism. Even now, their young men are eager to travel to unknown worlds to spread their beliefs. With the impetus of a restoration which they would surely look upon as miraculous, their zeal might know no bounds."

"It's possible, Commander. But perhaps the Sternverein could put such fanatics to good use. That was the first thought that occurred to me when I learned of the relic."

Cormasson nodded but did not reply. Leaning forward, he said, "Perhaps I should hear the soundscribers now. Is all the information here?"

"Yes, Commander. Channel C of the one of the left is my collated account. The rest is source material, coded for origin."

"Good. You've done well on this mission, Zuern."

She thanked him and left him alone. He played her account through, listening carefully, then turned to the source material she had drawn on. From time to time he stopped to dictate notes into a small soundscriber of his own. When he had heard all the sources, he listened once again to Zuern's collated version.

Afterward, Cormasson returned to his cabin, dimmed the lights, and sprawled on his berth, thinking on all he had heard. What had seemed a fairly straightforward mission had suddenly shown suggestions of a dangerous new dimension. This relic, should it be found, might turn a planet of harmless holy men into a nuisance, perhaps even a threat, to the Sternverein. On the other hand—as Zuern had suggested—it might help make them manipulable and useful in the further-ance of the Sternverein's goals. It was impossible to be certain which result was more likely.

Of one thing Cormasson was absolutely certain: if the relic was to be found, it must be found by the Sternverein. But since he could do nothing to initiate the search until this mission was completed, there was no point to worrying about it now. First came the securing of Peter's Rock. With that completed, the way to the relic might be easier than it now appeared.

On Peter's Rock, the newcomers settled into the routine of daily life and quickly became part of the community. Court-ships began, and marriages soon followed. At the end of two years, most of the men and women from the *Garrashaw* had married into old settlers' families.

The starfarers took up a variety of duties on their new homeworld. The majority—fourteen of the men and five of the women—became formal instructors in the monastery, sharing their knowledge of alien cultures with the future priest-voyagers and introducing the priest-ministrants to new techniques of healing and counseling, preparing them for the *Garrashaw*'s return, when they would at last be taken to new worlds with their message. Others became foresters, quarriers, or farmers. Two men left, with a novice ministrant, to explore the abandoned sites of the breakaway settlements. Two others entered the long course of study to become priest-scholars.

The older settlers found these newcomers to be hard workers and good companions. At first, their ways seemed strange. But they were so friendly, so willing to explain and demonstrate and answer questions, that the natives soon warmed to them.

The ship-settlers, as they were called, said very little about their organization or the white ship that brought them, but they spoke freely on every other subject. They knew songs and stories from a hundred worlds. They had seen and heard things that the homeworlders of Peter's Rock had never even imagined. In every field of daily endeavor, they seemed to know tricks and secrets that made the work easier and the results better. It seemed that they could endure greater extremes of temperature, live on less food and drink, and still work harder than the natives. And when the work was done, they were ready for play.

Wrestling was a favorite pastime on Peter's Rock. In the centuries since planetfall, it had been refined to near perfection—or so the homeworlders believed. The people from the *Garrashaw*, it was soon found, knew grips and holds that made one man or woman the match of three. But they did not hoard their techniques; they shared them freely and took genuine pride in the homeworlders who were the most apt pupils.

They even introduced new pastimes. The townspeople had always stayed close to their homes and fields. Few but the foresters had ever traveled out of sight of the monastery. But at the urging of the ship-settlers, they began to range over their planet and learn its ways and resources. In a short time it became commonplace for little groups to set out for an entire trisept's roving with no more than an extra day's food and a spare tunic against the night chill.

The only weapons on Peter's Rock before the coming of the *Garrashaw* were ancient firearms, now beyond repair from long disuse. The ship-settlers brought with them long-barreled pistols they called *ripguns,* and a seemingly endless supply of ammunition. They were all expert marksmen, and they practiced regularly on a range they built just beyond the outermost quarry. At first the natives avoided the place, but in time a few grew curious. They were invited to try their hand, and with the coaching of the ship-settlers, began to develop skill with these weapons. The word spread, and before long nearly a score of the townspeople were regular visitors to the range, and a few had acquired pistols of their own—gifts from their new friends.

Abbot Gossard found this last development disturbing, but kept his doubts to himself. The weapons were, after all, being used only for sport and were providing pleasure and companionship for many. His knowledge of Old Earth history inclined him to think that weapons of any sort were likely to be put to mischievous use sooner or later; still, Peter's Rock was not Old Earth. This was a new planet, with new ways.

The ship-settlers worked hard and earned their leisure. Whatever personal reservations he might have, Gossard told himself, they had the right to enjoy their traditional pastimes. But on days when the wind carried the sound of firing from beyond the quarries, the abbot spent extra time in prayer.

V. _____

Roharr: The Second Mission

Now that two of their number had actually begun the work, the priest-voyagers began to overcome their sense of novelty and settle into a routine. With one voyage behind them, they felt like seasoned starfarers. They recalled Enskeline's words—incredible when he spoke them back on Peter's Rock—that space travel was one of the most boring achievements of human science, and found themselves agreeing. At drivespeed, they had no sensation of motion. Nothing could be seen beyond the ports in the flat grayness: they might have been painted over. There was only the regular rotation of meals and watches, the constant confinement, and the utter sameness.

The run to Roharr was uneventful, as Enskeline had predicted. The priest-voyagers devoted their free time to prayer, meditation, and study, with an occasional boisterous theological debate that left Faranaxx awed and Enskeline grumbling about a headache. Scragbones scrupulously avoided them.

When they passed the three-quarter mark, interest in Roharr began to quicken. Quarrier and Fielden were delegated to ask Captain Enskeline to brief them on their destination. Enskeline complied with scarcely a complaint. He welcomed the opportunity to talk and be listened to.

They assembled in the ship's mess, as before, but now with a bit more elbow room. The very fact of that extra room reminded them of their companions on Sassacheele and threatened to make the meeting too solemn for Enskeline's taste. He rubbed his hands briskly and plunged ahead.

"I've been to Roharr, so I can tell you about it. First thing you ought to know is that Roharr is a beautiful, big world.

71

Biggest one you've reached so far, but only a little bit more gravity than Peter's Rock. You won't feel as though you're walking around with a ten-kilo weight in each boot," he said, smiling at his little audience. They smiled faintly in return, but said nothing. He went on, "It's mostly water. Three continents, about two-score major islands, and hundreds of little ones with nobody living on them. From space, it looks as if someone broke up all the land and scattered it over the planet very carelessly. Travel is mostly by water, so I hope you can all swim and nobody gets seasick."

"Everyone learns to swim on Peter's Rock," said Quarrier.

"That's good. Roharrans don't think much of anyone who can't swim."

"What sort of people are the Roharrans, Captain?" Dallamer asked.

"Plain Earth human. You won't see anything like Wishbone on Roharr, unless it's just passing through. One thing, though—you were all white on Peter's Rock, weren't you?"

"All those who remained with the monastery were," said Dallamer.

"Well, all of the races of Old Earth are represented on Roharr. And since intermarriage is strongly encouraged—it was mandatory in the early years—there are probably a few mixtures nobody on Old Earth ever saw. You won't look strange to them, but if anyone on Roharr looks strange to you, don't make anything of it. They don't much like that. They're friendly, but there are some things they just don't like."

"What do they believe, Captain?" Torris asked.

Enskeline thought for a moment, then shrugged and said, "Anything they like, as far as I know."

"Do you mean there's no single planetary faith on Roharr?" Torris sounded uncomfortable asking the question.

"It's not like Peter's Rock, Rever. Most places aren't. A planet like Roharr, with twenty million people on it, all of them different from each other, isn't going to have everyone believing the same thing. I know there are Mechanists there, and Poeites, and Neo-Romans, and Reformed Ecumenical Dispensed Christians, and . . . Children of Earth, and—"

He was silenced by an eruption from the priest-voyagers, all of whom, after initial stunned silence, cried, "Who?"

"What are they?" "What do they believe?" and similar questions. He waited until the uproar died, then said simply, "Wait until you get to Roharr, and then find out for yourselves."

"But you must know, Captain," said Fielden.

"Yes, you've actually met some of those people," Dallamer said.

"I've met them all. But we didn't talk religion."

"Didn't you *ever* discuss it?" Fielden asked incredulously.

"Not once. Just because something is important to you, Rever, that doesn't make it important to everyone else. You'd better learn that."

"But it *is* important! We're bringing the message of God to these people, Captain!"

Enskeline looked at Fielden for a moment, then at the others. He shook his head uneasily. "That's what you say. And you believe it. But maybe you ought to think of how it sounds to others. You're telling people that the god who created the universe picked Earth—a wasted world, a world they've all forgotten to be the birthplace of his son. Some people are going to laugh at you when you say that. What will you tell them then?"

Fielden flushed but controlled himself. In a calm voice, he said, "God works in eternity, Captain. He is not bound in time, as we are. If he chooses to spread His word from world to world over many ages, some world must be the starting point. Why not Earth?"

Enskeline scratched the base of his topknot as he pondered this answer; then he nodded. "Good point, Fielden," he said. "But people may not stay to hear it. If you don't realize that, you'll have a disappointing time ahead."

"We understand that, Captain," said Quarrier in a placating tone. "But surely you realize how the Roharrans' beliefs concern us. If we're going to bring the faith to them, it would help greatly to know what they think about the ultimate questions."

"Perfectly reasonable, Rever—to someone from Peter's Rock. But the people of Roharr haven't spent the centuries praying, and they don't spend much time at it now. They worry about other things. Always have."

"Do they believe in a god?" Quarrier pressed him.

"I suppose some do. Maybe they all do. They don't go around talking about it all the time, I know that," Enskeline said with obvious impatience.

"What about your own beliefs, Captain? You said once you were a Mechanist."

"I pretty much follow the thinking of the Finite Mechanists. But I don't feel like talking about it. If you want to practice on somebody, practice on each other. Listening to you preach isn't part of my agreement."

"I was merely curious," Quarrier said.

"Be curious about Roharr, if you like. But not about what I believe."

"I'm sorry, Captain. Please tell us more about Roharr."

Mollified, Enskeline went on to describe the people and the customs of their destination, drawing on his own visits and the observations of other travelers, carefully surrounding every statement with a protective hedge of qualifiers. He explained the chief problem: the time dilation resulting from travel in the drivespeed range made it difficult to keep abreast of developments on the worlds one visited. What was a short absence for the starfarer might be anything from a few seasons to generations by planetary reckoning. The only certainty was that two friends parting—one remaining behind while the other went into space—would never meet as coevals again.

"Do you mean that our friends on Peter's Rock are old now?" Fielden asked.

"Not old. I'd say . . . well, if we'd returned directly from Sassacheele, you'd have noticed a difference in your friends. They'd look like their own older brothers and sisters."

"But we've only been gone . . . scarcely twenty trisepts!"

"Twenty trisepts aboard the *Rimjack,* Rever. A lot more than that downside."

"Is there no way to escape it, Captain?" Quarrier asked.

"None at all. You can control it a bit, but you can't avoid it. Depends on how much risk you want to take and how much pain you can stand—and how good a ship you're in. The time dilation takes place during acceleration and deceleration; the faster you get in and out of drivespeed range, the less time differential. Trouble is, the faster you accelerate and decelerate, the harder it is on the drivecoils and the more painful it becomes. Beyond a certain range, it kills you."

"The time lag doesn't seem to bother you, Captain."

Enskeline shrugged. "It's the price you pay for coming out here. I think it's worth paying. I'm sorry I didn't make it clearer back on Peter's Rock, though. You talked then as though you understood."

"Zacher gave us a general idea . . . nothing like the true extent."

"Too bad. Not much you can do about it now."

"We're not complaining, Captain. We don't intend to go back, so it doesn't really matter."

Enskeline nodded and resumed his description of the economic structure of Roharr's chief continent. There was no more talk of time dilation aboard the *Rimjack*.

Their first view of Roharr verified Enskeline's words: it was a beautiful planet. It came to life before them, a perfect sphere of deep blue, studded with land masses of rust and brown, dark green and gray, shrouded with shifting whorls and swags of pure white cloud, a jewel hung against the black breast of space. Onward they sped, the bright world drawing them ever closer, until in a queasy instant they underwent the reorientation from *onward* to *downward* and felt themselves falling into the thick white cloud mantle that billowed beneath them, obscuring the surface. Into that tenuous white sea they plunged, emerging over a calm ocean spangled with sunlight and pebbled with islands. They crossed into darkness, and as they passed over a continent the priest-voyagers cried out with joy and relief at the network of lights that blazed below them. Heading sunward, they recrossed the terminator and began their final descent to the landing ring on Roharr's major continent, Ermacene.

This was a far different planetfall from the one they had experienced on Sassacheele. The landing ring was only one of nine arranged in a circle about three kilometers in diameter. The ground surface was smooth hard rock, absolutely flat, covered with thick lines in various bright colors. Enclosing the ring complex was a high fence of metal in which only one gate was visible. Towards this gate they walked, Enskeline in the lead, the crewmen from Peter's Rock just behind him, and the priest-voyagers next, with Faranaxx lumbering at the end, carrying all their belongings. Scragbones had remained aboard the *Rimjack,* on first ground watch.

From the ring complex to the metal fence was about a kilometer's distance. Since the gate was in the portion of the fence farthest from their ring, the men of the *Rimjack* had a long walk to it and plenty of opportunity to observe their surroundings.

The first thing they saw was a white ship three times the size of the *Rimjack.* It stood on the ring diametrically opposite the one on which their ship had locked. At the sight of it, Enskeline shook his head and muttered something the others did not hear.

"Did you say something, Captain?" Torris asked.

"Not to you, Rever," Enskeline said sourly. He strode on for a few paces, then stopped abruptly and pointed at the white ship, where figures dressed in black were moving about with apparent purpose. "See those blackjacket musclemen? You keep clear of them, do you hear? Have nothing to do with them."

"Who are they?"

"Sternverein security troopers. Their mission is to wipe out the free traders so the Sternverein can have all trade in the galaxy to itself. But we're too smart for them. And too fast."

"Will they try to harm you, Captain?" asked Dallamer nervously.

"Not on Roharr. But keep away from them all the same. If you can't avoid talking to them, don't say you came here with a free trader or they'll look on you as an enemy."

"Why do they want to be rid of free traders? Surely the galaxy is big enough for all of you," Torris said.

"They don't think so. If you ask them, they'll tell you that all they want to do is encourage trade, expand it, make it safer. . . . But I've seen their work. They clear the spaceways of pirates and slavers, it's true, but they're more dangerous than the crowd they eliminate. Avoid them," Enskeline repeated, and then walked on, leaving the priest-voyagers to think on his words as they hurried after.

To their left and behind them, the ground extended flat and unbroken to the horizon. Out there, beyond the limit of their vision, was the sea. The coastal plain continued inland for some distance, but the hills marked the horizon before them.

They were covered with vegetation in a hundred shades of green, with patches of bright red scattered in the lower reaches but more frequent at the higher altitudes.

The city began just beyond the fence and extended as far as they could see; for all they could tell, it might have reached to the foot of the mountains. There were more buildings in their immediate view than existed on all of Peter's Rock, and many of them were large. Nothing could be seen to match the great monastery, but nearly half the buildings were larger than any other edifice on their homeworld.

The architecture seemed to follow no pattern. There were square buildings, cylinders, cones, tentlike structures, domes, and even two spheres, one much larger than the other. Most roofs were flat, but a few were sharply pitched; some overhung the building line by a precarious margin, while others ended flush with the walls.

As they walked on, marveling at their surroundings, the starfarers noticed three uniformed people awaiting them just inside the gate. Two were gold-colored, one was black. All three were women. The priests exchanged apprehensive glances; Enskeline's story of different races, which they had half-doubted, appeared to be true. As if he had read their thoughts, Enskeline dropped back to walk in their midst.

"Just a reminder to all of you—you're going to see things on Roharr that you never saw on Peter's Rock. Be prepared. If it's too much for you, go back to the *Rimjack* and wait for me there. We're lifting off in thirty-seven planetary days," he said.

"Where shall we stay? What will we do here for thirty-seven days?" Torris asked, an edge of panic in his voice.

"I'll find you a place for the first few nights. After that, you're on your own." Enskeline looked at the wide-eyed faces surrounding him, grinned, and said, "You wanted to find out what the Roharrans were like, didn't you?"

"Yes, but not . . . we didn't . . ."

"Well, now you can. You've got enough time to see all of Ermacene City and the biggest upland towns. Remember what I said—don't go upland without a guide. You have to ride haxopods to go that far, and you have to be shown the way. The haxopod is a miserable, vicious, sneaky brute, but the guides can handle them. Agree on a price before you leave, and don't pay in advance.''

"We'll remember, Captain," said Quarrier.

"All right. You can visit one of the nearer islands—there's a lot to see on Boolo—but there won't be time to see the other continents. They're not very interesting, anyway. Ermacene is the center of everything on Roharr.''

"Is there a central church of any kind, Captain?''

Enskeline shrugged. "If there is, no one ever told me. I don't think there's any such thing on Roharr. You can ask at the stayhouse.''

By this time, they were almost to the gate. Enskeline smiled and waved to the three women, who returned his greeting readily. Their manner was friendly even as they questioned Enskeline closely and inspected everything Faranaxx carried. The sight of the books Enskeline had brought to trade impressed them visibly; their treatment of him became almost deferential.

The women spoke rapidly, with a great deal of gesturing. Enskeline seemed to have no difficulty in communicating, even to the extent of matching their free gestures with his own. The men from Peter's Rock looked on uncomfortably, returning the women's smiles but reluctant to venture speech. They had understood about half of what they had heard, just enough to appreciate the shift from surprise to incredulity to mild amusement when Enskeline described their mission.

Still smiling, the women waved them past, extending a welcome to their world. The priest-voyagers and the two crewmen made clumsy, stammering responses, sending the women into peals of laughter.

As they walked down the broad paved strip that led to the city, Enskeline said, "For people who intend to preach, you're mighty reluctant to open your mouths.''

"They spoke so quickly, Captain," said Torris. Fielden added, "And their gestures . . . We've never seen people move around and wave their hands so when they speak.''

"Oh, yes, the gestures. I should have remembered. They're a part of the language here.''

"They are?" Fielden asked, his voice showing his concern.

"The words are the most important part; they should be no

trouble to you. But gestures can change the meaning of words. Just like the tone of your voice.''

Morosely, Fielden said, "It will take us a lot more than thirty-seven days to learn how to speak with these people.''

"It's not that hard, Rever. They'll know you're off-worlders as soon as you open your mouths, and they'll make allowances.''

Quarrier laughed ruefully. "Maybe we'd do better if we kept our hands behind us when we talk.''

"Don't do that, Quarrier. It means you don't trust the person you're speaking to.'' The priest-voyagers exchanged a dismayed look at this bit of information, but Enskeline cheerfully assured them, "Just *tell* them you're offworlders. They're a nice friendly people here, believe me.''

"But what if we make some unintentional gesture of insult?'' Quarrier asked.

Enskeline swept the group with a glance, and shaking his head, said, "I don't understand you at all. You go to a bleak, empty world like Sassacheele—you meet a race that can't even make sounds—and you're all excited and happy. But you come to a beautiful world full of humans like yourselves, friendly, speaking a language you can understand, and you act as if you were surrounded by perils.''

"Captain, we want the Roharrans to like us and listen to our words. We're afraid we might turn them against us by accident,'' Quarrier said.

"All right. Keep your arms folded whenever you talk, and tell people . . . say that on your homeworld anyone who gestures when he speaks is put to death.''

"But that's not true!''

"No, but it will work. Now, no more questions, please, and no complaints. I want to get you settled, and then I have business to attend to,'' Enskeline concluded, stepping out purposefully.

Enskeline's business took him to a cluster of pale-colored domes in the center of the city, known as the Industrious House of Kamparongsang. He was pleased to find that little had changed since his last visit. The bright, fragrant bushes which adorned the grounds were taller and thicker, shielding the buildings even more effectively from the eyes of curious passersby, but the buildings themselves were just as he remembered them.

He identified himself to the small, silent old man who sat by the public door. The old man smiled a toothless grin of welcome and signaled to a youth to conduct Enskeline inside. They passed through cool, shaded rooms furnished in subdued elegance, and came at last to the inner garden, where the master of the house waited to greet his visitor. He was a stout man, very pale of complexion, with long jet-black hair and quick eyes dark as beads. At the sight of Enskeline, his expression became joyous.

"Kamparongsang Seven Domorie welcomes his friend Jod Enskeline to the house that he must consider his own," he said, stepping forward to clasp the trader's hands, one by one, in both of his. "Anxiously have we awaited your return."

"I've been away from Roharr a long time, even by ship's reckoning. How long is it, planetary?"

"Eighty-six years, my friend. More than a hundred of our tenza. As soon as I learned of your arrival, I examined the records. I knew you would soon be visiting the house of Kamparongsang." Domorie signaled to the servant, who bowed and left them; then to Enskeline he said, "Be seated, please. I have long looked forward to this day. My father often expressed his wish to meet you. His father, Six Domorie, spoke much of you."

"He was a good man and a good friend," Enskeline said, settling on the long low platform opposite his host. "Six Domorie was always fair to me, and he gave me good advice as well."

"I never knew him. My father told me what he said of you."

"Is your father still living?"

"He lives on in the name of my eldest son, Three Butyuga, as I will live in the name of my second son. I am head of the Industrious House of Kamparongsang now."

"It will be a pleasure to deal with you, Seven Domorie. I've brought rare goods with me. You'll be pleased to see them."

"There will be ample time to speak of business, Enskeline. First I must see to your comfort. Will you stay in my house on your visit to Roharr, and consider it your own?"

"I'll be honored to stay with you."

Domorie smiled with unfeigned happiness—hospitality was considered a great virtue on Roharr—and signaled for his servant. Enskeline was ushered down a latticed corridor to one of the smaller domes, where a suite of rooms awaited him. He had stayed here on his last visit, and it looked to him as though the rooms had been kept as he remembered them through all the years of his absence. All was as he recalled it, even the placement of the cushions and the light plaques on the curving walls.

He stripped and bathed, luxuriating in the warm scented waters. When he rose to dress, he found that his traveling outfit had silently been removed and replaced by loose trousers and a tunic matching the colors of the House of Kamparongsang. He was indeed being treated as an honored guest, and he did not doubt that Domorie's inbred desire to be a good host had been stimulated by the information that Enskeline's trade goods consisted of authentic Old Earth books.

Enskeline rested for a time, awaiting the formal request to dine that would come only after sundown. Lying on the soft platform, gazing idly up at the play of reflected light on the domed ceiling, he thought of the woman who had shared this suite as his companion on his last visit. Zalorra was her name. She was a beauty, dark-skinned and pale-haired, with wide blue eyes. Now, if she still lived, she was a very old woman who had long ago forgotten him and all the others she had companioned in her long career. The woman who agreed to serve as his companion this time would also be an aged crone when he next visited Roharr, and his host would be a descendant of Seven Domorie; yet Enskeline himself would be only a few years older than he was now.

He sighed and closed his eyes. In quiet times like this he was tempted to reflect on his life, touching more cultures and races and civilizations than most men knew existed, yet never being fully part of any; always visiting, always on the periphery of life, never fully entering any world.

He sat up abruptly and shook his head in irritation. This was not the time to be thinking of pleasure or philosophizing. There was business to be conducted and information to be sought. Everything else came after . . . even Zalorra.

A formal dinner with a Roharran trader was a long, leisurely affair, as intricate and precisely patterned as the steps of the ritual damura dance. Everything was a part of the experience. The color and intensity of light, the temperature, the shape and texture of the utensils, all changed with each new dish, and the bowl of blossoms in the center of the table was replaced nine times before the last course, a snow-white goblet of hot, sweet black krennabar, was placed before Domorie and his guest.

Though he had eaten a heroic amount and a vast variety of food, Enskeline felt no sense of satiety. Indeed, there was still a mild edge to his appetite, and he knew that this, too, was a calculated element of the dining experience. He and his host would stroll for a time in the private garden; then they would return to the house to discuss business. But first they would eat small, crisp biscuits filled with tart setta seed and drink thick, sweet daarberry wine.

The traders of Roharr were a self-possessed breed, and the House of Kamparongsang was one of the most imperturbable among them. But when the trading was done, Seven Domorie was beaming like a child on its nameday, sitting cross-legged on the platform by the soft light of dawn, a book open on his ample lap and others spread around him in easy reach of his hand. Enskeline sipped his daarberry wine, patted his round and still comfortably filled belly, and smiled on his host like a kindly uncle.

"I knew you'd be pleased to see them, Domorie. They're the oldest I've ever seen or heard of," he said.

"And in such fine condition, Enskeline!" Domorie marveled. "They have been well tended. And the others are in the same condition, you say?"

Enskeline nodded. "Every bit as good as the one in your hands. They were part of a library kept by holy men on a world they call Peter's Rock. They brought hundreds and hundreds of books out with them."

Domorie looked at him, hungry-eyed. Enskeline smiled at the unspoken question, and said, "I may be able to get more, and I'll bring them first to the House of Kamparongsang; I promise you that, my friend."

"You have made us the most important trading house on Roharr, Enskeline. In all his life, my grandfather saw only one book. My father saw none. Now I possess all these at one time!''

"And your son, or grandson, will possess many more when I visit next, if I'm successful. But to get those books I must have something to trade with the holy men, and I don't know where to seek it. I need your help to get information."

"You need only say what you ask."

"It's a long story. Basically, I need two bits of information. I have to know if a certain driveship landed on Roharr—it would have been about two hundred tenza ago, as near as I can figure—and if it did, I want to know where it went."

"I assume that this ship held something that the holy men want."

"Yes. They want it badly enough to give a lot of their books for it. Can you help me?"

"I will speak with my wife and daughters this day, Enskeline. If the information exists, you will have it."

By long Roharran tradition, all matters relating to driveship traffic were in the hands of women, as were banking and agriculture—and, it was said, assassination. Men were in charge of all trade and maritime affairs. There were exceptions, for Roharr was an easy-going world where people did much as they pleased—but generally the tradition was honored. The Kamparongsang women were as influential in the driveship professions as the men were in trade. Enskeline knew that he could depend on their help.

When the servant had refilled their tiny winecups, Domorie dismissed him and Enskeline gave a full account of the schismatics' flight and their theft of the relic. Domorie listened without speaking a word or making any gesture beyond a nod now and then.

"So that's the story," Enskeline concluded, covering a yawn. "That scrap of cloth is the most valuable thing in the universe to those holy men. It's touched the body of their god. And the chest they keep it in may be worth even more than the books they gave me. It's encrusted with precious stones from Old Earth; most of them have never been found anywhere else; they're priceless."

"You speak of great wealth. The books would bring a fortune by themselves. The gems of Earth would bring perhaps even more," said Domorie.

"And we might get it all," said Enskeline, grinning.

"Yes, all. No one else knows of this, I take it?"

"I'm sure the missionaries with me are aware of it, but I don't think they'd mention it to anyone. It's a painful episode in their history."

"But is there a possibility that they seek it?"

"No. I think they really expect that it's going to be returned to them by some miracle. That's the way they think, Domorie."

"Good. You may be sure I will tell no one. The secret is safe between us."

Domorie reached out to clasp Enskeline's hands, one after the other, in both of his in the Roharran gesture of welcome and gratitude. Enskeline returned the gesture. Then, for a time the two men sat in silence, smiling at one another like boys after some successful prank, bemused by the thought of the immense wealth that might one day be theirs. Enskeline laughed softly and sipped his wine. Domorie at last broke the silence.

"You are a true friend to offer to share this fortune with our house, Enskeline."

"Your grandfather was good to me, Domorie. If it hadn't been for him, the blackjackets would have gotten me long ago."

Domorie gestured reassuringly. "The men of the Sternverein will not trouble you while you stay with us, Enskeline. They have learned to walk softly on Roharr since your last visit."

"That's good to hear. I saw a white ship on one of the rings when I arrived. I told my passengers and crew to avoid the blackjackets, just in case. The last thing we want is for that lot to find out about Peter's Rock."

"Indeed, yes! But I think you need not concern yourself with the Sternverein. They are not welcomed on Roharr."

"All the same, they're here."

Domorie responded with a slow gesture, the Roharran equivalent of a careless shrug. "They come here from time to time to remind us of the perils of the universe and the advantages of cooperation with the Sternverein. But their tales of horror do not frighten us, and their blandishments do not tempt us."

"I'm happy to hear that someone is resisting them. The

Sternverein seems to be having considerable success on all the worlds I've heard of.''

"We hear this, too. I must not overstate our position, though. We do not resist them openly or bluntly reject their proposals. They are powerful, and willing to use their power to attain their ends. We of Roharr are like a coy lover who never surrenders, yet never strays quite out of reach. We give them nothing, but encourage them to hope.''

"Very delicate tactics, Domorie.''

"We realize this. But the Sternverein will not last forever. Even now, at the height of their power, internal rivalries weaken them. If we can keep them off Roharr long enough, they will fade away.''

"I hope I live to see that day.''

Domorie took up the decanter and refilled both cups with daarberry wine. "One last drink, Enskeline: to the fulfillment of your hopes. Then you must rest," he said.

They drank and parted. Enskeline walked through the cool, darkened halls to his quarters, feeling pleasantly relaxed and filled with anticipation.

When Enskeline awoke the next morning, he started up at the sight of a slim figure reclining on the platform by the garden window. He had not expected her to be ready so quickly. The sun gleamed warmly on her smooth brown skin and haloed her pale, gold-white hair. "Zalorra," he said in a hushed voice.

"I am here, Joddor," she said, using the intimate form of his name, rising and coming to his arms. "Long have I waited for your return.''

He felt his heart leap at the sight of the tears of unfeigned joy and love in those deep blue eyes. "Zalorra," he said again. "I've thought of you all the time I was away. You're lovelier than ever.''

"I have thought of no one but you, my Joddor," she murmured, taking his face between her cool hands and brushing his forehead with her lips. He pulled her close and drew her gently down beside him.

They rose from the platform at midday to bathe, then dined in the filtered light of afternoon. The days and nights that followed were like a long, sweet dream for Enskeline. He knew that Zalorra—whatever her real name might be, to him she would be only Zalorra—had not been born at the time of his last visit to Roharr. In all likelihood, even her grandparents were not yet living then. She was a companion, trained and experienced in her profession; when Enskeline returned to Roharr, she took up the role her predecessor had played generations ago. While he stayed, she would be his Zalorra, giving him her total love and devotion, sharing memories she had painstakingly learned from the records in the Dome of Companions. When they parted she would weep, and her tears and her sorrow would be real. Her memories of their time together would be added to those at the Dome, and soon she would begin preparing herself for her next companion. When Enskeline returned again to Roharr, his beloved Zalorra would be waiting, her youth and beauty and passionate devotion untouched by time.

Hers was a profession respected on this world. Companions offered to lonely starfarers, isolated from all other relationships by space and time and the unalterable laws of nature, the sensations of love and a life with someone who cared and waited faithfully for every return.

Enskeline surrendered totally to the sweet illusion. For a time he knew no world beyond the private one in which he and Zalorra lived out their love. Her soft breathing at his side was the last sound he heard as he drifted off to sleep; her face was his first sight upon awakening. Domorie was discreetly absent; the servants were invisible yet superlatively efficient; the *Rimjack,* Peter's Rock, and even the prize he pursued were quite forgotten in this happiness.

But events intruded on his sanctuary. One sultry afternoon Zalorra woke him from a light sleep. He reached out for her, but she took his hand and said, "Your host has a message of importance for you, Joddor."

He followed her glance to where his clothing lay neatly folded. Atop it was a black-and-gold blossom, a tasamma flower, used as a symbol of news.

He drew her gently to the platform. "We'll see him after dark, for dinner, Zalorra," he said. "I think I know his message, and it can wait until then."

"The tasamma's stalk is broken, Joddor. The message is urgent," she said, tugging at him.

He rose and found that she was right. Frowning, he began to dress, all the while speculating on what message might induce Domorie to disturb his peace. Once he had started thinking of the possibilities, they seemed to multiply—his ship, his crew, passengers . . . the blackjackets . . . the fugitives. . . . it might be good news, but was more likely to be bad. He embraced Zalorra and went directly to the main dome.

Domorie was waiting. His face bore an expression of solicitude. "Forgive this intrusion on your peace, Enskeline. One of your crewmen arrived with an urgent message."

"You did right to summon me, Domorie. Was it Faranaxx?"

"Not the Quespodon. A human. He is here," Domorie said, motioning to a servant who left the room at once and returned with Isbinder.

"Scragbones is dead, Captain, and Faranaxx hasn't been back to *Rimjack* for nine watches," Isbinder blurted. "I didn't want to trouble you, but I didn't know what else—"

"Trouble me? *Rimjack* is my ship, Isbinder! Why did you wait nine watches?" Before the distraught crewman could answer, Enskeline demanded, "Was it blackjackets who killed Scragbones?"

"No, Captain. He killed himself."

Enskeline closed his eyes and sighed deeply. "Lixian honor," he said.

"That's right. Captain. He said that when he was planetside, he learned that one of his broodmates had avenged his disgrace. I didn't understand much of what he said, but then he asked me and one of the women at the port to act as his family and see that his things got back to Lixis. Then he . . . he just sort of . . . shivered himself to death, Captain! He squatted down and trembled until I thought all his bones would break; and then he died."

"He terminated himself. I've heard of it before."

"It happens often on Roharr," Domorie said. "Many Lixian exiles visit this world, and all inquire about the status of their honor on the homeworld. When their honor is restored, they are prepared to die."

"He gave us things, Captain: a little bottle of his blood, and a name-disk. He made us promise we'd get them to Lixis somehow."

"Your path lies far from Lixis," said Domorie, glancing at Enskeline. "If you entrust those objects to me, I will see that the promise is kept."

Isbinder complied willingly. When he had given the bottle and the disk to Domorie, Enskeline asked him about Faranaxx.

"I don't know, Captain. When he missed his third turn at watch, I knew something had to be wrong. And now, with Scragbones dead and just Waghorne and me, we'll have to—"

"Did you check with the main gate?"

"Yes, sir. No messages from him, or about him."

"Faranaxx isn't bright, but he's dependable. Something's happened to him. He'd never miss a turn on watch intentionally," said Enskeline, talking half aloud, half to himself.

"We will make inquiries. Faranaxx will be found," Domorie said.

"I'd better get back to the *Rimjack* with Isbinder."

"Perhaps it would be best if your crewman went ahead and you joined him later," Domorie suggested.

Enskeline took the hint. He sent Isbinder to the ship. When he and Domorie were alone, he asked, "Do you have information for me?"

"The ship you seek came to Roharr one hundred eighty-four tezas ago. It remained only long enough to take on supplies and left as soon as they were aboard."

"Did you learn the destination?"

"They seemed to have no destination in mind, but I learned something that might be helpful. The captain inquired about planets with Earth colonies. At that time the only such planet in this sector was Huttoi."

"There's been trouble on Huttoi, hasn't there?"

Domorie made a gesture to indicate uncertainty. "There has been conquest, but I have heard nothing of trouble. The Altenorei and their servants simply occupied the planet. The Hutt seem to have accepted the occupation without offering resistance."

"How long ago, Domorie?"

"It is difficult to be exact about such things. The conquest almost certainly occurred after the time the ship of fugitives would have reached Huttoi."

"Any more information?"

"I regret to say that I could learn nothing more."

"You've told me a lot, Domorie, and I'm grateful. I think I'd best get to the ship now and look over the situation for myself. There won't be any trouble over Scragbones's death, will there?"

"We understand Lixian ways, Enskeline. The woman who witnessed his death is of this house; her report will satisfy the ring officials. But it might be well to be cautious until you know what befell the Quespodon."

"I didn't bring a weapon. Do you have one?"

"We seldom use weapons in the city. I will have you watched whenever you leave the house. Do you object?"

"Not at all, Domorie. That's probably the best way. I'm no fighter."

Despite Domorie's apprehension, Enskeline's walk to the ring complex was untroubled. He inspected the *Rimjack* and found everything in order.

Scragbone's body was laid out in the main cargo hold, the only place in the ship where his corpse could lie at full length. Waghorne had covered it. Enskeline lifted the cover and saw an unfamiliar look of peace on the dark, wedge-shaped face of the Lixian. He sighed, laid the cover back in place, and told the crewmen to gather their belongings.

When he had sealed the *Rimjack* and arranged for a guard, he took his companions to report on Scragbone's death. The formalities were completed with an ease that would have surprised him had he not already known the influence of the Kamparongsang women in port affairs.

Outside the ring area he drew Isbinder and Waghorne aside and gave them a generous supply of cashcubes. "I'll send a man from the trading house. He'll take you where it's safe. Relax and enjoy yourselves for the next eleven days. Report back to the *Rimjack* on the twelfth morning, ready to work. We have a long trip ahead of us. If I can't find Faranaxx and get a replacement for Scragbones, we'll all be working extra hard," he said.

"Will the priest-voyagers still be coming along, Captain?" Isbinder asked.

"As far as I know."

"Maybe we could train them to do some of the work—if you can't get a replacement for Scragbones."

"We might have to. I'd rather get an experienced spacehand, but if I can't, we'll have to do what we can. Listen, if you see Faranaxx, or hear anything about him, get word to me immediately. Don't try to do anything on your own."

"Yes, Captain," they said.

"Have a good time. But remember, once you set foot on the *Rimjack*, you'll be working. Be ready for it."

The remaining days on Roharr passed quickly. When Enskeline made his last farewell to Zalorra and started for his ship, sorrow at leaving her was mixed with deep concern for his other problems.

He had learned nothing of Faranaxx. The Quespodon had disappeared without a trace. Enskeline was not a hard master; had Faranaxx wished to leave the *Rimjack*, whatever his reason, Enskeline would not have prevented him. Faranaxx knew that well, and his silent disappearance was for that reason ominous. A busy port city like Ermacene, with strangers constantly arriving and departing, had its share of predators. Those who dealt with slavers knew that a strong Quespodon would always fetch a good price. Thieves found it safest to conceal their crimes by murdering the victims.

The worst part of losing both his experienced crewmen was that he could not risk replacing them, and that meant backbreaking work for all hands on the way to Huttoi. Domorie had been unyielding on that point the very day they had learned of Faranaxx's disappearance, and Enskeline was forced to agree. A new spacehand, however sound his credentials, simply could not be trusted on a mission involving treasures of such magnitude. Enskeline would have to be his own bridgeman, and trust that his new crewmen had learned their duties well enough to carry on unsupervised.

He strode to the ring area with a frown on his face, deep in thought, muttering to himself now and then. The sweet taste of Zalorra's lips was still on his own, and her fragrance still clung to him. He would have preferred to savor his memories of her without distraction. But now he was no longer the lover returned from the stars; he was captain of the *Rimjack*, bound for Huttoi in search of riches beyond imagining.

Loud cries broke into his musing. He looked up and saw the four priest-voyagers waiting by the ring gate, waving and calling an eager greeting. He returned their salute and hurried to join them.

"I didn't expect to see four of you. Have you changed your minds? Coming on the *Rimjack* to find another world?" he asked.

"We're staying on Roharr, Captain Enskeline," Torris said. Our very first efforts have been blessed with great success."

"Got some people to listen, did you?"

"The Grand Selector of Felill has invited us to settle there, and bring our message to all his people," Quarrier said, fairly bursting with eagerness. "There are thousands of people on the island, and many more visiting to trade. By the grace of God, word of our mission will spread quickly on Roharr."

"I'm glad for you, Revers. Just be careful of the blackjackets. I don't think they care much what people believe, but they may not like to see anyone else become influential."

"We seek no worldly power, Captain," said Quarrier.

"They do. It makes them touchy."

"We're in God's hands, Captain. He'll protect us," Torris said confidently.

"I hope so. Ask him to look after us, will you? We need all the protection we can get. Scragbones is dead and Faranaxx has disappeared. We'll all be serving as crew on this trip."

Dallamer and Fielden exchanged a quick startled glance. Fielden said, "We'll be glad to help if we can, Captain." He sounded very uncertain.

"I won't ask the impossible. Waghorne and Isbinder have learned their way around the *Rimjack,* and I know the ship like I know the back of my own hands. We may need you to relieve us now and then, that's all."

The priest-voyagers said their farewells, and Enskeline led Dallamer and Fielden aboard the *Rimjack.* Waghorne and Isbinder were already aboard. The cargo was stored, and the *Rimjack* was cleared for liftoff.

Enskeline delayed for a time, looking out beyond the ring gate, hoping to see the bulky figure of Faranaxx hurrying through the crowds. But he saw no sign of the Quespodon. He left a message with the gate guards, instructing Faranaxx to go to the Industrious House of Kamparongsang. Domorie would see to it that the Quespodon got a decent berth or find him appropriate work downside. Enskeline could do no more.

Late in the morning, the *Rimjack* lifted off from Roharr and vanished into drivespeed, bound for a destination known only to Enskeline. Fielden and Dallamer were exuberant, filled with the prospect of beginning their mission at last, buoyed by the example of their comrades on Sassacheele and Roharr. Isbinder and Waghorne were sweat-drenched and bone-weary, but proud. They had done the work of four crewmen, and done it well enough to win Enskeline's praise. They were experienced spacehands at last.

Once the *Rimjack* was safely into drivespeed and locked on course, Enskeline gave all his thoughts to Huttoi. There he might find the greatest treasure in the galaxy—or bitter disappointment. Then again, it might turn out to be just one more step in a pursuit that would draw him ever onward, to his last breath.

VI. _____

Peter's Rock: The *Sthaga-Renga*

Five peaceful years and seven trisepts after the departure of the white ship, the third visitors came to Peter's Rock. On the last Penanceday of Lent Minor, a squat driveship with a scorched and scurfy hull made a fast, purposeful descent on the landing ring. Scarcely had it locked in when a ramp licked forth. Out of the ship poured a band of humans and humanoids who broke into clusters and set off with deliberate speed, some to the town, some to the monastery, with others on the flanks and to the rear of their comrades.

They were a strange-looking lot, and their appearance grew stranger as it became more distinct. Some were dressed in a fantastic rainbow array; a few wore armor; others were nearly naked. Tiny creatures no higher than a child's waist scurried in twos and threes alongside hulking figures taller and broader than anyone on the planet.

There were males, and females, and creatures of no determinable sex. Some of the newcomers were jet black with golden hair; one was dead white with a brilliant, blazing red mane that flowed like a cloak about his bare shoulders and fell to his waist; others were mottled like pale marble; some were covered in a coat of soft, shining fur. A few looked much like the natives of Peter's Rock, who stood amazed as the strangers fanned out and approached them. Low-slung, sinuous creatures loped silently by the side of some of the humans, and a white birdlike thing perched on the shoulder of one of the black men.

A pair of field workers were the first to speak with the starfarers. They laid down their long-handled hoes, raised their open hands in welcome, and stood smiling as four visitors from the ship encircled them.

"Welcome to Peter's Rock," said the elder worker.

No one replied for a time, though the newcomers exchanged glances when they heard the greeting. A tall man, human in appearance, with a high crest of stiff black hair rising from his otherwise shaven head, at last stepped closer and said, "Pidarok? Make say Pidarok, you here?"

"Peter's Rock. This planet is Peter's Rock," said the field worker slowly, gesturing to encompass their surroundings.

"Pidarok, so." The starfarer said, returning their smile of welcome. He inhaled deeply and let out a long breath. "You Pidarok, good so. Strong good so," he said approvingly.

The homeworlders smiled awkwardly at the others, then turned to one another, uncertain how best to continue. The two loping creatures settled on their haunches at the crested man's side. They had long, slender muzzles and big, wide-set eyes. Their teeth were the teeth of predators. They sat attentively, making no sound but their soft breathing.

The starfarer poked one farmer in the chest and pointed to the monastery. "Him there, you say monserry?" When they returned a look of puzzlement, he said, "Him up there, monserry? Long back come high-talk prayer-man go *Rimjack*?"

"The monastery, yes, that's the monastery up there!" the younger field worker said excitedly. "You've met one of our voyagers, then!"

The starfarer clapped the thick forearm of one of his companions, a burly black man with a lank fringe of deep yellow hair, and said happily, "Him there, monserry, just so like Jammasha tell you! Strong plenty book, and nobody to stand up, only sojai dirt-scuffers like him-him here." He laughed aloud, and with a quick step forward, thrust his hand sharply against the chest of the older man.

"What are you doing? What do you want here?" the man demanded, staggering backward, nearly stumbling.

A short, sharp cry of pain came from the next field and was followed by the long, choked-off scream of a woman. The younger worker stooped to snatch up his hoe, but the starfarers' leader sent him sprawling with a kick that grazed his temple. As he scrambled to his feet, the black man reached out and seemed to brush his hand across the young worker's throat.

The head dropped free and fell to the ground while the body tottered erect for a moment. The killer ducked out of the bright jet of blood that fountained up from the trunk, and the others laughed at the sight.

The older worker turned and began to run straight down the furrow he had been working, heading for the sanctuary of the monastery while he shouted a warning of the invaders. The loping beasts, who had been lapping the blood of the fallen man, set off in pursuit at a word of command; simultaneously, two of the starfarers, tiny humanoids covered with soft gray fur, took aim at his back and let fly with short, broad-bladed knives. One hit below the left shoulder and the other sank into the runner's spine just above the waist. The man gave a single cry and staggered before the beasts struck, hurling him to the ground. One closed his narrow jaws around the man's neck. There came a crack, loud enough for the four invaders to hear. The man twitched for a moment, then was still. From the distance came another sharp cry, quickly cut off.

"Good work, all you," the starfarers' chief said. "Come along, follow Jammasha now to monserry."

Jammasha's party had grown to nine by the time it reached the top of the mountain and stood before the gateway to the monastery. Below them, tiny figures moved across the fields, while others pursued. A plume of smoke rose from the town, then a second. Shouts and cries came faintly to their ears.

Out of breath from the climb, the black man pushed back his golden hair and looked disapprovingly at the rising smoke. "That's sojai work, that burning. Top sojai." Turning to their leader, he went on, "This world's leng guka, like you say. We need a long rest in a nice place. We could pick it clean good and slow, take our time and stay a while. Don't be leng guka if these sojai burn it all down."

"You strong sojai, make say 'stay a while,' " Jammasha answered scornfully. "Quick take monserry book, quick get off. Other him-him maybe come, give trouble."

"The others won't give us trouble. There's no need. Enough here for fifty ships, Jammasha," said the black man.

The white creature on his shoulder unfurled leathery, translucent wings and then delicately furled them again. It turned two of its red eyes on Jammasha and gazed at him, unblinking.

"Jammasha no talking other ship be friend. Talking

blackjacket. Say quick-quick take and go. Blackjacket, him-him
no friend.''

At the mention of their enemies, the group exchanged
apprehensive glances. The black man said, ''Quick-quick
take and go, like you say. We're ready.''

''Good so,'' Jammasha said. He turned and led the way
through the gaping entry.

Inside, the monastery was dim and silent. The little band of
pirates walked warily, weapons ready for instant use, but they
saw no sign of life and heard no footsteps except their own.
Past one empty chamber after another they went, ever inward,
deeper into the monastery.

''Where are the books?'' asked one of the Quiplids.

''Monserry book-hold down-down,'' Jammasha said, pointing to his feet. ''Need find some high-talk man, make him
show where be.''

''There's a way down,'' the other Quiplid said, pointing to
a staircase that opened at the end of a side corridor.

The steps descended into blackness. Digging in his waistband,
Jammasha drew forth a small handlight and switched it on.
With the glowing disk held overhead, he led the others down
until they reached the foot of the steps. They were now in a
wider corridor, from which side passages opened, and in the
third of these passages was another long staircase. When they
descended this, they found themselves in a great open space,
its arched roof lost in darkness, the lower portion faintly lit by
a round window of many colors in the wall ahead of them,
the far wall of a room where small lights burned. To one side
of them was an unbroken wall of living stone; set in the other
wall was a pair of high doors.

''Him here, like be book-hold place,'' said Jammasha.

He dimmed the handlight slightly and stepped forward,
toward the room where the lights shone. As he approached, a
figure took up a stand in the entry, hands half-raised in a
gesture of peaceful supplication. The pirates stopped and
quickly scanned the space all around. At a hiss from its
master, the white creature spread its wings and soared up into
the dark. But no attack came. There seemed to be no one on
this level but themselves and the single brown-robed figure in
the doorway.

''Who you be?'' Jammasha demanded.

"I am Abbot Gossard. I bid you welcome to Peter's Rock and the Monastery of the Holy Sepulcher," the dark figure said, without moving.

"Good so. Him here be book-hold place, you say?"

"If you seek our library and our books, they are behind those doors," the abbot said, gesturing to the high doors. "You are welcome to take what you need."

"That's why we came," said one of the pirates, laughing.

"We offer you no resistance. We wish to harm no one and to see no one harmed," the abbot went on, speaking slowly, reassuringly, but with great urgency in his voice. "We ask only that when you have taken the books you wish, you will leave us in peace. In God's name we ask this."

"Nobody stand up, you say?"

"There will be no resistance, if that is your question. Such is not our way."

"Good so," Jammasha said, coming closer, peering past the abbot's form into the half-lit chapel, surveying it with rapid glances. "Him here, be no book-hold, you say?" he asked casually.

"This is the founder's chapel. The library is in the other room."

Jammasha's hand rested on his waistband for a moment, then flew out and jabbed twice at the abott's chest. Gossard gaped at him, staggered backward, rubbing slowly at his chest while blood oozed between his fingers. Then he fell backwards and lay still.

"High-talk prayer-man lie to Jammasha." The pirate leader pointed to a long table that stood on a raised platform at the center of the chapel. Upon it, opened, lay a massive book covered in red, its pages edged in gold.

"It's only one book, Jammasha. You said we'd find a whole roomful," said one of the others.

"Other more be around. We look." Pointing to the black man and one of the Quiplids, Jammasha said, "You-you, go look where high-talk man say be book-hold."

They had scarcely begun to tear apart the chapel in their search when a wild cry of joy and amazement resounded through the high hallway and echoed in the chapel. Jammasha and the others needed no explanation. They abandoned their work and raced headlong to the other chamber.

Beyond the open doors they saw rank after rank of books packed closely in rows, one above the other, reaching almost to the high ceiling. Books of all sizes, bound in all colors, in all the forgotten languages of Earth—a treasure lost since the time of the great exodus. It was the greatest accumulation of books that any of them had ever seen, beyond anything they had ever hoped to see, enough to buy every one of the crew a ship and crew of his own and a lifetime of pleasure. In their wildest dreams they had never imagined such wealth in a single place, unguarded, theirs for the taking.

Half drunk with the suddenness of their exultation, they reeled into the library and began to tumble the books in heaps on the floor, laughing wildly, shouting wordlessly, thumping one another on the back, clapping their hands. In the din of their celebrating, they did not hear the doors close at their backs with a soft click.

A man stepped from behind the farthest bookshelf to stand at the end of the aisle facing them. He was dressed in the same plain brown robe as the abbot, but he carried a long-barreled pistol, the deadly ripgun that was the standard weapon of Sternverein security troops.

"Who you be?" Jammasha cried, and the others were at once alert and silent, weapons drawn. "How be high-talk prayer-man make with ripgun, you say!"

Jammasha started forward, and the flattened fan-shape of the muzzle came up to point at his chest. He stopped short, hands raised in surrender, and glanced to the side where he could take shelter from the devastating fire of the ripgun. There he saw another armed man at the end of the aisle, weapon raised. From the startled voices of the others, he knew that every aisle was covered, and the loud crash and cursing at his back told him that the doors were shut firmly behind them.

"Sanchon Jammasha, master of the driveship *Sthaga-Renga,* the Justiciars of the Court of Mercy have found you guilty of piracy. The sentence is death," the man facing them recited. At the last word, he aimed.

Jammasha sprang forward, groping for his blade as he moved. He had not taken his second step when his chest was blown open and he was flung to the ground, a corpse. One of the Quiplids had attempted to hurl a knife. He was blasted into a bloody scrap of fur. The flying white creature, diving on one of the troopers, exploded in a red spray. Then all was still. The other stood rigid, hands atop their heads. They had heard the death sentence pronounced on Jammash alone, and they clung to the only hope they saw—surrender.

The door behind them opened, but they dared not turn. Deft hands disarmed them. Rougher hands pushed them into the hall, where men and women dressed in brown, armed with ripguns, lined them up against the stone wall.

The man who had pronounced sentence stood over Jammasha's body. A young woman entered and reported to him.

"The abbot is dead," she said.

"Which one did it?"

She pointed the muzzle of her ripgun at the corpse. "They all swear he did."

"How did Gossard get back in here?"

"He must have known an entrance he never told us about."

The man grunted in agreement. "Do you think he ever suspected what we were doing?" When she shook her head in uncertainty, he went on, "I told him we'd get the townspeople to safety in the forest and no one would offer resistance to the pirates. He and the monks were to go to the caves in the quarry."

"Maybe he thought he could convert the pirates."

"Maybe he did. Well, now we'll have a new abbot. I think it should be Ollenbrook. The Commander said he had a much better attitude than old Gossard."

"Can we manage it?"

"After this, we can manage anything we want," the man said confidently. "Have you any word from town?"

"It's all over. We lost six, they lost twenty-two. We killed all the loping beasts. They mauled two townspeople badly before we got them."

"Prisoners?"

"We have thirteen in town, and the seven outside," she said.

"Did we lose any of ours?"

"No. The six who died were townspeople. The ones we trained fought well."

He nodded, satisfied. "The prisoners have hard work ahead of them. Get two in here to clean this mess up, and have the others brought to town. They'll dig the graves and rebuild everything they've destroyed. They'll leave this place better than it was before they hit.''

"And then?"

He gave a quick, faint smile. "Then we'll relocate them."

For three days monastery and town mourned the death of Abbot Gossard and their companions with profound sorrow. All but the children and the infirm observed a strict fast for that beloved man, and many performed acts of self-mortification to manifest their sorrow. The great bell in the tower of the monastery tolled each hour with deep leaden groanings, as if the lifeless metal itself were moved to woeful utterance by his brutal slaying and the deaths of their fellows.

Then, at dawn on the fourth day, all the bells on Peter's Rock burst into merry music to celebrate the seating of the new abbot. The election of the vigorous young Ollenbrook came as a surprise to the townspeople, who had anticipated the choice of someone older and more mindful of tradition. But when it became known that Abbot Gossard, with his dying breath, had urged the election of Ollenbrook, the logic of the choice became apparent.

Ollenbrook was a close friend of the people from the white ship. He had personally instructed several of them in the elements of the faith. Being a younger man—the youngest abbot since the great schism—he was more favorably inclined toward the suggestions of the newcomers than the cautious Gossard had been.

Through the long hot summer, under the eyes of stern and watchful guards, the captives rebuilt and replanted. When all had been restored, a delegation from the town, led by three of the ship-settlers, urged that a second landing ring be built. A group of monks, and some of the townspeople, wanted the pirate ship to remain on the ring, arguing that as long as it did, another raider could land only at considerable risk. The ship-settlers pointed out that the *Garrashaw* was to return, and this precaution would make it difficult for their friends to land, as well as their enemies. Without the *Garrashaw,* no new priest-voyagers could carry the faith to the stars. Abbot Ollenbrook listened carefully to both factions and decided on a compromise. The second ring would be built, but the ring complex would be placed under permanent guard by the ship-settlers and those townspeople they had trained for such work. Thus Peter's Rock would enjoy the opportunity for peaceful commerce while preserving security.

The principle of the landing ring was simple, requiring no advanced technology for its construction. Provided they could measure accurately, make and work simple alloys, and anchor the parts securely, even a primitive race could construct a serviceable landing ring. It was strenuous work and was assigned to the captives, under close supervision. While the work went on, the pirate ship—renamed the *Marystar* in honor of the trisept of its liftoff—was sent into orbit around the planet as a training ship for some of the settlers. Abbot Ollenbrook thought it altogether fitting that the vessel that had brought death and suffering to Peter's Rock should serve as an instrument to carry the faith to other worlds.

On the last Almsday of Third Pentecost, having spent two full trisepts in slow orbit of the planet, the *Marystar* gently descended and locked securely into the new landing ring. In the celebration that followed, even the captives were participants: they were allowed a measure of wine in recognition of their work. Whatever their crimes, they had built the ring well.

Now, with the work done, the question of their fate became timely. Some had adopted the faith of Peter's Rock. There were those among the monks, and even a few townspeople, who expressed their hope that the converts would be accepted by the community. They had shown repentance, their advocates argued, and deserved forgiveness. But there were many who felt that a year's constructive work and an outward show of contrition were small atonement for the lives taken in the pirate raid. The final decision rested with Abbot Ollenbrook. He took much thought over it. At last he summoned Saxe Rannlock, leader of the ship-settlers, and asked his advice.

"I've thought about it myself, Abbot, and I've discussed it with some of the townspeople and the monks. I think the best solution is to isolate them—send them into exile in some remote part of the planet," Rannlock said as they sat at dusk in the abbot's quarters.

"That possibility never occurred to me," Ollenbrook confessed. "I fear I have much to learn."

"A problem like this has never arisen on Peter's Rock until now. There was no reason for you to think about it."

"True, Rannlock, but no excuse for me. I find myself unprepared to deal with so many matters. I'm fortunate to have you and your companions here. You give me the benefit of your experience, and it's so much greater than mine. If it had not been for your presence on Peter's Rock . . . We owe you much, and our debt grows."

"This is our chosen home, Abbot. When we help you, we help ourselves and our children as well."

"Regarding your suggestion: where could these pirates be exiled? Would it not be better to build some place to hold them?"

"I think not. As I said, I've given this some thought. We could not trust them to build their own prison, obviously. Therefore it would require our own labor, which we can't spare. This world needs workers, and a man in prison is a wasted worker. But exiles, on the other hand, must build their own shelters, raise their own food—eventually, they become a productive community. This seems to be the best solution for all of us."

Ollenbrook thought for a time, and then said, "I can see no objection to the idea. But where would the place of exile be?"

"I can think of at least four possibilities. Are you familiar with the maps we've been making?"

The abbot sighed and made a weak gesture of frustration. "I know of the work, but I've had no time . . ."

"No need for you to study them. If you wish it, I'll take care of this."

Ollenbrook looked up. The expression on his pale, drawn face was that of a man delivered from a wearisome task. "I would appreciate that, Rannlock. I have so much to do, and you know more about these things."

"I'm happy to serve. If there's anything more I can do, please tell me."

"Perhaps . . . perhaps, if you think it wise, you would train more of the townspeople as defenders. If another raid should come— You may think me fearful, but I was much shaken by Abbot Gossard's death and by the wanton destructiveness of the raiders. I've forgiven them, and I pray each day that God will forgive them, but I cannot forget the horror of their deeds. If another attack came . . .''

"We will be ready, I promise you."

"And if it could be done without the taking of life. . . . We must not meet violence with violence."

"That's our wish, too."

"Then I place the safety of the monastery and the settlement in your hands, Rannlock," said the abbot with obvious relief, rising and smiling up at the other man. "I trust you to bring the captives to a place of exile."

"I'll choose a site and outfit an expedition at once. I'll report to you personally when the prisoners are secured and see to it that you're protected while I'm gone."

Rannlock was prompt to fulfill his word. On the second morning after his visit with the abbot, he left the settlement at the head of a small caravan. The sixteen surviving prisoners, each carrying a heavy pack, were lined up under the eyes of twelve ship-settlers, all of them armed. They were to leave for a nine days' walk to the seacoast, where they would be conveyed to a remote, fertile island and left there without boats or the means to build them. They carried farming tools and seeds and extra clothing: all they needed to fend for themselves and survive. Some of the settlers were present to watch them depart; a few even called out to wish them well.

For two days they traveled across the low, rolling hills and wooded groves that surrounded the settlement. Then they reached the uplands. Soon they were crossing bare stony ground, with a steady breeze in their faces and enough chill in the air to liven their pace. There was a good bit of talk; prisoners and guards chatted freely, in almost a friendly manner.

On the seventh day of travel they came to a crevasse. It was not wide, but it was very deep. Rannlock dropped a firecube into it. The flame diminished and finally disappeared without a sign of impact. They followed the crevasse for a time, then Rannlock called a rest halt.

The prisoners dropped where they stood, exhausted by their burdens. They were so weary that they did not notice their guards moving off and lining up about seven meters away. Rannlock's voice roused them instantly, bringing them to shocked awareness.

"Prisoners, hear. As crew of an outlaw driveship, you are guilty of piracy. The Justiciars of the Court of Mercy have condemned all pirates to death," he proclaimed.

The pale man with the long mane of bright red hair sprang to his feet and shook his fist. "Liars! We're to be taken into exile!"

"Your exile is at the bottom of that crevasse. You'll have no second chance to destroy worthier people than yourselves," said Rannlock.

"Stinking blackjacket assassins!" one of the others cried.

"Prepare to execute sentence," Rannlock ordered, stepping into line with his companions and raising his ripgun.

"Let's get them!" the pale man shouted, springing forward. The others clambered to their feet, close behind him.

"Execute!"

Nine of the prisoners were hurled over the edge of the crevasse by the ripgun missiles. The rest were sent tumbling and sprawling, torn and broken by the terrible impact of the Sternverein's weapons. The roar of the volley dissipated, and soon all was still.

Rannlock checked the bodies one by one for signs of life, following the prescribed routine, though he knew well that nothing of flesh and blood could survive a short-range burst from a ripgun. These weapons were designed to destroy anything they were turned upon. With his inspection completed, he ordered the rest to secure their weapons.

"Over the edge with these," he said.

"What about their packs?" a woman asked.

"Everything goes over. Use their water bags to wash away the bloodstains. There's to be no trace of this lot. As far as anyone is ever to know, they're exiled on the Isle of Penitents."

The women, Galien, his second-in-command on this mission, saw to it that the order was carried out. When all was done, and they had reassembled for a rest, she spoke to him privately.

"This was well done, Saxe. Is there a chance that anyone might reach the Isle of Penitents and find no sign of the exiles?"

He shook his head. "I was on the expedition that discovered it not long after we arrived, and I can tell you that no one's going to set foot on that island for a long time. I was raised on a water world and spent most of my early years on a boat; but I never encountered currents or reefs like the ones around the Isle of Penitents. We very nearly lost our boat going out, and again coming back. No one among the original settlers would dare the trip.''

"Then the secret is safe,'' said Galien.

"It is. I don't think Ollenbrook would question us, in any case. He's so glad to have us here to defend him and solve his problems, he wouldn't dare risk offending us.''

Galien nodded. "This mission has gone well.''

"Because of the Commander's planning. Cormasson worked it all out. He knew there'd be a raid, and he knew the effect it would have on these people. It's gone exactly as he said it would.''

"When it comes to getting inside an enemy's mind and working out just what they plan to do, Cormasson is uncanny. He can outguess anyone.''

"And not just an enemy. He read the monastics like a screen. Told me how to get Ollenbrook into the abbot's post and how to handle him afterward.''

"We're lucky to serve under a man like that.''

"Cormasson will be returing in about a year. We ought to have a good situation report for him if things keep going as they've gone so far.''

"We surely will. And at first . . . I have to admit, when I first saw the monastics and heard them, I thought we'd meet opposition. Nothing violent, of course, but I expected much less cooperation, or at least a grudging attitude toward us and our efforts. It's one thing to bring the Sternverein to people who have nothing, but these people believe that they have everything!''

Smiling drily, Rannlock pointed out, "They don't have driveships.''

"No. That's our advantage. But they've held to one belief for centuries. They care about the driveships only because with them, they can spread their faith. That's the only thing that really matters to them: their religion. I was certain they'd reject the Sternverein as . . . as a kind of rival . . something competing for their followers' loyalty.''

"Better for them they didn't. The Sternverein wants this world.''

"I know that. I'm surprised we've taken it so easily, that's all,'' said Galien.

"Thank Cormasson for that," Rannlock said, climbing to his feet and stretching lazily.

"Where do we go now, Saxe?" Galien asked, rising at his side.

"We'll stay out for a trisept, then head back. I have everything we'll need cached at a campsite near the sea. We can relax for a time. We've earned it, I think."

The year passed without further incident. No new visitors came to Peter's Rock, and there was little talk of the pirates. People preferred to forget that day of horror, though they remembered the lessons it had taught.

A new and different spirit came over the mild folk of Peter's Rock. The guards on the landing ring were vigilant at all hours. The people of the village, encouraged by the abbot, learned the tactics of the ship-settlers and familiarized themselves with their fearsome weapons to the extent that almost everyone on the planet—even some of the monks—became capable of defending their world in the event of a new attack.

Now and then, on special days, the ship-settlers put aside their plain working garb and donned their black uniforms for a ceremonial parade. They made an impressive sight. The onlookers, accustomed to the splendor and pageantry of their own festive days, were fascinated by the austerity and precision of the starfarers' rituals. Curiosity grew, and the men and women from the white ship were urged to talk about their organization and describe its history and traditions. At first reluctant, they eventually acceded to their neighbors' wishes. In a very short time the songs and wisdom of the Sternverein were almost as familiar on Peter's Rock as were the ways of the monastery.

On the day the *Garrashaw* returned, the garrisoned men and women were present at the ring, uniformed and in tight formation, to greet their comrades and their commander. Abbot Ollenbrook and his prior stayed to the side, observers of the welcoming ceremony rather than participants in it. All around the ring area people of the village gathered in loose, mobile clusters. To them, the return of the white ship was an occasion for celebration. They were safer than ever now; their protectors were present in full force.

Ollenbrook looked on with mixed feelings. All his life he

had studied and pondered the question of evil; but his intellectual exercises had not prepared him for the reality that the pirate raid had brought to Peter's Rock. He had been badly shaken by that experience, and he could not forget his fear. He wanted these warriors of the Sternverein, with their iron discipline and their unimpassioned fidelity to duty, to stand between him and the horrors that threatened invisibly overhead. Their weapons intimidated him; their cool efficiency made him conscious of his own inadequacy; but they were strong and brave, and with them on this world he was safe.

He watched Cormasson pass down the ranks of uniformed ship-settlers, greeting each one warmly, exchanging a few words, nodding with approval, now and then smiling in that sudden way. Watching Cormasson, the abbot felt a momentary doubt. It would be so easy for these people to seize the monastery, the village, everything on this planet, if they so wished. No one could resist them, and few would see any reason for resistance. It could all be theirs, the work of centuries surrendered in one helpless gesture.

Ollenbrook was immediately suffused with shame. This was an unworthy suspicion. The Sternverein had saved them all from certain destruction. The ship-settlers had become exemplary members of their society. They had never failed to show respect for his office, always assisted willingly, and given beyond asking. He had only to mention a need, a problem, a difficulty, and Rannlock or Galien or one of the others was on hand to help. To suspect such goodness was a sign of his own infirmity.

He frowned and rubbed his brow, as if to erase the outward signs of his inner weakness. He could feel his prior's sidelong glance of concern, but he ignored it and fixed his eyes on Cormasson, thinking on the words of welcome he would say to him.

Cormassion was pleased with his troopers. They had performed superbly. To judge from their appearance and their greetings to him, they had thrived on this mission. Most of them had families by this time and had extended their influence in the community. Seven were in charge of the priest-voyagers' training for the forthcoming journey; two had themselves progressed more than halfway to ordination as priest-scholars. He was proud of their work, and he told them so.

Abbot Ollenbrook greeted him cordially. As they walked to the monastery, Ollenbrook said, "No doubt you've heard of Abbot Gossard's death."

"I have, and it saddens me. He was a good man," Cormasson replied.

"He died for the faith."

"So I gathered. I hope you'll be able to give me a full account. I did admire Gossard. From what my people say, you were a good choice to replace him."

Ollenbrook, with a deprecatory gesture, said, "I fear I'm a much less effective abbot than my predecessor. I have a great deal to learn."

"You seem to know the most important thing for a leader to know. You know when you must do a thing yourself and when you can entrust it to others. I've seen men and women trying to rule whole worlds without knowing that, and those worlds were badly ruled. Peter's Rock is well ruled, Abbot. Don't undervalue yourself."

"You are kind, Commander."

"I say what I see."

"I thank you. Will you remain long on Peter's Rock?"

"Not long, Abbot. In truth, there's little for me to do here. I'll leave supplies and equipment. I have a few more of our people who wish to settle here—if you have no objection."

"How could I object? Your people have helped us in many ways. Had it not been for them, we might all have been killed or enslaved. Everything might have been lost."

"I'll be getting a full report on the raid from my people. I would greatly appreciate hearing anything that you or anyone else from the monastery might be able to add."

"Of course, Commander."

"After that I'll be ready to lift off as soon as is convenient for your priest-voyagers."

Ollenbrook brightened as these words. "Then you will take our missionaries with you this time?"

"That's what I agreed to do, Abbot. We can take fifty-two aboard the *Garrashaw,* and as the word is spread among the white fleet, you'll have other ships coming to Peter's Rock to take more of your people."

The mission of the monastery was to begin in earnest. Ollenbrook was so moved by the prospect—and by shame at his doubts about these brave and generous starfarers—that he could not speak. He clasped Cormasson's hand, nodded, and walked on at a faster pace, eager to welcome the men and women of the *Garrashaw* with all the hospitality at his command.

Rannlock and Galien reported to the records center of the *Garrashaw* where Zuern awaited. Cormasson soon joined them. He took a seat and listened without interrupting while they reported on events during his absence. Only when their lengthy preliminary report was complete did he speak—to praise them for their work.

Zuern then took over, questioning them in close detail, playing and replaying the soundscriber transcription as she checked response against response, expanding here, compressing there, collating the successive layers of material into a third account. Cormasson watched, silent once again as he observed the troopers, savoring Zuern's expert skill as she wove raw data into a tight, cohesive account of the mission.

At last Zuern switched off her machines and said, "I have all I need for the moment, troopers. I'll see you again when I've checked it over. There may be a few points to clear up." Turning to Cormasson, she asked, "Does the Commander have anything to add?"

"I do, Zuern," said Cormasson, rising and taking a seat directly facing the troopers. "I listened very carefully, and I heard no reference to the relic that was carried off by the dissidents who deserted Peter's Rock."

"I made none, Commander," Rannlock said. Galien added, "Nor did I."

"Have you heard such an object mentioned by anyone?" Cormasson asked.

Rannlock frowned in concentration, and at last shook his head. "They speak of those people very seldom, Commander. Schismatics, they call them."

"I know what they call them. I'm concerned with the object they took when they left Peter's Rock."

"Was it some kind of image? A picture of a face?" Galien asked abruptly.

"It may have been. Tell me what you know."

After a momentary pause to collect her thoughts, she said, "When we had cleared the monastery of all known pirates, I took a squad through from top to bottom to make sure all was secure. I had four troopers, three of the settlers we had trained, and a monk to guide us. We were in the chapel, where Gossard had been killed. The pirates had done a lot of damage, and the monk was very disturbed by it. He spoke of desecration by the shedding of blood. Apparently some ceremony would be required before the chapel could be used again as a holy place. One of the settlers said something. . . . I can't recall his exact words. He was trying to comfort the old monk; he said that maybe it was by God's grace that the schismatics had taken the reliquary away with them. I think *reliquary* was the word he used, Commander. It's unfamiliar to me."

"Go on, Galien."

"Then he started to say that the pirates, in their ignorance, would probably have destroyed the shroud bearing the sacred image—I'm sure of those words, though they made no sense to me—thinking that the value was all in the reliquary. The monk told him to say no more. He seemed upset that the man had even mentioned these things."

"Anything more?" Cormasson asked.

"No, Commander. I never heard any further reference to shroud or reliquary from anyone."

Cormasson turned to the other trooper. "And you, Rannlock—have you ever heard anyone mention these things, even indirectly? Think hard. It may be very important."

"No, never. But I recall something, a very small incident. It may be all imagination, Commander . . ." Rannlock said, looking uneasy.

"I'll judge for myself."

"Just after Ollenbrook became abbot, we visited the chapel. About a dozen monks were working on repairs. When we entered, there was a sudden silence; then they resumed their talk. It was a very small incident; at the time, I thought nothing of it. But it seemed as though they changed the subject as soon as they saw me enter. As if there was something I mustn't hear. I can't be sure of this, Commander, but taken with what Galien said, it may be significant."

"It may, Rannlock. Can either of you recall anything more?"

Rannlock turned to Galien. "You mentioned something to me when we had disposed of the last pirates. You said you had never expected Peter's Rock to be brought over so easily. Perhaps you should tell the Commander."

She nodded, and turning to Cormasson, said, "I was speaking of a suspicion I felt at the very beginning of this mission when I first went among these people and learned their ways. They're united in a very firm belief. Not all believe with the same intensity, of course—some of the villagers scarcely believe at all—but there really is no alternative point of view on Peter's Rock. In a way, Commander . . . it's hard to explain exactly, but this world reminds me of Occuch."

"Explain, Galien."

"Everyone on Occuch belongs to the Sternverein. We're all loyal to it, and that binds us to one another. These people are the same about their faith."

"Why did this trouble you?"

"It occurred to me that if strangers came to Occuch and tried to tell us that there was a different way—a better way—of looking at things, they wouldn't get very far. They'd probably meet strong opposition. But we were made welcome on Peter's Rock, and listened to."

"Can you think of reasons why?" Cormasson asked.

"They need our driveships, of course. But they could pay for passage. They don't need to be friends in order to use our ships, they just have to avoid being enemies."

"They want our protection, too," Rannlock pointed out. "Ollenbrook was badly frightened by that raid, and he's not the only one."

"But they were friendly and receptive from the very beginning, long before the raid," Galien said.

"I understand your thinking, Galien, but can you support it with anything tangible? Have you seen or heard anything that makes you doubt the sincerity of these people in accepting the Sternverein?"

"Nothing at all, Commander."

"Do you still feel this way?"

She paused before saying, "No. I think they genuinely

respect and trust us. I suppose I simply didn't expect things to go so smoothly.''

Cormasson rose and said, ''For the present, I'm assuming that that's the true explanation for what you perceive. This has been an almost perfect operation. It's only sensible to look closely when things go so well.''

''Will that be all, Commander?'' she asked.

''For the present, yes. When Zuern has taken all the individual reports and collated them, we'll meet here to hear the final version. If nothing turns up between now and then to justify suspicion, we'll consider Peter's Rock to be secure for the Sternverein.''

Zuern was busy for much of the next trisept, interviewing each of the ship-settlers, questioning, checking, building individual bits of data into a supplement to Rannlock's and Galien's earlier accounts. When her work was done, Cormasson heard it through. It contained not one reference to the relic or the schismatics' ship, not even a suggestion that they might exist.

The commander was troubled. Gossard had mentioned the relic at their first meeting, but never again. It seemed that now its very existence was being carefully concealed; such absolute avoidance of all mention could not, to Cormasson's mind, be fortuitous.

He racked his brain for the reason why the shroud was being kept secret from the Sternverein while the monks showed perfect trust in every other way, but he could come up with nothing. There was no sign of doubt or suspicion anywhere, from anyone. Ollenbrook had placed the very survival of the planet in the hands of the Sternverein—why, then, did he withhold the existence of the shroud? Cormasson pondered long, and concluded that the answer lay with the abbot. He visited Ollenbrook the following day. He came directly to the point.

''In my first meeting with Abbot Gossard, he spoke of a relic taken from Peter's Rock by your schismatics. Since then, I've never heard the relic mentioned. I've come to ask you why,'' he said.

''I don't understand, Commander,'' the abbot responded.

''I'll speak more plainly. Men and women of the Sternverein

have risked their lives to save the monastery and the people of Peter's Rock. We've proven our good faith many times over. Yet it appears to me that you conceal the existence of your greatest treasure from us as if we were thieves,'' Cormasson said coolly.

"No, Commander! Believe me, that is not the case, not at all!'' Ollenbrook said, greatly perturbed. He half rose, then fell back in his seat and looked at Cormasson imploringly.

The commander gave him a smile of reassurance. "If you say so, Abbot, I believe you. Can you tell me the reason, then, for the silence on this subject?''

"It was not intentional, Commander, I assure you. We trust you completely. The fault is mine. All mine.''

Cormasson made no response. He waited in silence for a time, and Ollenbrook, without raising his eyes, said, "You must know, Commander, that I became abbot suddenly. It was a great surprise to me to learn that Abbot Gossard named me his successor in his last moments. He knew my failings.''

"Perhaps he saw a strength beyond those failings.''

"Perhaps he did. I have not yet discovered it in myself,'' Ollenbrook said. He sighed, then went on, "I took office in a difficult and fearful time. I was utterly unprepared. I knew of the shroud and its taking, but my knowledge was vague. It was all so long ago; surely the shroud is lost to us forever. It seemed to me that to speak of it at all would be to increase the danger of future attacks on Peter's Rock. There would be more death and suffering. I told myself that it was God's will that the shroud was taken from us, and that no amount of talking would bring it back.'' He raised his eyes. "In truth, Commander, I feared its return.''

"Understandable, Abbot. It would be a terrible responsibility, even with my troopers here to protect it and you.''

"So I told myself. Did I do right?''

"I cannot judge that. Tell me, Abbot—did the trader and the missionaries who left with him know of the relic?''

"The priest-voyagers must have known, but they would not speak of it carelessly. Whether or not Enskeline was told, I cannot say. I doubt it.''

"Why?''

Ollenbrook frowned. "He was said to be a fair man, honest in his dealings with Abbot Rudlor. So say the records of those times. But he was a trader; his interest was in gain, not in things of the spirit. Knowledge of the reliquary in which the shroud reposes might have aroused avarice in him. I can only say that, in Abbot Rudlor's place, I would not have told him.''

Cormasson rose. The abbot looked up apprehensively. "Thank you, Abbot, for speaking so frankly. I will say nothing of this talk, or of the shroud, to anyone.''

The talk with Ollenbrook confirmed Cormasson's decision. If the shroud still existed, it must be found and taken for the Sternverein. Its hold over Ollenbrook, who knew it only as a remote legend, was proof enough of its power. Its religious significance was a matter of one's belief; its material worth was probably exaggerated; but its potential for danger, should it fall into the wrong hands, was too great to be ignored. The shroud could become a threat to the peace and order the Stenverein was imposing on world after world.

There were those in the Sternverein—in positions remote from combat—who scoffed at the danger of fanatics. Cormasson, who had fought against the white giants of Hingwoll III, knew better. Given a belief, a banner steeped in legend, and the dim half-truths of a patchwork history, a clever leader could rally the gullible and use them for any purpose. The Sternverein stood for order; all who opposed it threatened that order. Nothing that might aid the enemies of order could be left unguarded.

He departed on the *Garrashaw* with his mission fixed in his mind: find the shroud. He left behind him a planet and people under the growing influence of the Sternverein.

VII. _____

Huttoi: The Third Mission

The *Rimjack* was the only ship locked in the six-ring complex on Huttoi. The complex was large and generously staffed with people who appeared to have little to do. Nevertheless, Enskeline and his passengers and crew were kept waiting two full days for permission to disembark, and they waited the better part of another day in a five-sided shedlike building in a remote corner of the port area for an official to clear them for trade and travel on the planet.

Enskeline had not been on Huttoi before, but he had a general knowledge of the planet's recent history. When he had learned, on Roharr, that it was to be his next destination, he set about seeking more detailed information. There was little to be had. Sometime about a century ago by Roharran reckoning, an alien race called the Altenorei had occupied Huttoi. By all accounts, the occupation had been peaceful; in effect, it was a mass resettlement from the overcrowded Altenorei homeworld onto sparsely settled Huttoi, where a small human colony comprised the only higher life form.

The Altenorei were a race of thinkers, not workers. Work was left to a subject race, the Nandra. The day-to-day running of affairs on Huttoi was entirely in the hands of the Nandra, and it was they who dealt with any visitors. The Nandra were said to be humanoid in appearance, devoted to their masters, and contemptuous of all offworlders.

The port official came to the building where the crew of the *Rimjack* had been waiting, a human trailing close behind dressed in garments as dark and loose as the Nandra's. The Nandra was indeed humanoid in appearance. Enskeline's first impression was of great elegance and grace.

115

The Nandra had an elongated face, hard-featured and blue-tinted, with markings of rank on its high, narrow forehead. Pendulous, fleshy palps fringed its long ears, which were set close against its head. Its manner was that of someone performing an unpleasant task against his better judgment; alien features did not conceal the Nandra's distaste at the sight of the visitors. It set to work at once without greeting or explanation, signaling to the human to begin.

The human interpreter—presumably a Hutt—hurried through the questions. He seemed to be paying little attention to the responses and did not bother to translate every one for the benefit of the Nandra. Enskeline was cautious in his replies, suspecting that the Nandra might understand starfarers' pidgin very well but prefer to listen to visitors with its knowledge unrevealed.

The interpreter spoke to all five. Waghorne and Isbinder clearly did not interest him, but he probed the priest-voyagers with more searching questions. Fielden seemed naturally to fall into the role of spokesman, while Dallamer remained deferentially silent. When Fielden told of their purpose in visiting Huttoi, the interpreter stopped him and turned to confer inaudibly with the Nandra. After a brief exchange which appeared to annoy the Nandra, the interpreter addressed Fielden in a petulant tone.

"Your language is meaningless to us. Explain your intentions in a clear statement."

"We wish to bring the word of God to the people of Huttoi."

"Do not speak of this world as Huttoi. Its name is Tenorrask, to honor the homeworld of the Masters," said the interpreter. "And who is this god, that you wish to bring us his word?"

"The Supreme Being. The Creator of all things."

Coldly, contemptuously, the interpreter said, "The name of the creator of all things is Valatule, not 'god.' Valatule reveals Itself only to the minds of the Altenorei. Our Masters graciously share the knowledge with the Nandra and their servants. It will not please us, or the Masters, to have offworlders speak of their superstitions."

"Do you forbid us to speak?" Fielden asked.

"You may speak of anything you wish. The Nandra do not learn from offworlders, and you will never be admitted to the presence of a Master. I tell you that it will not be pleasing to the Nandra. That is enough to say.''

Enskeline thought it best to get off this subject. "May we travel freely?" he asked.

"You may travel wherever Hutt are permitted to travel. Keep to the lowlands. All elevated areas are restricted to the Nandra. You require permission of the Port Overseer to enter them. This permission is denied. You may enter only five-sided buildings. Do so only in the company of at least two Nandra. You are never to enter a building with any other number of sides. Under no circumstances are you to attempt to see or speak with one of the Masters. Do you understand what I say?'' the interpreter demanded in a sharp, angry voice.

"We understand,'' Enskeline replied.

"Then leave us and go about your work.''

"What about our ship?''

"Your ship is nothing to us. If you are fearful of thieving Hutt, secure it in some suitable way. Nandra do not stand guard over offworlder vessels.''

"What about Hutt? Can I hire a few Hutt to guard my ship?''

"Speak no more of Hutt. We do not deal with them.''

"Aren't you of the Hutt?''

The interpreter flushed and glared at Enskeline. The trader noticed a quick flicker of the Nandra's narrow, down-drawn eyes and wondered if this was a sign of amusement at the lackey's annoyance. The interpreter pulled his loose outer garment about his shoulders, drew himself up, and said, "My family have assisted the Nandra with the Masters' work since the Masters first came to this world. The Nandra, who are privileged to speak to the Masters, do not lower themselves to learn the speech of other races. When it is necessary to speak to Hutt, or related races, I am privileged to serve as interpreter. I am accepted by the Nandra, and my services are valued. They do not consider me Hutt. I am not Hutt.'' He cast a hateful glance at the five starfarers, then stepped to the other side of the Nandra. The interview was over. The Nandra and its human follower stalked away without a backward glance.

"Welcome to Huttoi,'' Enskeline muttered.

"He doesn't like us very much, does he, Captain?" Isbinder asked.

"I don't think he likes himself very much, either. Can't blame him for that," Enskeline said, looking after the human in Nandra attire, striding behind his alien master. "The Nandra don't think much of anyone but themselves and their Altenorei masters. I knew that, but I didn't expect to find turncoat Hutt doing their work for them. Renegade humans are always nasty to deal with."

"Perhaps we should take our message first to the Hutt," Dallamer suggested.

"They might listen to you," Enskeline said. "But you can be certain that if the Hutt accept your message, the Nandra will reject it."

"What do you suggest, then?" Fielden asked.

"I have no suggestions about your preaching. That's your business. But I think our first priority is to find a place to stay; the Nandra certainly won't offer us hospitality. Then we'll eat, clean up, and get some rest. And then we'll see what we can find out."

What was easy to suggest proved difficult to accomplish. There were no Hutt in the settled area near the rings; it appeared that few had followed the example of the interpreter. Places where Nandra lodged were forbidden to all offworlders. Those establishments that did deign to offer shelter charged exorbitantly for dirty lodgings and foul food and ignored all complaint. After three wretched days of this, Enskeline, his crewmen, and the priest-voyagers took stock of the situation.

"I can't hold my temper much longer, Captain," said Waghorne. "The next Nandra who downtalks me, I'll put my boot in his stupid blue face."

"You'd probably be killed on the spot."

"I wouldn't die alone. I'd take Nandra with me," Waghorne said fiercely.

"Yes, and then the Nandra would kill all of us. And that interpreter would look on and cheer. You have to learn control, Waghorne. Like these two," Enskeline said, nodding to indicate the priests.

"I'm no holy man."

"Neither am I, but I want to stay alive and do business. If

you're going to live a starfaring life, you have to learn to control your anger. If you can't do that, you won't last."

"The Nandra are not evil, Captain, they simply see things in a different way," said Dallamer. "In time, we'll come to understand one another."

"First you have to get them to listen to you."

"That will come in time. God brought us to Huttoi for a reason, Captain. We must not lose faith."

"The *Rimjack* brought you to Huttoi, Rever. It can bring you to another world if this one turns out bad. I know it wasn't part of the agreement," he said, raising a hand to forestall their objection, "but I wouldn't abandon you on Huttoi if you wanted to leave."

"We'll stay, Captain. But we thank you for your offer."

Fielden said, "Rever Dallamer and I have been discussing the possibility of bringing our message to the Hutt. What do you think of that, Captain?"

"I don't think you have much choice."

They were all silent for a time; then Isbinder said, "Captain, something bothers me. About the port and the landing rings. I can't figure it out."

"What do you mean?"

"These people don't seem to want us on their planet. We're human, so they say we're Hutt and treat us like dirt. But you told me that nearly all free traders are human, and most blackjackets are human. Isn't that so?"

"That's right, Isbinder."

"Then, it doesn't make sense. They dislike all humans, and they don't seem to like anyone else any better. They don't want to trade, or even talk. But they keep the rings ready and have a staff waiting around the port even when the rings are empty. Why, Captain?"

Enskeline scratched at the base of his topknot. "Maybe . . . maybe they want everything ready in case another ship should come from the homeworld," he suggested, not sounding very confident.

"But you said that was all over long ago," Waghorne pointed out.

"Yes. Yes, it was. Well, maybe . . . maybe they . . ." Enskeline frowned, pondering the question, then suddenly tensed. "Slavers," he said in a low voice. He glanced at the

others. The fear in his eyes was naked for them to see. "The
Nandra may be keeping them clear for slavers. And you can
be sure that any slaves the Nandra are selling will be taken
from among the Hutt—humans like ourselves."

"Captain, slavery was abolished centuries before anyone
left Earth!" Dallamer exclaimed.

"What happened on Earth doesn't mean anything out here,
Rever. Slavery is practical on some worlds. There's profit to
be made, so there are slavers."

"That interpreter was Hutt. He couldn't possibly be involved in enslaving his fellow humans, Captain."

"You should know history better than any of us, Rever.
Do you really believe that?"

Dallamer turned away, silent under Enskeline's cold, knowing eyes. The others were suddenly uneasy.

"Let's get off this planet, Captain," said Waghorne, glancing about as if he expected to see a gang of slavers rounding
the corner of the building.

Isbinder added, "The *Rimjack* isn't guarded. We can slip
aboard and be off before dark."

The priest-voyagers exchanged apprehensive glances but
remained silent. Enskeline was in command; what he decided
would be followed. They trusted his wisdom.

Enskeline tried to gather his wits. The threat of slavery was
only a conjecture. Perhaps he was jumping to a rash conclusion,
but he found the circumstances suggestive despite the lack of
any proof. To be taken aboard a Daltrescan slave ship was
tantamount to a death sentence. And that death was certain to
be painful and degrading. The crewmen had the right idea:
leave Huttoi at once.

But the schismatics might have come here. The reliquary
could be somewhere on this world, waiting for him. If they
left now, it might be lost to him forever.

"We came to Huttoi for a reason. We won't let ourselves
be frightened off," he said as boldly as he could manage.
"We'll join the Hutt as soon as we can."

"Wouldn't we be better off on our own, Captain?"
Waghorne asked.

"Not when there's only five of us. If we can join with fifty
or sixty Hutt, we'll be safe. Daltrescans don't attack unless
they have heavy odds on their side. But first we're going to

the *Rimjack*, all of us. We'll need supplies and trade goods. You'll all be carrying heavy packs for a few days."

The short Huttoi day was almost over when the five left the *Rimjack* secured on her ring. Each man carried supplies for eight days and four Skeggjatt medical kits like the ones Enskeline had traded on Sassacheele. The Hutt were humans—early colonists like the settlers on Sassacheele. Now that they were reduced to wanderers on a world dominated by others, medical supplies seemed the most practical thing to bring them.

Enskeline also brought a case of twelve short-range ripguns, smaller versions of the deadly personal weapon of the Sternverein security troopers. At a distance of up to ten meters they could tear a full-grown man—or a Daltrescan—to pieces. Their force and accuracy dropped sharply at longer ranges, but Enskeline did not plan to fight a war. He wanted only to defend himself and his companions if it should become necessary. Daltrescans, he knew, would not press an attack against superior weapons.

He gave one ripgun to Waghorne and one to Isbinder, instructing them how to prime and fire. He thought of giving weapons to the priests, but recalled some of the shipboard debates about war and the taking of life and decided to wait. The ripguns would be handy, should they be needed, and immediate danger was a persuasive force.

They traveled as long as the light permitted, passing through a dense forest of low, large-leafed trees. Vegetation grew thickly on Huttoi, but nowhere did it grow very high. They camped for the night at the edge of the open lands beyond the forest, but made no fire. Enskeline knew of no dangerous animals on Huttoi and saw no sense in advertising their own presence. They took turns keeping watch through the night.

Next day they began to cross a great savannah. Thick green grass, striped with broad bands of yellow and red, reached to knee height. Scattered about the plain, singly or in clumps of three or four, were low trees. In the light, the travelers saw the uniform left-hand spiral of the trunks and the intricate patterning of the leaves, each about the size of a man's torso.

"The vegetation is not very different from that of Peter's Rock. Grass, trees, flowers. . . . I'm sure there must be edible grain and fruits on Huttoi, too," Fielden observed.

Dallamer said, "It's much like the growth on Roharr, as well. Remember the plain of Felill? It was similar to this."

"Your friends will find the lowlands of Sassacheele much like this, too. Those early colonists looked for worlds that reminded them of home. Why settle where you have to live under a dome and walk around in a pressure suit and respirator when there are worlds where you can live as you've always lived?" said Enskeline.

"No need, when God's bounty is endless," Dallamer said.

Enskeline smiled drily. "The statistics help, too. In a galaxy with billions of planets, there are bound to be many that resemble each other."

"That's true, of course. But do you see nothing of God's plan in all this, Captain?"

Enskeline had done his best to avoid discussing his personal beliefs with the priest-voyagers. He believed in very few things, and even in those his belief was halfhearted. Defending his beliefs against someone else's was something he had no desire to do. It seemed a waste of time. Now, faced with a direct question, having no shipboard duties in which to take hasty refuge, he had no other alternatives but to respond, walk away, or trudge on in silence. He chose to answer Dallamer's question.

"I'm a Mechanist, Rever. I don't know who's running the universe, or how it's being run, or why. I can never know. It seems to be working, and that's enough for me. But one thing I'm sure of: whatever is running it is not at all like a human being. Not one bit. If it were, the whole universe would have fallen to pieces long ago."

The two priests began to speak at once. Enskeline said nothing, waiting for them to sort out their responses. Fielden spoke first. Whatever he may have felt, his manner was composed, his voice calm.

"God is *not* a human being, Captain. He is a pure spirit."

Enskeline looked at him accusingly. "Now, Rever, I've heard you say that your god turned himself into a man. Isn't that so?"

"God assumed human nature, it is true. He became man in order to redeem us."

"Well, I hope you won't take offense at this, either of you, but if your god chose to become a human being, I don't think much of him or of his choices. I've seen a lot more humans than you have, and even more of their handiwork; and I wouldn't want to live in a universe run by a god who wants to be, or look, or act like a human.''

"How can you say that, Captain, when you're human yourself?"

"I didn't have any choice. But your god did. There're a lot finer creatures in this universe than human beings. Just think of that interpreter—he's human. Your god could have turned himself into a third-stage Onhla. They live for ages and can communicate with everything on their planet, living and dead. They protect their people and do good for them.''

"Have you seen these beings, Captain?" Fielden asked.

"There are no more. Humans wiped them out.''

Dallamer said, "You judge humans harshly," but in his voice was a note of sadness.

"No, Rever," Enskeline replied staunchly. "I'd never betray them, or sell them out to slavers, but I have no illusions about the human race. I've seen too much. It was humans who founded the Sternverein. They claim to be making space safe for trade and travel, but all I've ever known them to do is steal and kill more efficiently than the spacetrash they hunt. These slavers we're running from—the Daltrescans—humans taught them to be slavers. It's been like that everywhere colonists from Old Earth set down.''

"Surely there are decent humans, Captain. In your travels you must have encountered good people.''

"A few," Enskeline admitted. "Zacher was a good lad, and a good bridgeman. But I find fewer good people each time I look. The bad ones keep killing them off. I don't much like being around humans, to tell you the truth. Up to now, I've always had a mostly alien crew on the *Rimjack*, and I did it by choice.''

They walked for a time in silence. Enskeline began to feel uncomfortable. All he had said was true, but it was only a general principle. He disliked humans, but he had come to like, and even respect, the men with him. At last he said, "I ought to tell you, though, that the people on Peter's Rock, and all of you who came out with me, are a lot better than the rest of the humans I've known. I didn't expect you to be, either.''

"Why not, Captain?" Fielden asked.

"Any time I've heard humans start talking holy, they were getting ready to do something bad to someone. But you seem to believe what you say and live up to it. I never saw that before."

"We try, Captain. We don't always succeed," Dallamer said.

"What's it really like on Peter's Rock, Rever? Do people get along? Is there ever any fighting or killing?"

Dallamer appeared shocked by the question. "Never, Captain! Even at the height of the great schism there was no thought of violence."

"People stole your ship, though. And your relic," Enskeline pointed out.

"They were careful to injure no one. In their own consciences, they must have believed that they were doing good."

Enskeline thought of the ripguns in his pack. "How about you, Rever? Do you think you could kill someone?"

"No. I could not."

"Not even a slaver? If a gang of Daltrescans popped up right in front of us and you knew they wanted to make a slave out of you, wouldn't you fight?"

"I would try to flee."

"Suppose they hunted you down and trapped you. If you had a weapon in your hand, wouldn't you use it to save your life and your freedom?" Enskeline persisted.

"It is not for me to say that another intelligent being deserves to die so that I may live."

"What about you, Fielden?" Enskeline asked the other priest.

"Life and death are in God's hands, not mine."

Enskeline shrugged. "I hope the Daltrescans know that. It wouldn't hurt for the blackjackets to learn it, too. Is there any chance your god might get the message to them?"

"We will carry the message to the best of our ability, Captain," Fielden said.

Enskeline sighed and walked ahead. At least he had learned that it would do no good to arm the priest-voyagers. The extra ripguns would probably be better used as a trade item among the Hutt, anyway—provided they had something worth trading for. Enskeline knew of nothing particularly valuable on Huttoi and would not have made planetfall but for Domorie's word of the lost ship. Huttoi was not a popular world among free traders.

But here he was, on a world where the dominant race looked upon him as little better than an animal; where slavers might even now be pursuing him; bereft of his trusted and experienced alien crewmen; in the company of humans, in search of other humans. Danger upon danger, hardship upon hardship, and all for the sake of a treasure that might be forever lost or actually hidden half a galaxy away.

At this very moment, Enskeline considered, he could have been taking his ease and pleasure on Roharr, spending his days among those who honored him and courted his influence, passing his nights in Zalorra's arms. The books from the monastery had made him wealthy. He could become a full partner with Domorie, or even start his own trading house. Others could take the *Rimjack* star-hopping while he took the profits. There was no need at all for him to be here, chasing rumors and staking his life on the flimsiest of chances. It was foolish. It was close to madness.

Yet, he could not turn back. His present wealth was a handful of dust compared with the riches to be gained from the reliquary and the monastic library. The monks would give all they had to regain that sacred cloth of theirs—and thank their god for the privilege. Enskeline would be the richest man in the galaxy—richer than even the fabled Leddendorfs—and be honored forever on a world where dwelt the only colony of fellow humans who did not disgrace the name. The people of Peter's Rock were really quite decent folk, he thought.

Of course, their religion was a lot of nonsense. Gods and men all mixed up together, and nobody daring to lift a hand to defend himself, even against slavers. They talked of loving everyone as a brother—even those who did them harm. It was all well and good to talk that way on Peter's Rock, but the rest of the galaxy was different. There were other things, too—things he had heard the priest-voyagers discussing among themselves on the *Rimjack,* that no sensible Mechanist could hear without smiling. It was really amazing, Enskeline decided, that a people so innocent, so out of touch with the realities of

existence, could survive for so long. One might almost believe that that god of theirs, who could not even prevent his own
death, was somehow protecting them.

He laughed quietly and shook his head, as if to clear it of
such foolishness. The presence of the priest-voyagers for all
this time was starting to affect him. He set his mind to the
immediate problem: find the Hutt.

On their fifth day of travel across the savannah they came
upon a trail and followed it. Enskeline was beginning to
worry less about the danger of slavers. There had been no
sign of pursuit. He wondered if he had panicked at an imagi-
nary danger. The real problem now was of being lost out here
with supplies running low and no idea where the Hutt might
be found.

The trail was well-worn, and there had been no attempt to
conceal it. Enskeline found that reassuring. The Hutt did not
appear to be living in fear; that would make them easier to
find, and to deal with. If they still spoke a recognizable
dialect of English, communication would be no problem either.

He knew very little about the Hutt and their ways. They
were descendants of one of the earliest groups to leave Earth
in the years of exodus. Originally they had lived by agriculture,
but after the Altenorei conquest they became nomads. From
that time on, the planet and its people became more and more
an enigma. Visitors to Huttoi were few, and their visits
gained them little knowledge and less profit. The Altenorei
were remote, never revealing themselves to offworlders. No
one knew what they looked like or how they lived. The
Nandra did not condescend to exchange information with
inferior races, and they looked on all other races as inferior.
The Hutt were elusive.

Late that day the five starfarers came upon a village, open
and unguarded. It was a simple settlement: two rows of
steep-roofed shelters, about twenty to a row, facing each
other across a wide central space. Every third shelter was
enclosed with walls made of tightly woven grass mats, over-
lapping in layers. The rest were open on all sides. In front of
the enclosed shelters stood poles on which were hung pen-
nants of all shapes and colors. Enskeline had no idea of their
significance.

Halfway down the central street, at its widest point, Enskeline saw what he had been hoping to see. A ring of stones two meters in diameter stood at the midpoint of the street and the settlement. The ring was empty: the Hutt were at peace and ready to trade.

By this time, the starfarers had been noticed. Several villagers had stepped out from the open-sided shelters and now stood looking at them. Two of the men carried what appeared to be short javelins, but they made no show of hostility. They seemed to carry them as staffs, not as weapons.

Enskeline turned to the others, who were all glancing uneasily at the growing crowd of villagers. "Do just as I say, and I don't think we'll have any problems. Walk behind me, in a line. When we get to that ring of stones, take two medical kits out of your pack and lay them inside the ring. Then step outside the ring and wait for the Hutt to make the next move. That's how they trade."

"Will they understand us, Captain?" Waghorne said.

"I'm pretty sure they still speak a dialect of English."

The priest-voyagers exchanged a hopeful glance. The crewmen smiled. Enskeline noticed that the women in the crowd outnumbered the men. If this was the situation among the Hutt, their stay might yet turn out to be pleasant.

Enskeline swung the pack from his shoulders and drew out two of the medical kits, leaving two for later trading. The others did likewise. Replacing the packs, they took two kits under each arm and, at Enskeline's word, followed him with confident steps as he proceeded down the broad village street, past the silent watchers, to the ring of stones.

When ten medical kits lay within the ring, Enskeline turned to the villagers and said, "We come in peace to trade these goods. Do you understand me? We want to trade."

A woman stepped forward and looked carefully at the five starfarers. "Are you family, or cluster? Where is your ground? Where are the women?"

Enskeline was pleased to hear her speak a form of English, but he was uncertain of her meaning. "We come from the *Rimjack*," he said. "There are no women among us, and no more men."

"*Rimjack* is no grassland settlement. Are you from the valley, or the ocean shore, or the sandy wastes?"

"We are not from Huttoi. Not from this world. *Rimjack* is a driveship. We come from another world. Do you understand?"

"We know of other worlds. Our first settlers came from another world, long ago. The Altenorei and their servants came from another world. There are many worlds," the woman said.

"I and these men with me are descended from settlers who came from Earth, as your first settlers did."

The woman looked more closely at the crewmen and the priest-voyagers. She was a handsome woman, with strong features and long dark hair streaked with white; but her eyes were as cold and unrevealing as lenses.

"Why so many of you, and so little to trade? Why do you come to our world? Speak truly," she said.

Enskeline noticed more men and women with javelins. They still made no menacing move, but they were on all sides now. "I am the only trader. These two men are my crew on the *Rimjack*," he said, pointing to Waghorne and Isbinder, who stood to his left. "They come with me because the Nandra offer those from other worlds no place to stay, and no food. They will return to the *Rimjack* with me, and we will leave Huttoi together." Gesturing toward the priest-voyagers, he said, "These men wish to stay and speak to you of things they believe."

The woman raised her open hand. Enskeline took this as a signal for his silence. She said to the priests, "Is this true? Do you wish to stay on Huttoi?"

Both said, "We do."

"This is a good world, but there is hard work for all. Are you willing to work, or do you come only to talk?"

"We will work. I'm skilled at growing things, and Rever Dallamer is skilled at building. We both know something of healing," Fielden said.

The woman pondered for a moment, then asked, "Are you good hunters?"

"We will learn to be," said Fielden confidently.

"Among us, men hunt and build and help to grow food. Our healers are all women, but your skill is welcome. I tell you again, though—Huttoi is a hard world. The weak and the unwary do not live long."

"We know that life can be hard. We hope that our message will help you to endure."

"We endure," the woman said. Her tone made the words as final as the closing of a port. To Enskeline, she said, "First, we trade. When trading is done, we feast. The hunters have done well. It will be a good feast. Then you will tell us about other worlds." Turning once again to the priest-voyagers, she added, "And you will tell us something of your message."

"And you will tell us of Huttoi, and the Hutt," Enskeline said.

She paused for an instant, then her expression softened and she said, "I will tell of the Hutt."

The Hutt proved to be unsophisticated traders. Once Enskeline had shown them the contents of the medical kits and explained their use, they made no attempt to conceal their eagerness to possess them. Then arose the problem of exchange: the Hutt appeared to have nothing of value to trade. Their clothing was simple and drab; they wore no decorations or ornaments; their tools and weapons were crude makeshifts. In the entire village there seemed to be no item of any real value. The woman, Josta Bothossa, who was village leader, went through an inventory of all their possessions, but to no avail.

"We could give you food," she said at last. "We would fill your ship with good food, all you can hold."

"It would go bad. There's no place to store food. I have a ration-producing unit; that's all I need."

"There must be something we can exchange," she said wearily. "We must have those healing boxes, but we cannot take them without a fair trade."

Enskeline judged that the time had come to broach the subject that had brought him here. He looked around to make certain none of his companions was within earshot, then said, "If you can help me learn something I want to know, I would accept it as trade."

"Only information? Nothing more?" she asked warily.

"Nothing more. The information would be very helpful to me, and it can be of no use to you. I want to know about a ship that may have landed on Huttoi. . . ." He paused, frowning at his realization that he knew nothing at all of the Hutt system of calculating time. "It landed, I think, just before the coming of the Altenorei. It was a large ship, with many aboard, from Roharr.''

"You speak of long ago. My parents were not yet born. The memories are few, and far back," Josta Bothossa said thoughtfully.

"Can you help me?"

"It will take time. I must reach back to Yansa's memories, from the time before Haxila, who led the village before me. Are you willing to remain with us for a time?"

"As long as I must."

"Good," she said, brightening. "Few children have been born to us in recent times. We need your men. I hope they will assist us."

"I'll speak to them about it," Enskeline said.

While the feast was being prepared, he sought out the priest-voyagers and took them to where they could speak privately. He had already ascertained Waghorne and Isbinder's enthusiastic willingness to cooperate with the women of the village, but he was not certain what obligations and restrictions Fielden and Dallamer had placed upon themselves. He did not want to offend Josta Bothossa or her village.

"I have to find something out," he said. "Back on Peter's Rock your abbot said that the priest-voyager's is a celibate ministry. I think I understand what that means, but would you explain it to me?"

"It means that a priest-voyager does not marry," Dallamer said.

"Never? Not under any circumstances?"

"There might possibly be conditions . . . ." Dallamer said hesitantly.

Fielden interjected, "Understand, Captain, that we've taken no vow to remain celibate. Since we're the first ever to leave Peter's Rock, it was realized that we might encounter . . . unusual circumstances . . . customs unknown to us."

"But we promised to observe the tradition to the extent that it was compatible with our mission," Dallamer quickly added.

"I think I understand. You haven't actually sworn to have no relations with a woman."

"Not sworn, no, Captain. But the tradition . . . the custom . . ."

"Of course, Rever. But you could father children without

forsaking your beliefs, if it were essential to your mission; isn't that so?''

Fielden and Dallamer exchanged a startled glance. Fielden asked, ''Why do you raise this question, Captain? It seems a peculiar time for you to become interested in our vows.''

''I'll be blunt. For the health of their race—for its survival in the long run—the Hutt need fresh genetic material. That means us. It means all of us, yourselves included.''

''There are men among the Hutt, Captain,'' Dallamer said.

''But not enough of them are of the proper age, and in the proper physical condition, to father healthy children. The males have not survived well on this world. That means there's been a lot of inbreeding, and it eventually will mean the end of the race. I'm not exaggerating. I've seen it happen on other worlds. It happened on Sassacheele. A small colony cuts itself off from all outsiders, and after a few generations it begins to rot away from inside.''

''No outsiders came to Peter's Rock before you, Captain, but our people did not degenerate,'' Fielden objected.

''Your original colony was much larger and you had a greater variety of genetic stock among the settlers. The Hutt are all descended from a few families.''

''But you're not speaking of marriage, Captain,'' said Dallamer.

''There is no marriage among the Hutt, Rever. They do what they must to keep from dying out. If you think it's holier to be extinct, there's not much point in talking. Do whatever you think is right, but if you hope to be accepted among the Hutt and to have your message heard and believed, then you'd better help them to stay alive.''

They stood silent for a time. Then Fielden sighed and said, ''We must take time to think, Captain. We've never considered such a possibility. We must reflect, and pray for guidance.''

''I understand. I'm sorry to cause you worry, truly I am. But I want you to know what the Hutt expect of you.''

''We thank you, Captain,'' Dallamer said.

Enskeline left them alone and returned to the village, where the promised feast was still in preparation. Josta Bothossa was nowhere in sight; his crewmen, too, were not to be seen. He settled in a shady spot and watched the villagers at work, thinking with cool detatchment about the situation into which he and his companions had been placed.

He sympathized with the priest-voyagers, even though he could not understand their inability to accept another world and its people on its own terms. Holy men, whatever their particular beliefs, seemed intent on making life difficult for themselves and those around them. Here they were, realizing the fulfillment of every lonely starfarer's dream, and all they could think of was reasons why they should not enjoy it.

Enskeline sighed and leaned back, stretching his legs. Like all dreams come true, Huttoi had its flaws. There had been a decline in the level of civilization, surely; the Hutt who left Earth had not been a band of nomadic hunters. This village of women, each ready to welcome him to her bed, was not a world of bejeweled and scented beauties with shining hair and soft limbs. The Hutt women were hard, sun-browned, and marked by toil, with calloused hands and feet and dirt ground deep into their roughened skin. Their features were pleasant, but work and weather had left marks on even the youngest.

And none really cared for him—for the individual man, Jod Enskeline; nor did they really care for any of his companions. There was no passion here, only the immemorial yearning of bodies to be filled with new life. He and the rest were merely carriers of the seed that gave the Hutt the promise of new generations.

This knowledge did not anger him or injure his vanity. Men who had crossed the immense emptiness, seen dying stars and decaying civilizations, and walked amid ancient ruins of stupefying grandeur had no room left for vanity. They took their little victories wherever they could, knowing that the next world might be a place of horror or the last one they would ever see. Life was a brief journey through assorted pains and pleasures; death was final. The universe was incomprehensible and, as far as the individual was concerned, meaningless. Enskeline found that an acceptable explanation. There was no comfort in it, no satisfaction; but at least it did not posit a malicious supreme will, while it did correspond with his own personal experience. In the proper mood, he even found it rather amusing.

He fell into a light sleep, from which Josta Bothossa woke

him. The feast was ready. He took his place at her side, and without further ceremony they all fell to.

The food was well-cooked but bland. The only seasoning was a coarse, reddish-brown granulated stuff. Enskeline applied a cautious pinch of it to his meat and nearly gagged at the acrid bite it caused. He ate the rest of the meat unseasoned.

Afterwards, at Josta Bothossa's bidding, he told of his travels, gave news of other worlds and colonies, then called upon the priest-voyagers to speak. The Hutt listened attentively as Dallamer and Fielden explained their faith, but they asked no questions. In the silence that followed, Enskeline asked Josta Bothossa to tell the history of the Hutt.

Their story was typical of most early Earth colonies. They were refugees from a war-maddened, poisoned planet, in this case a band led by a social reformer named Hutterston, a woman of charismatic forcefulness. Trusting her implicitly, her followers had crowded more than four hundred people aboard a driveship designed to hold fewer than two hundred, bringing only the bare minimum of supplies. Their landing on this pleasant, temperate, water-rich world damaged the driveship severely. They had no means of repairing it and lacked even the knowledge of how to begin. They also soon realized that they had few of the basic tools for building a civilization. In rejecting the technological glut that had brought old Earth to ruin, they had rejected as well the technology that might have enabled them to build a new and better Earth here.

Their tight little society collapsed and fragmented. Families wandered off to settle in other regions. Edible foods could be grown, edible animals roamed the grasslands, and the waters held edible life. Subsistence was possible, and it was all the settlers asked.

For a long time, there was no trade or barter between the separated groups. What they caught or grew separately, each group separately consumed. The concept of producing more than was needed, of storing a surplus for trade or exchange, was slow to develop. Also, without a need for inventories or accounts, writing fell into disuse. Among some groups it died out entirely. Important facts were committed to memory and passed down from the head of each family to her successor.

In time, contact was reestablished among the survivors, and some joined into larger clusters to share their skills and lighten their labor. Soon after this came the Altenorei and the Nandra.

"We saw lights in the sky, but we knew nothing of their coming," said Josta Bothossa. "Later, we learned that their ships had landed on the far side of Huttoi, in a barren place where Hutt had never gone. One day, in the time of Janta, my mother's mother, a man came to us. He was Hutt, but he was strangely dressed in dark clothing that hung loose around him. Others were with him, dressed in the same manner, but they were not men. He called them Nandra and said that he and they both served another race called Altenorei, who were now the masters of this world. He told us that we need fear nothing from our new masters as long as we did not intrude upon the Altenorei."

"Has anyone ever seen the Altenorei?" Enskeline asked.

"Never. We can see from a great distance the square towers where they dwell. They never leave those towers. We were able to see only the Nandra, and we always spoke to them through a Hutt who served them. In Janta's time, and in the early days of Haxila's leadership, we went to their settlement, but we go no more. They treat us as worthless things."

"The Nandra don't look strong. Has anyone ever resisted them?" Waghorne asked.

"We are too few to resist them. Our weapons are too weak," said the woman. "The Nandra have weapons that kill silently and leave no mark. We have no defense against them."

Enskeline thought of the ripguns that were still in his pack. A small force armed with them could wipe out the Nandra port installation in a single stroke. But he said nothing of the ripguns. He had not come to Huttoi to start a war. Instead, he asked Josta Bothossa if slavers had ever been known to visit the planet.

"Never to our knowledge," she replied. "Except for the ships of the Altenorei, I know of only four driveships to come to Huttoi. There may have been others, but I have never heard a memory of others."

"Can you find out more?"

"In the morning I will go with my daughters to revive the deep memories from Janta's time. Be patient, Enskeline. I will find what you seek." Josta Bothossa rose and signaled to a dark-haired young woman who sat nearby. The woman approached and held out her hand to the trader.

"I am Lossian of the Bothossa," she said.

"You will stay with Lossian for now, Enskeline," said Josta Bothossa. "Is this agreeable to you?"

Lossian was a tall, big-framed woman. She looked at Enskeline with cool, appraising eyes, making it clear that she had no great desire to share her bed with him. For his part, he would have preferred the yielding softness of Zalorra. But Lossian was here, and Zalorra was far away.

He took her hand and said, "Agreeable, and an honor."

The men of the *Rimjack* were looked upon as a cluster—a grouping of families—and accepted into the life of the Bothossa village. They had arrived at the warm season of the long, mild Huttoi year, and they adapted easily to the languorous pace of daily life. The Hutt considered it a hard life, but to the men of Peter's Rock it was no more than they were accustomed to. The days passed quickly and pleasantly.

Waghorne and Isbinder were at ease in the village at once. The commonplace skills they had acquired on Peter's Rock, still fresh in their memories and ready to hand, were lost knowledge among the Hutt. Waghorne had worked for a tanner and cobbler, and Isbinder came from a family of smiths. Both men had a good knowledge of carpentry. They found their skills needed, and set to work happily.

Dallamer and Fielden spent the mornings hunting. In the afternoon, while the other hunters rested, they worked with the women gathering wild grain, or helped the crewmen in their tasks. After an initial period of reserve, the Hutt had become receptive to the missionaries' message, and the two men seemed always to be at the center of a discussion. Enskeline did not ask them how they had decided on the problem—to them, at least, it was a problem—of their celibacy and the needs of the Hutt. It was not his business. Whatever course they had taken seemed to have offended no one.

Despite himself, Enskeline spent a good deal of time puzzling over his exact relationship with Lossian. She was civil to him, helpful in answering his questions, solicitous for his comfort. But in their moments of intimacy, tight in one another's arms, she did not speak to him or even whisper his name. Her body responded to his without reserve, but she never yielded control of her feelings.

Then, one afternoon as he sat idly watching the villagers come and go, Enskeline realized the truth: no Hutt, man or woman, could risk forming an intimate personal bond with one of the opposite sex. The natural desires of the individual had to be subordinated to the needs of the group. Survival was the foremost consideration. There were no subunits in the family Bothossa, no bonds to supersede loyalty to the family. Children knew which individual had borne them, but considered themselves children of the larger family, and were reared as such.

He recalled the cold words of Josta Bothossa: *We endure.* So they did, but at a terrible price.

Enskeline thought differently of the Hutt after that, and of Lossian; his feelings for her deepened, though he knew he must never reveal them. He could not help pitying these people for the price they had to pay to survive; but he admired their fortitude in paying it. They endured.

Josta Bothossa was gone for sixteen days. She returned looking weary and aged, having undergone an ordeal of fasting and hypnotic trance to free the oldest memories passed on to her by her predecessors. She was unable to speak to Enskeline when she returned, but she sent a daughter to tell him that she had the information he sought.

She received him in her shelter the following evening. Her face was thinner. Her eyes, ringed in shadow, seemed larger and brighter than they had before. She summoned him close, for her voice was faint.

"At the beginning of Yansa Bothossa's fourth year of life, a driveship from a world called Pitorok came to Huttoi. There was sickness aboard. Many had died. The family of Kellima spoke with one from the ship, but they did not go near him. They did not board the ship for fear of the sickness," she said.

"Was there anything of value aboard the ship?"

"The traveler said that they had with them a cloth that bore the face of God."

Enskeline shut his eyes and swallowed. He took a deep breath to calm himself.

"Is this what you sought?" Josta Bothossa asked.

"It is. Can you tell me where the driveship went when it left Huttoi?"

"That was not in Yansa's memories. But it was told to the family Kellima. You will learn it from them."

"Thank you," Enskeline said fervently. "You've traded fairly. I'm grateful."

She said nothing. Her eyes closed, her breathing became slow and regular. Enskeline slipped quietly from the shelter.

Four days later, Enskeline left for the upland village of the Kellima. A boy named Ber-Somias, youngest of the Bothossa males, went with him as guide. At Josta Bothossa's urging, Enskeline took two of the medical kits. He brought his own ripgun, concealed, purely for peace of mind. He took no weapons to trade.

Ber-Somias was an intelligent lad, observant and willing to talk. Enskeline found him good company on the long, almost featureless trail across the grasslands. He pointed out each small grove of the trunk-twisted trees as if it had a distinct appearance; to Enskeline, they were all identical. He told of an encampment on a sheltered hillside, a hunt for weepalo in a long ravine, a flooding of a little stream, and his flow of talk made the time pass quickly. After a few days travel, Enskeline began to feel as though he, too, were on familiar ground.

On their ninth day of walking, they climbed a long, shallow rise. Ber-Somias was silent for once, but he had a mischievous expression that led Enskeline to anticipate a surprise. Near the crest the boy could contain himself no longer. He raced ahead, shouting for Enskeline to hurry and join him.

The rise ended abruptly, dropping to a broad flat plain, like a dry riverbed. It was about three kilometers across at this point. To Enskeline's right it widened steadily from bank to bank; at its farthest point the open space was ten kilometers across. To his left, it narrowed to a slit.

"We're safe crossing now. Sometimes the killwind comes

through that narrow opening, and then you mustn't be down there," Ber-Somias announced.

"What's the killwind?"

"When the weather changes very quickly from hot to cold, a wind comes down the valley beyond that opening. It blows so fast it makes the stones fly. The little ones dig right into you, and the big ones can smash your bones, they blow so fast. We lost a hunter down there once."

"Does the killwind rise that suddenly? No warning at all?" Enskeline asked. The three kilometers to the far side suddenly seemed an endless distance.

"It comes out of nowhere, everyone says. The only thing to do if you're caught in it is to get behind a big rock, if you can reach one. If you're in the open, strip off all your clothes and roll them into a bundle, then lie down flat as you can behind the bundle. But that doesn't work so well. You have to hold the bundle to keep it from blowing away, so the stones smash your fingers. Then you can't hold it any more."

Enskeline looked down, then studied the narrowing walls that led to the deadly opening. "Are you sure we're safe?" he asked.

"Never a killwind in this weather. Come on," Ber-Somias said, starting down the steep cliffside.

At bottom, Enskeline moved out anxiously. Ber-Somias showed no great concern for a swift crossing, so Enskeline drew the boy into conversation to try to force him to keep pace.

"Is the killwind the only dangerous thing on Huttoi?" he asked.

"It's the only really dangerous thing, I guess. False-fruit will kill you if you eat a lot of it. Looks just like tussery, only it's poisonous. Ponberries will make you sick, but you generally get better."

"There aren't any big fierce animals, are there?"

"Nothing bigger than the loopers, and they're harmless. Chittercats will attack if you try to take their young, but they've never killed anyone. The snuffties and gleepers run if you shout at them. The only really dangerous things are the towers."

"What towers? I never saw a tower."

"The Altenorei towers—big square things where the invaders live," the boy explained. "Try to go too close, and you die. You just fall dead; and there aren't any marks to show what killed you."

"Have many people died that way?"

"Not for a long time. We keep away from the towers now, and nobody bothers us."

Enskeline grunted thoughtfully. This world was a puzzle. He thought of the mysterious Altenorei, going about some incomprehensible mission in their towers, unseen and unknown, while the Hutt lived their primitive lives in the open spaces, much as their remote ancestors had done on Earth so long ago. And between the two races stood the Nandra, subservient to one, despising the other. He had never encountered a situation like this. He wondered what the future held for these three races. For all his harsh views of the human race, his sympathy was with the Hutt. Logic told him that their hope of surviving was small, but he admired their toughness, their tenacity, their ability to sacrifice for the sake of the future. The missionaries of Peter's Rock were like that too. Perhaps, Enskeline reflected, if he had met these people earlier, he would now have a different opinion of humanity.

When they reached the other side, Ber-Somias turned to Enskeline and said casually, "I told you it was safe to cross. It's only when the wind changes suddenly that there's danger."

"I'll remember that. Is there any other way of crossing, just in case I'm here when the weather changes?"

"The killwind gets worse as you head up the valley. Far down, it's not so dangerous; but then you have to travel through swamplands, and there are no trails. We don't go there."

"I'll just hope that the weather holds," Enskeline said with a sigh of resignation.

On this side of the ravine the ground was more irregular. Soon the groves began to grow larger and closer to one another. By the third day of travel they were in a forest. The trunks of the twisted trees—spinneries, the boy called them— were thick here. Some were more than a meter in diameter, but they were still stunted. Enskeline saw none that reached above four meters in height. The broad leaves spread out into a canopy that shaded everything below. The two travelers walked on a soft, yielding green carpet that gave off a faintly sweet aroma as it was crushed underfoot.

"Sweetmoss," the boy said when asked about the scent. "The loopers eat it. It makes their meat taste good."

Enskeline could see no vestige of a trail, but Ber-Somias made his way ever deeper into the spinnerie forest with as confident a stride as if he were on a broad highroad lined with markers. They walked an entire day and the following morning up a gentle rise. Then Enskeline saw sunlight ahead. Soon he was looking down into a shallow valley where threescore shelters stood. They were sturdy structures, built of stone. Cleared paths, fences, and gardens were visible from the valley rim. A lake lay at the center of the valley, dotted with small islands. Boats moved slowly over the smooth water.

"This is the Kellima settlement. It's a cluster, biggest on Huttoi. This is where I'm going to live," Ber-Somias said, looking eagerly down on the scene.

"Aren't you going back to the Bothossas with me?" Enskeline asked, alarmed at the prospect of trying to retrace his way alone.

"Not me. They'll send a male of their own in exchange, though. He'll help you find the way back."

A trading ring stood at the center of the Kellima village, but there was no need for Enskeline to make use of it. Once Ber-Somias had presented him to Maxen Kellima as an offworld cluster-leader, he was an honored guest.

The feast of welcome was held in a large stone building. It was solidly built, with a long narrow table running down the center, and benches on either side and at the ends. The workmanship of building and furnishings was skillful. Clearly, this was a permanent settlement, and had been here for a long time—perhaps from the earliest days on Huttoi. Enskeline felt encouraged. The chance was good that history was preserved in such a place.

Maxen Kellima, leader of the cluster, was overwhelmed with gratitude for his gift of the medical kits. When Enskeline asked her about the visitors to Huttoi, she took him herself to the locked chamber where written records from the colony's past were preserved. He was given free access to everything, with the promise that any material of interest to him, however lengthy it might be, would be copied out by Maxen Kellima's own daughters, who preserved the knowledge and practice of writing words by hand.

The records were written in dark ink on long strips of hide scraped to translucent thinness and flexible as leaves. They were kept in rolls. Enskeline soon accustomed himself to handling them easily. The writing varied from scribe to scribe, but it was always careful and perfectly legible. Some words were unfamiliar, but he was usually able to deduce their meaning from the context.

The earliest entries were exhaustively detailed. As time passed, and the settlement established its ways, entries became conventionalized and often perfunctory, as routine incidents and commonplace events were noted again and again. But the entry that Enskeline sought stood out when he unrolled it as vividly as if it had been set down in letters of fire:

> On the sixty-fourth day of the ninth year of the leader Mermora, came to Huttoi a driveship bearing humans from another world.

Enskeline threw back his head and gave a great sigh of relief. He read the words again, laughed to himself, then looked around the chamber before going on. He feared the next words almost as much as he burned to learn what they said:

> Our leader Mermora, with three observers and three to guard them, went to the ridge where awaited the visitor from the ship, a male. He warned them to keep far away. Plague had taken many aboard the ship, he said, and he did not wish to infect fellow humans.
>
> Close to ours was his language, but often hard to understand was his speech, for his excitement. When he told of the sickness, Mermora offered our help. He did not accept, saying that the ship must go on, to bring the holy shroud to a world . . .

Enskeline stopped reading. He could feel the fluttering of his heart. He held out his hand and saw that it was shaking. Taking a deep breath to calm himself, he rose from the hard bench, walked once about the chamber, then settled himself and read on:

*. . . where all the races of the galaxy might see it,
and know its truth, and worship his god. When Mermora
asked of the holy shroud, what it might be, the man said
that it was a cloth that bore the face of his god. When
Mermora asked what world he came from, he said they
had all fled Peeta-rok when others who had once believed in their god betrayed him. From us the man of the
driveship wanted nothing but information that would help
him find the way to a planet named Desshe. When
Mermora told him that our own driveship and all charts
and records had been destroyed, he left us. He was seen
no more.*

Enskeline read to the end of the roll before stopping. There
was no more about the schismatics' ship. He had found what
he sought, but his new knowledge had raised new mysteries.
The ship had been bound for Huttoi; but after making the
dangerous landing—unaided by a landing ring—and finding
humans, the schismatics had lifted off almost at once. Something must have happened during that long journey to cause
such a drastic change of plan.

Perhaps the plague had sickened their minds as well as
their bodies, or perhaps the sight of dying companions had
driven the survivors mad. Such things had happened more
than once to those unprepared for the long empty spaces
between the stars.

But where was Desshe, and how had they learned of it?
There must have been a planetfall, some other contact, between Roharr and Huttoi. Enskeline had spent his life in
starfaring and was familiar with the names of most of the
settled worlds; Desshe was unknown to him. It might have
been an approximation of some muttered alien word barely
heard by the Hutt and garbled further by the scribe. Even so,
Enskeline could recall no world with a name similar to it.

More information could be found on the *Rimjack*. And at
least he was not seeking blindly now. He had a destination.
Wherever Desshe was, he would locate it and track down the
reliquary. He had a momentary vision of a great ship filled
with corpses speeding outward from the known worlds, taking its treasure and its mystery into the void beyond the rim
of the galaxy, moving ever faster into the silent unknown.

"No!" he said aloud, slamming his fist down on the hard planks of the table. He shook his head to drive out the desolating image. He would not fail. He had traced the schismatics to Roharr and thence to Huttoi. He would follow them to Desshe and beyond, as far as they had fled—to the end of the universe, if he must.

He stayed in the Kellima village forty-one days, reading the annals and learning more about the ways of the Hutt. Of the aliens, he could discover nothing. Settled as they were, seldom straying far beyond their pasturelands, the Kellima folk knew the Nandra and Altenorci only as names entered generations ago on a scroll long unread, spoken of now only by the old. They did not represent invaders, or enemies, or anything to be feared or resented. To most of the Kellima, they were scarcely real.

When Enskeline spoke of the men who had come to Huttoi with him, Maxen Kellima expressed interest in hearing the message of the missionaries. Enskeline promised he would send one of them to the village upon his return.

His new guide was a youth named Ber-Kember, about the same age as Ber-Somias. Ber-Kember was being sent to live among the Bothossa in exchange for their male. Like Ber-Somias, he seemed to accept the departure from the people and scenes of his childhood with equanimity. In this he was no different from the villagers. As he left them, presumably never to return, there was no sign of emotion on any face in the Kellima village. He might have been going for a morning's stroll or a swim in the lake. Enskeline thought once more of the hard price the Hutt had agreed to, and were paying, for survival on this world.

Whether they followed a different trail, or took the one on which he had come, Enskeline could not tell. It did not much matter to him now, for he planned to be gone from Huttoi for good soon after they reached the Bothossa. He had learned all this world had to tell him.

Ber-Kember was a quiet lad, far more interested in observing his surroundings than in talking to his companion along the way. They walked in silence for the most part, confining conversation to their rest and eating times. The Kellima had provided them with a generous supply of dried looper meat and dried fruit. Since water was abundant in this part of Huttoi, they carried only a single small flask between them.

The day before they reached the ravine, Ber-Kember found them a rare treat. They had stopped to rest and refresh themselves by a brook, under the shade of a trio of spinneries. Enskeline was just dozing off when Ber-Kember waded into the water, shaded his eyes, and began splashing downstream.

"What is it?" Enskeline shouted.

"Butterberries!" the boy called back, without turning.

He returned in a short time with two handfuls of round yellow fruit. "Best food on Huttoi, everyone says. There aren't any more around the village. Loopers eat them, roots and all. Take some," he said excitedly.

The butterberries were about a size to fit through the loop of his thumb and first finger. Enskeline bit down cautiously on one, then gave a low cry of sheer delight. The flesh was creamy, rich, and delicately sweet, a treat for the most re-fined and demanding palate. Ber-Kember laughed delightedly at Enskeline's reaction and handed him two more. They ate their fill, rested, and then ate a few more before starting off again.

Late the next day they came to the ravine, at a point farther down this time than the starfarer's earlier crossing. The opposite bank was at least four kilometers distant. Ber-Kember stepped to the brink and said, "Let's get across before dark."

"Wait. There's a wind rising. The weather's been change-able these last few days. The killwind may come," said Enskeline.

"There have been no sudden changes. No danger of a killwind."

"It's a long way across, Ber-Kember. If the wind comes . . ."

"It won't. We'll run. Come on."

"No, wait. Let's go up a way, to where it's narrower."

But Ber-Kember was already scrambling down the slope. He paused at bottom to beckon Enskeline on, then set out at a slow jog across the rock-strewn flat.

Enskeline muttered irritably and started down after him. The breeze was a bit fresher down here, but it seemed to carry no threat of danger. If he had not been told of the killwind, he would have suspected nothing. He began to trot after the diminishing figure of Ber-Kember.

He had gone about a kilometer when suddenly a low howl rose far up the canyon, quickly becoming a shrill keening. In an instant the air was opaque with blowing dust and sand. He tried to shout Ber-Kember's name, but the wind tore words and breath away the moment he opened his mouth. The flesh of his face and hands felt as if it were being pricked by hot needles. He felt a sharp blow, then another. Small missiles whizzed by him, narrowly missing. The killwind was on him in full force now. He had lost all sense of direction, and under its driving power he was stumbling helplessly like a drunken man.

He tripped and sprawled headlong. His outflung hand fell on a raised surface. Dragging himself forward, he crawled behind a bit of boulder jutting up half a meter from the plain, and slightly more than that from side to side. He stretched out, hands over his ears, eyes tight shut, pressing himself to the ground while the stone-charged wind boomed all around him.

At last came silence. He pulled himself up, shaking off the coat of grit and stones that covered him from the waist down, and looked around. The air was still, the sky was clear, and all was calm. No sound disturbed the silence.

At first he saw no trace of Ber-Kember. He eventually found the boy's remains tumbled far down the draw by the fury of the killwind. Ber-Kember looked as if he had been mauled by beasts. His garments were in shreds, and his exposed skin was torn and furrowed. Pebbles and small chips of stone were imbedded deep in his flesh. His face was so gashed and battered that his features were scarcely recognizable.

Enskeline did not know the death customs of Huttoi. But he could not bring himself to leave Ber-Kember here as he lay, so he carried the boy's body to the far ridge, where he dug a shallow grave and placed him within.

Alone on the savannah, Enskeline was helplessly lost. The striped grass, the scattered clumps of spinneries stretched on to the horizon, trackless, unmarked, identical in all directions to the untrained eye. He sighted on the clump of spinneries farthest from the ridge and set forth.

That night he awoke from chaotic dreams to find himself soaked in sweat, shivering, and in great pain. His throat burned, his head throbbed, and every muscle ached.

He pulled himself erect and drank deeply from the water flask. Each swallow was agony to the taut muscles of his throat, but it relieved the burning. He leaned against a tree and tried to pull his jangling thoughts together. He had felt perfectly well when he had lain down to sleep. Perhaps the butterberries . . . But that was two days ago, and the water he drank had come from a clear, fast-running stream.

Sudden weakness made him sink to his knees and fall forward. He felt his heart race, then slow, then race even faster, until its pounding seemed to reverberate throughout his body. His throat tightened so much he could not even groan. He thought he was dying. But his mind was clear. This was the end, then, and there was no one to hear, no one to help him. No one would know what had become of him.

It was the risk every starfarer ran. Unknown worlds held unknown dangers; eventually a man's luck ran out. But Enskeline did not want to die. He thought of the missionaries' god, that god of healing and forgiving, and with failing breath he called upon his name. Then he sank into blackness and silence.

VIII. ─────────────────

Huttoi: A New Mission

Enskeline had been gone nearly sixty days when a visitor came to the Bothossa village. He stumbled into sight, haggard and starving, barely able to speak for thirst. He collapsed at the head of the street, pitching forward in the dust where he lay, still as a corpse. Dallamer and Isbinder took him up and carried him to a shelter, where Josta Bothossa and Fielden joined them.

"Who is this?" she asked.

"I don't know. Is he from another family? Perhaps he comes with word of the Captain," Dallamer said.

"That is Nandra clothing," said Josta Bothossa.

Isbinder blurted, "The interpreter! Remember, Dallamer? He's the one who treated us like dirt when we landed on Huttoi."

"You're right, Isbinder. Hard to recognize him. He must have been wandering out there for days."

"Maybe his masters turned him out."

"Maybe they did. Whatever happened, he's human and he needs help," said Fielden.

The interpreter called in a feeble, cracked voice for water. Fielden knelt and brought a shallow dish to the dry lips. When the man had emptied the dish, Fielden wiped his face and forehead with a cold, wet cloth.

"Kill . . . all!" the man whispered hoarsely.

"You need rest. We'll talk when you've rested," Fielden said.

"Kill them!" the man repeated, and then he was silent.

"Raving," Dallamer said softly to Josta Bothossa.

Fielden rose and stood beside them. "He must have gone

147

days without food or water, wandering under the sun, lost. I hope he recovers.''

"I will use the healing box brought us by your captain. This man will be well soon,'' Josta Bothossa assured them.

The men of the *Rimjack* talked only of the translator that day. Waghorne and Isbinder were openly pleased to see the arrogant turncoat sent begging to those he had scorned. The priest-voyagers urged them to be charitable toward the man, but the crewmen were not inclined to be forgiving.

"He turned on his own people, Rever, and sided with the aliens who stole this world. He acted like he was one of them, not one of us,'' Waghorne said.

"But he must have spent his life among the Nandra. He knew nothing of the Hutt,'' Fielden objected.

Waghorne made a contemptuous gesture of dismissal. "He knew they were out here, humans like himself, and you heard the way he spoke about them. And about us, too.''

"Whatever he may have done, he's suffered. I think the poor fellow's lost his mind,'' said Dallamer.

Isbinder agreed. He told the others, "All he can say is, 'Kill them.' He keeps repeating it. They must have done something terrible to him.''

"How do you know he means the Nandra? Maybe he means us,'' Waghorne said.

"What could he do to us?'' Dallamer asked, smiling at the absurdity of the situation. "He's half-dead, Waghorne.''

"I don't know what he could do, but it's nothing to laugh at. He may believe that he can win back favor with his Nandra by getting rid of the Hutt. And that includes us.''

"Waghorne could be right. I think this fellow should be guarded,'' Isbinder said, rising and stepping to his fellow crewman's side.

"Someone will be watching him until he recovers,'' Dallamer assured them.

"I didn't say *watched*; I said *guarded*. By someone with a weapon, ready to use it.''

"The Hutt know how to defend themselves.''

"They don't have anything like *this*,'' Isbinder said, taking the ripgun from inside his shirt. "If this turncoat means us any harm, I'll see that he gets no chance to do it. Are you with me, Waghorne?''

"I'm with you," the other crewman said, drawing his own ripgun.

"You can't go in and kill him!" Fielden cried.

"We're going to stand guard over him, Rever, nothing more. If he means us no harm, he's perfectly safe."

Dallamer laid a restraining hand on Fielden's arm and said to the others, "We believe you. But be careful. Where did you get those weapons? Do you know how to use them?"

"Captain gave them to us. He showed us what to do," said Isbinder. "Don't worry. We don't want to hurt anybody, but we're not going to let anyone wipe out the Hutt—and us with them."

The crewmen went to the shelter and explained their presence to Josta Bothossa. She reflected for a moment, then motioned for them to enter.

"He sleeps now," she said softly.

"But he kept saying, 'Kill them.' We don't know what he meant, but he might mean us, all of us. We want to make sure he can't do us any harm," said Isbinder.

"You are right. He must be guarded. Are those your weapons?"

"Yes. They'll stop him, and his Nandru friends too, if they plan anything," Isbinder said. Turning to Waghorne, he said, "I'll take first turn, if it's all right with you. I'm wide awake."

"I'll get some rest, then relieve you."

"I will have food sent to you," said Josta Bothossa.

Isbinder settled in a corner of the shelter where he could see the sleeping man clearly, and the others left him. Waghorne relieved him at the midpoint of the night. They went through three full watches each before the newcomer woke with a cry that snapped the watching Isbinder out of his light doze.

"What happened? Has it struck? Are we the only ones left?" the man cried, struggling to rise.

Isbinder rushed to his side and pressed him firmly down. The man sank back without the strength to resist and looked up with wide, frightened eyes.

"Nothing's happened here. Everyone is safe," Isbinder said.

"No! We're not safe here, none of us! There may be no place on Huttoi where we're safe," the man said.

"What's the danger? Tell me, and maybe we can do something. No—wait until the others are here," Isbinder said, rising and backing to the doorway.

He signaled to one of the children playing nearby and sent her to summon the village leaders and his shipmates. When she had left he returned to the newcomer's side and poured him a dish of cold water, which he gulped down.

"You . . . you were on the driveship," he said, pointing a shaking finger at Isbinder.

"That's right. You translated for the Nandra when we arrived."

"You can escape. There may be time to reach your driveship and escape. You can save some of these people."

"We'll leave when our captain returns. If anyone wants to come with us, we'll take as many as can fit aboard."

"You must go now. No time to waste."

"We're not abandoning Captain Enskeline. You may not think much of humans, but we—" Isbinder turned at the sound of footsteps. Josta Bothossa, Lossian, and Waghorne entered the shelter. Three women followed them. The priest-voyagers came close behind.

"He spoke of danger, said no one is safe. I thought you should all hear what he has to say," Isbinder said to them.

"There *is* great danger. The Nandra have been told to remove all inferior beings from this world. They're going to spread a plague that will kill all humans. I know this! I've seen the plague work on people! We will die, all of us," the man cried.

"How do you know these things?" Josta Bothossa asked him.

"I overheard two Nandra talking. There is a rite of great significance to the Altenorei. It's observed on all their worlds at certain times, and it's due to be observed on this planet. It cannot be performed properly while other intelligent life forms abide on the planet. . . ."

"So the Altenorei ordered us exterminated," Waghorne said coldly.

"No! The Altenorei are good; I swear they are!" the man said, sitting upright, holding out his hands in exhortation. "They ordered the Nandra to remove you from this world, but not to destroy you. It was the Nandra who elected destruction. They despise humans—I think because they fear us as rivals. The Nandra developed a disease that would strike down humans without affecting themselves and the masters. They tested it . . ." He fell silent and sat motionless for a time, benumbed. Then, with an anguished cry, he burst into tears and said, "They tested it on my children . . . watched them die . . . I never suspected, until I overheard. . . ."

"And then you fled," said Dallamer.

"Yes."

They looked at one another, then at the abject figure seated on the pallet, his head slumped forward and buried in his hands. No one spoke for a moment. Then Isbinder said, "He came from the Nandra—he might have brought this disease with him!"

The man raised his head and made a negative gesture. "No. The disease is carried by an airborne virus. It works quickly. If I had brought it, we would all be dead by now. I've been in this place some days, haven't I?"

"This is your third day among us," Josta Bothossa said.

"My children died in less than half a day."

"When do the Nandra plan to release the virus?" Fielden asked.

"It must be done soon, so that the Altenorei rites can begin at the proper time. The virus may be abroad now, on the winds."

Fielden turned to Josta Bothossa. "Do the winds blow from the Nandra base in the direction of the village?"

"I cannot say," she replied.

"I think we can assume that they do if the Nandra are using the winds to spread this sickness. We'd better move. Head for the sea," Fielden said.

"Soon, soon," the man urged. "Once the disease strikes, there is no escape. No one recovers. No cure exists."

"We'll find a cure," Dallamer said confidently. "First, we'd better be out of here."

"I will give the order. We proceed to the sea in the morning," Josta Bothossa said.

"Take me with you, please. Forgive me for aiding the Nandra and turning against my own people. I knew no other way."

"If you can travel, you may come with us," Josta Bothossa

assured him. Fielden added, "We'll help you. You came to warn us; we won't abandon you here to die alone."

They left him then, for there was much to be done and time was short. Everyone in the settlement worked furiously until dark, making ready for the long flight to the sea. Food was prepared and packed into rations. Several of the shelters were dismantled. Goods and equipment and weapons were gathered and made ready for the march. It was late at night before the Bothossa villagers, exhausted, settled down to sleep.

Next morning, only twenty-six awoke. The rest had died during the night, passing into death without a cry, without even an audible sigh. Josta Bothossa, Lossian, and all the village leaders were dead. Isbinder and Waghorne were dead. All the children were dead, and all but three of the hunters. The translator who had brought them warning also lay dead on his pallet.

Of those who awoke, seven more were dead by midmorning. Fielden and Dallamer did their best, but there was no helping the sick. A sudden weakness and dizziness struck them down, their throats constricted, and they died where they lay without making a sound. In most cases, there was no sign of pain, but even those who seemed to suffer made no outcry. The Nandra's disease killed as silently as the Angel of Death.

Fielden collapsed at Dallamer's side and died in his fellow missionary's arms. Dallamer laid him gently on the ground and arose, dazed. He looked around at the bodies of men, women, and children lying as if asleep. The sound of weeping came from one of the shelters and from those who knelt over the fallen. Even the impassive Hutt, made stoic by life on this world, could not experience such horror unmoved.

Dallamer stood watching for a moment, listening, smelling the cold scent of death on the morning air, and then walked off to a rise overlooking the village. His companions were dead. Enskeline was gone. It was likely that he, too, had fallen. With Fielden gone, the mission now rested on Dallamer's shoulders. But the mission now had no meaning. Dallamer felt that his zeal was gone, his faith extinguished. His mind was in a turmoil. He found himself thinking things he had never thought before. He stayed on the rise until late in the day, when a young woman, Belrinn, came to him with food and water.

"The dying has stopped. One more died after your comrade, but then no more," she said.

He drank some of the water and ate a bit of the food. He said nothing, but merely sat looking down on the desolation.

Belrinn went on, "We must assemble to decide what to do now. I am the new village leader, and I think your knowledge will be helpful. I want you to stay with me and teach me things from your world."

"How many are left?"

"Nineteen."

"Nineteen . . . out of more than a hundred."

"We will rebuild," Belrinn said with quiet confidence.

"Is that what you think?"

"The sickness has spared us. We can go where the Nandra will not find us and rebuild the family. We have survived sickness before, Dallamer."

"This isn't sickness. This is the planned extermination of all human life on Huttoi. The Nandra have skills and knowledge and weapons that are beyond your imagining. They'll seek us out and find us. No matter where we run to, they'll eventually kill every one of us. Do you understand?"

She looked away, confused by his words. "The Nandra have never harmed us before."

"That doesn't matter. They've harmed us now, and they'll do more when they learn that some of us have survived."

"Then we . . . we will hide, far away."

He reached out and took her hands in his. Holding her firmly, looking unflinchingly into her frightened eyes, he said, "You want my knowledge, Belrinn, and you'll have it. All the Hutt will have it. May I speak at the gathering?"

"Men may speak at a gathering. They seldom do."

"I have something important to say. There's one way we can avoid being wiped out, but it's a hard way, and we may all die in the attempt."

"What is this way, Dallamer?"

"Fight."

Her eyes widened in alarmed surprise. She tried to draw away, but he held her at his side. "We could never fight the Nandra! They have power—you say it yourself, Dallamer—vast power, and knowledge beyond ours!"

"This family alone can't fight them. But all the Hutt,

united, would have a chance. We have powerful weapons of our own, Belrinn. I know of two, and I suspect that there may be more hidden in the village. We could take the Nandra completely by surprise. We might drive them and their Altenorei masters off this planet and reclaim it for the human race. We can do it, Belrinn!''

"No man has ever spoken like this before, Dallamer. Even the bravest women would not dare to speak of fighting the Nandra.''

"I dare, Belrinn. Do you? Will the others?''

She looked at him thoughtfully for a moment, then said, "I dare, Dallamer. But only because of you. You are different from all other men.''

He pressed her hands and shook his head slowly. "I'm just like other men, Belrinn. It's taken me a long time to realize it, but I'm no different from my fellow men. I know that now.''

As they returned to the village, hand in hand, Dallamer went over in his mind what he would tell the survivors. Sitting on the hillside, looking down on that peaceful village turned at a single stroke into a golgotha, he had felt all his faith in a wise and just God go out in a sudden pounce of darkness, like a candle in a night wind, leaving only emptiness. There was no sense at all in what had befallen the Hutt, no reason for it; no reason for some to die and some to live; no reason for anyone to die at all. Why was he alive, and Fielden, a gentler and a better man, dead? Why had they been warned, when warnings were futile?

One day ago, he would have known the reason for all these events and possessed the answer to all his questions: this was the will of God. But now he knew that a being who could will such things was not a god but a demon. And if the God he had worshipped and believed in, the God of Peter's Rock, had indeed loved these people and wished to spare them, then that was no God at all but some petty godling whose will was subject to a more powerful one. That other, then, was the supreme power in the universe; and it was a wanton, willful, bloody force, a mindless engine of malice and destruction, a thing not to be worshipped but hated, defied, and opposed until a man drew his last breath. There was no sense to thinking of an afterlife. If an afterlife indeed existed, such a vile deity would as soon punish the good as the evil and would dispense rewards with all the caprice of an absolute tyrant.

Dallamer knew his own abilities. He had studied the violent, bloody history of his race. He had been trained to lead, to sway opinion, to persuade his bitterest opponents to hear him and follow his way, and all these powers would now be brought to bear on the Hutt. They had never faced anyone so well prepared or so determined. Hutt men were dullards; the women led, but all their own energy was focused on preserving the life of the family. The Hutt knew how to sacrifice; now they must learn to sacrifice for a new reason.

Dallamer reached up and gripped the crucifix that hung around his neck. He tugged at it angrily, but the strong cord bit painfully into his neck without breaking. He released Belrinn's hand, pulled the cord over his head, and flung the crucifix far into the tall grass. That symbol held meaning for him no longer. It stood for peace, forgiveness, reconciliation. For him, such things did not exist. His symbols now were the javelin, the torch, and the ripgun. He had a new message to preach, of a new kind of freedom.

Enskeline awoke in sunlight. His body ached in every bone and muscle. His throat was dry as ashes, with a sour taste he had never known before. But he was alive.

He sat up, and his head spun. He was so weak he could not rise. The flask of water lay on the ground nearby. He crawled to it and emptied it of the little water that remained. It took away the sour taste, but he was as weak as ever and filled with the pain of ravenous hunger.

In his pack was a little of the dried meat given him by the Kellima. He dug it out and tried to eat, but he had not the strength to chew it and the taste made his gorge rise. He spat out the meat and raised the flask to his lips, forgetting that it was empty.

He collapsed, despairing, close to weeping in his misery. But the thought that he was alive returned, filling his mind and giving him strength and will. He had felt death clutch him, but he had been spared.

No, not spared, he realized. That gentle term did not apply to his survival. He had been snatched from death on the very brink. With his last breath he had called on the missionaries' God, the God of Peter's Rock, the unfathomable being who was both God and man—and God had heard.

Now the tears came, but they were tears of joy, not sorrow. He had been saved from death; he would be saved from his hunger and his weakness, too, because God had entered his life and now nothing would be the same.

God wanted him. That was unmistakably clear. He had been guided to Peter's Rock, and on that isolated, unvisited world had been forged the first link in the chain that drew him here to Huttoi, where the hand of God had reached out to shield him from death. All his life, he had believed that chance governed the universe. Even his escape from the killwind he had credited to starfarer's luck. Now he knew the truth.

There was no such thing as luck. All things were foreseen, and the universe unfolded in time according to an inexorable plan. Men could not grasp this simple truth; so they spoke of luck, and chance, and closed their minds to the working of God's will. God was in all things, saw all things, knew all that was and all that was to be. God was in him, Enskeline, moving him, guiding him. God had work for him to do.

The certainty calmed him and gave him strength. He crept to the nearest tree and dragged himself erect. He leant against the tree for a time, then, resolute, he set forth. He stumbled, he fell frequently, but he always rose secure in the knowledge that something awaited him.

Toward evening, he found water and food. With a prayer of thanksgiving, he plunged his face into the cool waters of a stream and plucked a handful of butterberries from a low, scrawny bush. These were smaller than the ones Ber-Kember had discovered, and not as richly sweet, but they were delicious all the same.

He ate, drank again, and filled his flask. He was exhausted from his day's travel, but before settling down to rest by the stream, he prayed. Never before in his life had he prayed. He had often laughed at those who did, and even taunted the missionaries for calling upon God to solve their problems and grant them their needs. But now he prayed, in halting words, in phrases overheard and half-remembered. He prayed for Ber-Kember, for his lost crewmen Scragbones and Faranaxx, for the men of Peter's Rock and the success of their mission, for the Hutt, and for all on this world. Last of all, he prayed for himself, that he might be given the light to see his true purpose and the will to fulfill it.

In the morning he felt stronger. He prayed again and then set about looking for food. Near the butterberry bush was a clump of thickly leaved vines, low to the ground, with pale flowers. He recognized them as seterma, an edible tuber. He thanked God for bringing him to this place of plenty where he might rest and regain his strength while he prepared for his task.

A thick stand of spinneries rose near a bend of the stream. It was almost circular in shape. In the center was a clear space big enough for a man to lie down and stretch out in comfort. The huge leaves that overlapped above him, drooping almost to the ground to make a wall around him, would be a shelter in the cool season of Huttoi. Here was his place to stay: to pray and meditate and purify himself in preparation for the revelation that was certain to come.

Enskeline remained by the stream through most of a long Huttoi year. At the end of that time his appearance was much changed. He was gaunt; his garments hung loosely from his frame. The starfarer's clothes, though made of tough and durable stuff, showed signs of wear, and his boots were worn through. His skin was weathered, hair grew thickly on his once shaven skull, and a tangled beard reached to his breast.

But the greatest change was in his eyes, burning in dark hollows over his sunken cheeks with the light of a sacred flame. They were the eyes of one who had seen the unseen and known the unknown. In the long solitude, in the silence and the darkness, Enskeline had learned his destiny.

Once he had been a seeker of wealth and pleasure and all the tangible embellishments of mortal life. He had sought them with all his strength and all his will. Often he had possessed them. But the joy of possession was short-lived. Soon he grew sated, and was off searching once again. But now he sought the happiness that did not end, and he knew the way to earn it.

The Holy Shroud must be found and returned to Peter's Rock. Enskeline would gather a new crew representing all the races of Huttoi, and they would set forth to seek the shroud.

If none would come with him, he would seek it alone. With God to direct the search, he could not fail to find it. This would be the atonement for his squandered life, the justification of his starfaring skills, the fulfillment of the plan begun on Peter's Rock.

On a warm, bright morning late in the mild season, he left his shelter, striding confidently into the pathless grasslands with none but God to guide his steps.

Dallamer was a man like no other on Huttoi. When he spoke, the Hutt listened intently and vague memories stirred within them: old tales of men and women who refused to submit to the rule of others were remembered now, and repeated among those who heard him. Sayings of Hutterston were recalled and found to contain a new significance in the light of the offworlder's words.

As his influence spread, Dallamer's confidence increased. He looked upon the Hutt as clay in the hands of a potter. Latent strength was in them, but they needed shaping and hardening in the kiln of battle.

The Hutt had lived for generations on a world of few external dangers. The climate was mild, the planet held no large predators, food and water were easily available. The killwind was a threat, but it could be avoided. Accidents were always a possibility, to be sure, but no more so than on any other world, or even aboard the *Rimjack*. The women still faced the danger and the struggle of childbirth—and the Hutt women were strong, alert, and quick-minded. But Huttoi had allowed the men to survive in peace and security. The hunters did no more than chase down timid herbivores whose only weapon was their speed. Consequently, the men of the Hutt had lost the will to struggle. Their world had been snatched from them with an ease that rendered them contemptible.

Things became clearer to Dallamer. He had wondered at first how the Hutt males, physically strong and showing every sign of robust health, had come to be so diffident, slow-witted, and short-lived—the Hutt females' inferiors in every respect. Now he understood. Life was struggle; the men of Huttoi had never truly experienced life.

On Peter's Rock, Dallamer had studied the history of Earth, and he saw it now from a new perspective. The truth came upon him like a revelation. It was the struggle of uncounted generations that had brought the humans of Earth to the stars. To struggle was to live, and a race or a nation that ceased to struggle soon began to rot from within, corrupt, and die. He vowed to deliver the Hutt from this fate and to restore their mastery over Huttoi.

Dallamer and the Bothossa survivors moved across the face of Huttoi, spreading their new gospel. The Kellima, stunned by the loss of more than half their number in a single day, accepted Belrinn and Dallamer as their leaders without hesitation; they were relieved to have someone to guide them. Two other families of the savannah joined them in the Kellima village. While Belrinn stayed to govern the village, Dallamer ranged widely in search of Hutt families and gatherings. All that he found had been decimated, and none suspected the source of the plague. They were numbed and helpless to act.

Dallamer's words galvanized them. When he returned to the Kellima village—now the home of the new Bothossa gathering—he led nearly three hundred Hutt. In his train were aged leaders who followed him because they heard in his words a wisdom to supersede their own. Mothers followed him because he promised vengeance for their slain children. Hunters saw him as one who would teach them how to be men again, as once men were on Earth.

At the village, Belrinn organized the new gathering. With nearly five hundred, it was the largest assembly of Hutt since landing day, and its very size seemed to encourage all its members. Dallamer picked eighty of the most promising men and women and began to build his army.

He knew nothing directly of armies or military life. But he knew discipline and organization and methods of training, and he learned each day as much as he taught. By the time the cool season ended, his recruits were down to forty-three, but those forty-three were a force to be respected.

In all this time there had been no recurrence of the plague and no sign of Nandra interest in what the Hutt were doing. There was much speculation among the humans, but no certainty. No Hutt really understood the workings of the Nandra mind. It was impossible to tell whether the aliens regretted their slaughter of an unsuspecting race, simply assumed that all Hutt had perished, or were biding their time while they prepared a new and deadlier weapon. Under the circumstances, Dallamer saw no alternative but to strike quickly.

With no knowledge of Nandra strategy, no idea of their weapons or tactics, he worked out a plan that combined the maximum surprise with the best chance of survival and escape. With his forty-three he traveled by night until they were within sight of the ring complex. The *Rimjack* still stood dark and silent on her ring, unguarded. The square towers of the Altenorei rose beyond the ship, dwarfed by distance.

Three stayed at this spot. Their mission was to wait for word of the attack. If no word came by the following nightfall, they were to return to the village and announce that Dallamer had failed.

The rest worked their way closer to the ring complex; six went on ahead to scout. For all their courage, they had no real idea what to look for. They could not be certain that they would be able to recognize Nandra communication equipment or weapons even if they saw them; they could only hope to remain unseen and stumble upon information by chance. Dallamer knew this and accepted it. He knew, too, that it was better to risk the loss of six than of forty.

One by one, the scouts returned. Two had seen a lighted building filled with machinery around which many Nandra hovered. Two others had seen Nandra with a round device affixed to a forearm, but had no idea of its purpose. The last to return had actually entered an unlocked, unguarded building where Nandra were resting.

Dallamer divided his force into three groups, each armed with ripguns, knives, and javelins. One group was to attack the lighted building, the second to kill the sleeping Nandra, and the third to provide cover. With the first two objectives achieved, all three groups would proceed to secure the remaining buildings.

The attack was a massacre. Sixty-seven Nandra were killed in so short a time that two of the Hutt did not even fire their ripguns. Twenty-nine of the enemy died in the odd weblike apparatus in which they rested. Twenty-two more were cut down in the lighted building which appeared to be a communication center. The rest died as they emerged from the other buildings.

Only three Nandra made any attempt to resist. Their weapon

was the drumlike device worn on their forearms. These devices stunned several of the Hutt but seemed to do no lasting damage. One was wrested from the Nandra who wielded it and turned against the defenders. The effect was devastating.

When the brief tumult of battle was over and all was still, the Hutt looked at one another and at their leader with a wild light in their eyes. Their enemies lay all around them, dead at their hands. The taste of triumph was sweet. It gave them an appetite for more.

"What now?" one asked, looking about.

"Let's demolish this place!" a man cried, and the cry was taken up.

"The towers! Let's attack the towers where the real masters hide!" a woman shouted.

"No!" Dallamer cried, and they fell silent before his commanding presence. "We destroy nothing. Understand that. We're going to search this place and study everything we find that may tell us about the Nandra and their masters." In a more reasoning tone, he went on, "We had the advantage of surprise this time. We may not have it again, and we must seek other advantages. Knowledge of Nandra ways and Nandra weaknesses will be our greatest strength."

"Those weapons, Dallamer—they worked against the Nandra, but not against us," a man said.

"Then we've learned something important. The Nandra don't know that yet. We'll collect all the weapons we can find and bring them back to the village."

"What about the Altenorei?" a woman asked.

"We aren't going near the Altenorei towers until we learn more about them. No one among the Hutt seems to know what purpose the towers serve. We have no idea how they were built, or why, but we know that they're protected by an invisible power that kills. Until we can protect ourselves against that power, we can't move against the towers. We need knowledge. Let's get that first," Dallamer said.

They spread throughout the complex, searching, gathering every item that could be carried and bringing it to the building of machines. Dallamer went through the other buildings, studying their shape and contents and the method of their construction. All were irregular polygons, tightly and efficiently made, with smooth unbroken walls. High openings admitted light and air, but there were no openings to permit vision. All the buildings were the same height—about six meters—but their shapes varied. One large, shedlike building, the one in which the starfarers of the *Rimjack* had stayed, was five-sided. It stood completely empty. The building of machines and several smaller storage sheds were six-sided. The place where the Nandra slept and all the remaining buildings— one of them apparently a kind of mess hall—were seven-sided. The only feature common to all was that the longest wall of every building faced north.

These were far better constructions than the stone houses of the village, and Dallamer decided to make use of them. They were the first Hutt territory to be recaptured; they would be the home of the new Hutt nation. Living here, studying the machines that still clicked and purred in the lighted building, the Hutt would learn the ways of their enemies and the way to conquer.

The others were astonished by the audacity of Dallamer's proposal. Once they got over their initial surprise, however, they were enthusiastic. Such bold defiance of those who had stood over them unquestioned for so long a time was a tonic to their spirits.

Word was sent back to the village. The Nandra corpses were removed and buried, and then the victors examined their spoils more carefully. Dallamer found himself wishing that the interpreter who had brought warning had been spared: he would have been helpful. As it now stood, they were conquerors of a heap of mysterious artifacts and a building filled with incomprehensible machinery.

The drumlike forearm weapons of the Nandra were the first objects of their curiosity. The Nandra who had fallen before them were flaccid, as if their internal structure had been dissolved. Questioning the women and the man who had felt its effects, Dallamer was told that they had experienced only a momentary dizziness and nausea, which quickly passed and left no ill effects.

Experimenting with the awkwardly shaped weapons, Dallamer found that they had no effect on solid objects in their path, though the power passed through them. The weapon seemed to work by the effect of sound, or vibration, or both. Dallamer did not grasp the principle, but the effect was plain.

They now had two weapons that could destroy Nandra. And knowing this, he grew bolder.

Two small Nandra posts lay near one another within a long day's march of this complex. With their weapons and the element of surprise, which was still their greatest advantage, his small force could seize both.

These raids were even more successful than the first. The Hutt killed eighty-one Nandra, seized more of the drumlike weapons, and took two humans captive. The force was back at the scene of their first victory within two days of their departure.

Once they learned of the plague and saw the evidence of Hutt victory, the prisoners grew more cooperative, but they remained uneasy. Like the man who had brought warning of the plague to the Bothossa village, they had been born and raised among the Nandra. Their parents had served the Nandra all their lives. These two had come to look upon their fellow humans through Nandra eyes: as brutal subhumans unworthy to share a world with the sublime Altenorei masters.

They were able to tell Dallamer much about the Nandra, but nothing about the Altenorei. In all their lives, they had never seen one of the masters, and knew no one who had. Knowledge of the Altenorei was restricted to a chosen few among the Nandra and absolutely forbidden to any other race.

Gemmosk, the male captive, was the more talkative. His information was often helpful, but sometimes confusing and contradictory. The Nandra, Dallamer kept discovering, simply did not think along human lines. Even the grotesque Wishbones of Sassacheele seemed more human in their ways, once communication had been achieved.

The other captive, Erlor, was less helpful. She told him little, and that grudgingly, as if she believed he had no right to know. Dallamer listened to them both, first separately and then together. Only after two days of questioning did he tell them of his plan for them.

"Gemmosk, you will be attached to a group responsible for the investigation and classification of every Nandra artifact we possess. Each morning you will breakfast with Belrinn and me, and instruct us in the Nandra language. You will also teach the language to others we choose. Do these things well and you will be a valuable member of our force," he said to the man.

"I'll serve you well, Master Dallamer," said Gemmosk.

Turning his cool gaze on the woman, Dallamer said, "Erlor, I tell you only this: Huttoi is now divided into two armies, the Hutt and the enemy. You have until tomorrow at sundown to decide which army you serve in."

"I tell you now—I serve the Nandra."

"Take the time I offer, Erlor, and think deeply. You're human. Remember, whatever you choose, you'll always be human."

"I am not Hutt," she said defiantly. "Hutt are beasts. I saw what they did to the Nandra."

"You have been told what the Nandra did to the Hutt."

"I know what the Hutt claim. A disease, a plague . . . all a lie. The Hutt died because of their own ignorance and filth. Nandra would not stoop to kill such creatures."

Dallamer looked into her face, twisted with contempt and hatred for her kind. He sighed and signaled to the guards who stood behind her. "I regret your choice. We'll bury you beside your Nandra friends," he said, and turned away.

"Would you kill me?" she cried. There was shock and fear in her voice.

"You chose death yourself," said Dallamer without turning.

"Beasts! You're all beasts!" she screamed.

"Take her out. See to it that Gemmosk is present at the execution. Let everyone know," Dallamer ordered the guards.

Erlor was dispatched quickly while Gemmosk and nearly two hundred others looked on. The execution had a sobering effect on the Hutt. Far more than the killing of the Nandra, it underscored the irreversible nature of their struggle and the new attitudes it required. To be Hutt was no longer sufficient; one had to be loyal to the Hutt as well and willing to serve the Hutt cause, or one was numbered among the enemy.

Whether by conviction or because of the example of Erlor, Gemmosk proved a heroic worker. Under his tutelage, the Hutt became familiar with the tools and weapons of the Nandra, and learned to understand and operate their machines. Dallamer, Belrinn, and twenty others made rapid progress in the Nandra language. As they learned to decipher maps and to wring meaning from the messages that still came in on the communications machine, the Hutt learned of other small Nandra installations. One by one, they seized them. Still there was no counterattack, no retaliation. It seemed that a Hutt victory was inevitable; the Nandra gave no sign of caring, or even of knowing of their losses.

Then, without warning, the plague struck again. The effects were less severe, but still a terrible blow. In a single night one out of every five Hutt in the captured bases died, and more died the following day.

There was no doubt that it was the Nandra plague. The symptoms were the same, the manner of death identical. And in this visitation the Hutt lost strength disproportionate to their numbers. Dallamer and Belrinn died, and so did nearly half the fighting force.

Ormerand, sister of Belrinn, organized the burial of the dead, but she had no idea what to do next. Some of the Hutt cried for an act of massive retaliation, a wave of vengeance that would not cease until the Hutt alone lived on their reconquered planet. Others counseled prudence or suggested a treaty with the Nandra that might prevent further killing. A few slipped quietly away from the base in the dark of night, convinced that there was no safety but in flight and concealment. Ormerand did her best to keep the Hutt together and bring them to agreement, but each day they were more divided.

Then came the pilgrim.

He entered the settlement one morning and halted by the landing rings. For a time he gazed at the driveship that stood sealed against all intrusion on its ring. He wore strange garments, but a Hutt cloak hung over his bony shoulders, and Hutt sandals were on his feet. He had a long, tangled beard; he was the first bearded man the Hutt had ever seen. They gathered around him, curious, staring openly at this stranger. He paid them no heed, merely looked hungrily on the driveship, his lips moving silently.

He seemed to come abruptly out of a trance. He looked around, and at the first contact with his burning eyes many drew back. He spoke familiar words, but they came haltingly to his tongue.

"Who rules here?" he demanded.

"Ormerand is our leader," said a man.

"She does nothing. We have no leader," a woman cried.

"If we don't follow Ormerand, we'll have the Nandra back—is that what you want?" snapped another woman.

Two men spoke up in support of the first woman, and in an instant an angry shouting match was under way. The newcomer stepped between the opposing groups, silencing them with his daunting gaze.

"Where is Ormerand?" he asked.

"I'll take you to her," the first man said.

They walked through the settlement. The newcomer's eyes were fixed forward; all other eyes were drawn to his passing. A crowd began to form in his wake, and by the time he reached the building where Ormerand was to be found, a good portion of the Hutt were following him.

He pushed past the guard who backed away from him, staring at what seemed to him an apparition, and walked directly to Ormerand, who was deep in council with three of her advisers.

"There must be peace," he announced in a voice that carried to those who stood outside.

"Peace? Who says . . . who are you?" Ormerand asked at sight of the stranger.

"I am a pilgrim. A messenger. Hutt and Nandra must kill no more. The time has come for them to unite in a great undertaking."

"Whose message is this?" Tembraye, an adviser, demanded angrily.

"It is the will of God."

The message of the priest-voyagers had been lost in the turmoil of recent times. Ormerand and her council glanced blankly at the pilgrim and then at one another. Ormerand made a confused gesture. "Who is God?" she asked.

"God is the creator of all worlds and all life. Hutt and Nandra are His children, equally beloved by Him."

"The Nandra do not believe this. They show no love for us," Ormerand said.

Tembraye added, "They kill us with sickness that they send on the winds. Does your god know of this?"

"They kill you with sickness, and you kill them with weapons. You are all guilty. But this must end," said the pilgrim confidently.

"Who will end it? You?"

Ignoring the question, the pilgrim asked, "Who among your people speaks the Nandra speech?"

"Several of us know it."

"Gemmosk speaks it best."

"Yes, Gemmosk."

"Then send Gemmosk to me. We will go to the Nandra and their masters and make peace," said the pilgrim.

Ormerand and the others exchanged suspicious glances. From the crowd outside, some of whom had entered, a growing murmur of interest rose.

"You will make peace?" Ormerand repeated.

"I will," the pilgrim said.

"Perhaps he can," one of the men said softly.

"No!" cried Tembraye. "Why should we believe him, or trust him? He's a stranger, and he acts as if we must do anything he commands. He walks in here from out of nowhere, and you trust him as if he were our new leader. This might be the work of the Nandra." Turning to the pilgrim, he demanded, "Who are you, and who sent you? Tell us these things plainly before you presume to give us orders."

"I come from God, who governs all. He has sent me to make peace. With His help I will do so. While Hutt and Nandra slay one another, the great work remains undone."

"What great work is this? Tell us."

"First, peace. Send Gemmosk to me," said the pilgrim, unyielding.

"I am against this. The man could be dangerous."

Ormerand said, "Peace would benefit us. Even a short truce could work to our advantage." Turning to the pilgrim, she said, "We will give you conditions to bring to the Nandra."

"No conditions. Only an end to the killing at once."

"We will give back nothing we've captured," Ormerand said. Tembraye added defiantly, "We will return nothing, and we must have more. That is our demand. Huttoi is our world."

"All worlds belong to God. Your quarrel is foolish, and your killing is senseless," said the pilgrim calmly, as if he were addressing children. "Peace will benefit all. More important, it will give all the races of Huttoi the opportunity to join in a work glorifying God."

"Tell us more about this work," said Ormerand.

"When I return I will tell you what must be done. Tell me this: what has become of the men from space who came among you?"

"Dallamer is dead of the Nandra sickness," said Tembraye.

"What of the others?"

"We know of no others. If there were any, they must have died in the first coming of the sickness."

"Does a woman named Lossian live among you?"

"No. The name belongs to the Bothossa," said Ormerand. "None from that family survive. Are you of the Bothossa?"

The pilgrim hesitated for a moment, then said, "I knew them once. Before the sickness."

Gemmosk entered at this point, making his way through the watching crowd to the group within. He studied the pilgrim for a moment, then saluted Ormerand and said, "Some in the crowd outside say I was sent for, others say I was not. I came to find out."

Without waiting for Ormerand's reply, the pilgrim stepped to Gemmosk's side and said, "Are you the one who speaks the Nandra language?"

"I am."

"You must go to the Nandra with me."

Gemmosk looked at the pilgrim, gaunt, sun-darkened, with eyes that caught and held him; then he turned to Ormerand and the council. He appeared perplexed. "Only two of us? It would be very dangerous."

"You must."

"Do you have a new weapon? If you don't have some weapon I don't know about, we can't—"

"No weapon. We go to end the killing, not to kill," said the pilgrim.

"Wait, now. Is this so?"

Tembraye tried to speak, but Ormerand silenced him with a stern look and a firm gesture. "Yes, Gemmosk. This man says he'll make the Nandra stop killing us if we stop killing them, and I think it's the right thing to do. But he needs your help to speak to them."

"Nandra won't listen to a Hutt."

"They will hear my message," said the pilgrim firmly.

"A message, a great work!" Tembraye burst out angrily.

"You keep repeating those words, but you won't say what you mean!"

"I bring the Nandra the same message I bring you: learn to love, and seek God," the pilgrim said.

"Is that the great message? Do you think you need only say that, and the Nandra will heed you?" Tembraye asked with a laugh and an incredulous look at the others.

"The message is not mine but God's. The Nandra will heed it, and so will the Altenorei and the Hutt. The intelligent beings of this world must learn to love one another and live in harmony so they may be free to seek the face of God among the stars."

"Fine words, pilgrim. And what if the Nandra decide not to love you? What if they kill you as soon as you open your mouth?"

"They will listen."

Ormerand came between them. Gesturing for Tembraye to be silent, she asked the pilgrim, "Why are you so sure? Gemmosk tells the truth—Nandra do not listen to Hutt. Why do you say they'll hear your message from this one you call God and not kill you?"

"I do God's work on this world, and He protects me. He has cured me of the sickness and sheltered me from the fury of the killwind. He has delivered me from hunger and thirst. I do not fear the Nandra."

"No one recovers from the Nandra sickness!" Tembraye cried.

"By the help of God, I recovered."

His words caused a stir among the council of advisers and among the watching crowd. Such unwavering faith was foreign to the Hutt. They had known confidence for a time, after their initial successes, but the return of the sickness had shaken them. Here was one who appeared unshakable. They looked upon the pilgrim with increasing respect.

"I'll go if you wish it," said Gemmosk.

"Yes, go with him, Gemmosk, and do as he says," Ormerand said decisively. "Make your preparations. You leave in three days."

"How far is it to where the Nandra leaders are?" the pilgrim asked.

"Nandra have no leaders," Gemmosk told him. "They

decide on all things collectively. Any Nandra on this planet can speak to all others through the communicator.''

''Can you work the communicator?''

''No. We can sometimes hear the Nandra, but we don't yet know how to speak to them.''

''Then we must go to the nearest Nandra base. Where is that?''

Gemmosk thought for a moment, then said, ''The nearest one is in the hills, about six days from here. I know the way.''

''We must leave today. No need to think of supplies or shelter. We are in God's hands.''

Gemmosk looked to Ormerand. She nodded, and the translator shrugged and said, ''I'm willing.''

''Then you will leave this day,'' said Ormerand. ''Take food and water for two days. I insist on that.''

''I accept your kindness,'' the pilgrim said. He turned and left the chamber, with Gemmosk close behind.

They left late that morning and reached the Nandra base early on the sixth day following. The pilgrim walked boldly across the open upland slope to the six-sided building where the Nandra communicator stood. Gemmosk walked at his side, matching his steps.

Gemmosk felt no fear or doubt, only a great joy. On their journey together, the pilgrim had told him of his mission, and as he spoke on, Gemmosk recalled the things he had overheard during his life among the Nandra, when they discussed the mysterious Valatule, the all-creating Force that made itself known only to certain of the Altenorei. The pilgrim's God was not like Valatule. It was not remote, but near and protective; it spoke to all, and loved all; it was a being of light and life, not a whispering visitor to dark towers. To Gemmosk, this was a being far stronger than Valatule, yet gentler; and as the pilgrim spoke he felt belief enfold him like a warm current, surrounding him, filling him, giving him a certitude and peace he had never known before.

Side by side they entered the communicator building, and there they halted. The Nandra gathered around the machine rose and drew together apprehensively, but the two men did not advance. Instead they made the Nandra gesture of friendship and then Gemmosk, his heart pounding, announced that the Hutt at his side had come with a message for them.

When he paused, the Nandra spoke softly among themselves. One stepped forward and addressed them in a voice that rose and fell sharply, like dissonant music. The speaker was older than the rest, presumably senior among this group, and appeared from the markings that almost covered his forehead to be of high standing.

Gemmosk heard the Nandra out, then said, "He says we must go at once. No Hutt may enter this building. He's not threatening us. I think he's too surprised at the sight of us to know what to do."

"Tell him that the Nandra are to kill no more Hutt. He is to inform all the Nandra of this, and of the Hutt's promise to kill no more Nandra," said the pilgrim.

Gemmosk relayed the message. The Nandra responded almost at once; his response was brief.

With a sigh, Gemmosk said, "The Hutt must be removed so that the Masters can receive the word of Valatule. This is what must be, he said."

"Tell him that Valatule is no more. I bring a message from the one true God."

With a quick, eager smile, Gemmosk proclaimed the pilgrim's words to the Nandra. There was a long silence. The two humans could not interpret the Nandra's reaction. They stood their ground patiently, unmoving, awaiting the response.

The Nandra speaker, as if awakening to a crisis, turned and joined the others. The undulating voices of a score of Nandra speaking in chorus filled the interior of the building with grating sound, recalling to the pilgrim a music he had heard once among the Farraka on a distant world. But he drove the distraction from his mind and concentrated on the Nandra.

"Can you understand anything?" he asked Gemmosk.

"They're confused. I think they're also frightened. I can't tell exactly. . . . They're speaking about the Altenorei; a lot of their words are unfamiliar to me."

The Nandra conferred a long time. The humans wondered if they had been forgotten, but they did nothing to intrude upon the Nandra; they only waited. At last the one who had first addressed them detached himself from the rest, came over to them, and made the gesture of friendship. They returned it, and he spoke to them now in a slightly slower pattern of speech, as if he were speaking very carefully and wanted to avoid any chance of misunderstanding.

Gemmosk listened attentively, then turned to the pilgrim. "He asks what message your God sends. From the way he's speaking, this is a very important question."

The pilgrim reached out, slowly and deliberately, to clasp the slender three-fingered hand of the speaker. The Nandra shuddered at the instant of contact, but did not pull free. Looking straight into the Nandra's narrow eyes, the pilgrim said, "Nandra, Altenorei, and Hutt must be as brothers. We must join together and leave this world in a quest for the face of God."

Gemmosk repeated the message carefully. The Nandra made a short, sharp sound—like a human gasp of surprise—and replied briefly.

Eyes wide, Gemmosk said, "He wants you to go with him to the Altenorei!"

"Only me?"

After another brief exchange, Gemmosk said, "Yes. He says we'll both be safe. I'm not needed. The Altenorei understand all speech and—I mustn't be following all he says—he seems to believe that the Altenorei have been waiting for you. But that couldn't be!"

"Tell him I'll go with him."

No sooner had Gemmosk transmitted the message than the Nandra moved off, signing for the pilgrim to follow. He did so with only a nod of farewell to Gemmosk. The Altenorei tower was far from there, a splinter of brightness on the far horizon. Gemmosk prepared himself for a long, uncomfortable wait.

To his astonishment, three of the Nandra approached him, saluted him respectfully, and inquired after his comfort. It was the first time in Gemmosk's life that a Nandra had addressed him as a creature with needs, wants, and feelings—as an equal. Speaking further with them and the other Nandra, he found that he was being treated not merely with courtesy but with respect.

Gemmosk spent nine days alone with the Nandra, and was at all times treated as an honored guest. He was free to go where he chose. Any questions he asked were promptly and fully answered, except those touching on the pilgrim. On that subject his hosts professed ignorance, and he believed them.

When he showed interest in the communicator, they eagerly explained its workings to him. He could not understand the physical principles involved, but when they began to instruct him in the operation of the machine, he grasped it quickly. At the end of a single day's instruction, he was able to establish contact with the Hutt-occupied base he had left.

The reaction of his own people to seeing Gemmosk on the alien mechanism and hearing his voice as if he were present was almost comical. He was able, in a short time, to teach them how to transmit their own voices to him, and a two-way verbal exchange was soon in operation. They had grown concerned about Gemmosk and the pilgrim, and there was already talk of a rescue party. Gemmosk assured them that he was safe, was being well treated, and had no doubts of the safety of the pilgrim. When he informed them that the pilgrim had been taken to speak with the Altenorei, the Hutt were at first astonished, then incredulous.

"In all the time they've been on this world, not one of us has even seen one of the Altenorei," Ormerand marveled, "and this man was brought directly to them."

"But why?" came the voice of Tembraye.

"None of the Nandra here seems to know. All he did was take the elder's hand and speak to him, and the old Nandra wanted him to go to the Altenorei right away."

After a pause, Ormerand asked, "And are they truly treating you well?"

"Better than I've ever known Nandra to treat Hutt. This pilgrim is no common man. I think even the Altenorei will listen to him."

"Gemmosk . . . what does he want? What does he really want from us?" Tembraye asked.

"I think he wants only what he says: to seek the face of God."

The pilgrim returned at last, borne by two Nandra. He was more gaunt and hollow-eyed than before, and so exhausted that he was barely able to stand. Gemmosk ran up to him. At sight of the translator, the pilgrim smiled and said in a faint but happy voice, "It will be. The Altenorei have heard. We will all be one."

He could say no more. His Nandra attendants took him to a building where he rested. Gemmosk at once sent word of the pilgrim's return to Ormerand and the others, then went to his quarters to wait. Late the following day a Nandra came to bring him to the pilgrim.

The sight of him unsettled Gemmosk. The pilgrim was as pale as a man drained of all blood, so thin that his bones seemed about to burst through his translucent skin. While Gemmosk shuddered to imagine the ordeal he had been through, the pilgrim stirred and opened his eyes. At the sight of Gemmosk he brightened and reached out to take the translator's hand.

"Are you well? Did they treat you badly?" Gemmosk asked.

"I'm only tired. Very tired."

"Did you see the Altenorei?"

"No. No light. Altenorei shun light. We . . . communicated."

"You look very weak and pale. Was it painful?"

"No pain. Exhausting, but no pain. They looked into my mind . . . brought me into theirs. So much to exchange . . . such eagerness. The Altenorei are wise . . . ancient . . . seeking, seeking for ages . . . and I brought them the word they sought. It will be, Gemmosk," said the pilgrim, gripping the translator's hand tightly, then releasing him.

When Gemmosk left him, the pilgrim lay in a half-waking state, reliving the experience of the tower, those sensations that no other human had ever known. In a dry, cool darkness so profound it seemed to consume him, he had known an illumination that transfigured his mind with the wisdom of an alien race. In remoteness and utter isolation from his accustomed world he had found a warm communion with alien souls. Serenity and terror, fulfillment and despair had intertwined in his consciousness to elevate him to a state for which his mind held no words and which his present memory could only vaguely recapture, as one experiences remembered bliss or suffering in the intellect but can not relive it in the body.

He recalled the long, complicated chorus of ideas that flowed like an intricate harmony among those conjoined intelligences. The Altenorei were an ancient, far-traveled race with a store of wisdom exceeding human imagining. For ages they had pondered the great questions of existence, seeking the cause that lay behind all others, the truth at the heart of all truth. They had learned much; yet mingled with their profundity were ludicrous pockets of ignorance; their mellowed serenity could yield in an instant to childlike exuberance when faced with an unfamiliar concept. When the pilgrim had brought forth his message and drawn from his memory the intricate debates he had half-attended during the empty watches between planetfalls, and confronted them with God, the chilly air of the tower fairly rang with the joy of the Altenorei. They had waited here for a message from Valatule, and Valatule had failed them. But a strange creature, from a despised and unimportant subject race, had burst upon them with a message that glorified his kind.

The darkness pulsed with eagerness as the possibility spread among the Altenorei. If the Hutt spoke truly—and they found no deception in him—then their mission was clear. Somewhere the image of the true Maker of All existed and could be seen; for though the Altenorei could not see as the Hutt and Nandra saw, they did not doubt that their subtler senses could apprehend the image just as they now perceived the creature who bore the message. The ultimate truth, then, could be known.

The pilgrim lay back, sighed, and allowed himself to sink into sleep. The work was under way. All would come about as it must.

IX.

Roharr: The Urixi

Cormasson scrupulously observed the letter of his agreement with Abbot Ollenbrook. The *Garrashaw* touched down at three Sternverein outposts, and at each one priest-voyagers were permitted to remain behind in numbers that varied in proportion to the planet's population and its distribution.

On the third planetfall, Cormasson announced that he would be leaving the *Garrashaw,* placing the ship and the completion of its mission in the hands of Secondary Zuern. Together they plotted a return route to the main base at Occuch that would make possible a safe distribution of all the priest-voyagers. With this completed, Cormasson soundscribed a final report in Zuern's presence, which she sealed for delivery to Sternverein Command.

"The honor of bringing the *Garrashaw* to Occuch after such a successful mission should be yours," Zuern said when the report was finished.

"The honor isn't mine alone. We all contributed to the mission's success."

"Without your leadership and judgment, Commander, it might have been extremely difficult."

"It might still be, Zuern. The mission's not over until we're all back on Occuch and the relic is safely in Sternverein hands."

"You seem certain that it exists and can be found."

"I must act on that assumption," Cormasson said. After a thoughtful pause, he went on, "To seek such a precious object after so long a time, when it might be almost anywhere in the galaxy—this must appear to be madness. Yet I believe that I can find this shroud. These missionaries like to speak of miracles and surely, if I find their relic, they will call it a great miracle and speak of the Sternverein as an instrument of their god. But there are no miracles, Zuern. There are only events. And events follow a pattern that a logical mind can reconstruct.''

''I, too, am a Mechanist, Commander. But when I think of the variables, the unknowns in this pattern . . .'' Zuern shook her head helplessly.

''It's not as complex as you might think. I've been busy gathering information ever since we left Peter's Rock. I know what charts the schismatics must have carried, and I know their ship's supply capacity. I can estimate their tolerance for lightspeed travel. I'm certain they made a planetfall on Roharr.''

Zuern was suddenly alert. ''Didn't the trader bring two priest-voyagers to Roharr?''

''He did. And that strengthens my belief. Two of the priest-voyagers went on with the trader Enskeline to visit another world—we know that to be a fact. I believe that they were seeking the relic. They learned something on Roharr, and I must learn what they found out, and follow.''

''Do you think they were together in the search?''

''Impossible to say. I doubt it, but one never knows. It's possible that each was seeking clues to the relic unknown to the others.''

''A complicated business. I wish you success, Commander.''

''Thank you, Zuern. Take care of the *Garrashaw*. If all goes well, I might be waiting on Occuch to see you land.''

For this mission, Cormasson thought it wise to conceal all connection with the Sternverein. He retained his own name, but assumed a new identity. He knew the ways of free traders well enough to play the role convincingly.

On a holding ring remote from the main landing area stood a captured scout ship. It had been modified for long-range use, with expanded cargo space and a stasis tank for slow-life sleep. Sternverein troopers had taken it on its first flight, and here it awaited final disposition. Cormasson found the ship ideal for his purpose and requisitioned it.

He rummaged through the outpost's storage vaults to assemble the typical mixed cargo of a solitary free trader: small arms, medical supplies, art objects ranging from gaudy trash to an exquisite, authentic motion-painting; a cage of dormant light-dancers, specialized fabrics, precision tools—and, as his special prize, three of the books given him on Peter's Rock. For himself, he filled a locker with plain work clothes, dryworld and cold-climate gear, a Kepler lantern, and plentiful ammunition for his short-range ripgun.

When the ship was fully loaded and provisioned and had undergone a thorough inspection, Cormasson decided to name it in typical free trader's fashion. He called it the *Urixi*, after a small, long-legged beast known for its speed and ability to escape pursuers.

He met one last time with Zuern. She questioned him closely about his new identity, his history, and his cover story, then pronounced him satisfactory, He had no further reason to delay. He lifted off that evening, bound for Roharr.

He passed most of the long voyage in the stasis tank. When he was roused, three watches before planetfall, he was surprised at the extent of the changes that had occurred during his extended sleep. He had lost some weight, and his skin was very pale. His hair and beard had grown long and tangled. Once he was dressed in a stained, well-worn coverall and scuffed boots he looked like a typical free trader. There was a slight stiffness in his joints—especially in his back and shoulders—and his muscles tired easily. He considered this all to the good, since it kept him from slipping into his habitual military posture.

The Roharran port officials passed him with only perfunctory questioning. He was given twenty-four days landing permission and unrestricted freedom to trade in Ermacene City and on the nearby islands. Cormasson acknowledged the conditions with unfeigned satisfaction. His chief destination, Felill, was one of those islands, and twenty-four days was adequate for his purposes. Should the time prove insufficient, he had no doubt that he could find a way to extend his stay. Ermacene was a marketplace. One could buy anything here, including time, if one was prepared to pay.

For six days Cormasson made the rounds of the trading houses in the city, bargaining vigorously and getting the worst of it almost every time. This did not matter to him; he found that a man talks a bit more freely when he has brought off a profitable deal. His trading was successful in the way he had hoped: he had gathered precious information and had at last made the connection he was aiming for.

On his seventh day he met with a representative of the Industrious House of Kamparongsang, an elderly man with very black skin and a long topknot of snow-white hair. The man, whose name was Paja, was so gracious, so considerate of his guest's ease, so very discreet, that most of the morning was gone before the subject of trading was even mentioned. After a leisurely midday meal, at which it was impossible to discuss business, and a restorative stroll in the outer garden, they returned indoors. As they reclined on comfortable cushions, sipping a spicy hot drink unfamiliar to Cormasson, Paja first broached the possibility of a transaction between the free trader and the Illustrious House of Kamparongsang.

"News travels quickly in such a busy place as Ermacene," the old man said, "and the activities of a free trader on his first visit to our world are followed with interest. We are pleased that, having gained some acquaintance with our rival houses, you have chosen to visit the house of Kamparongsang."

"I never heard anyone speak ill of you. The other houses envy your success, but they respect you. I took that as a good sign."

"You do us honor, Suru Cormasson," said Paja, inclining his head slightly as he spoke the title of respect.

In all his dealings in Ermacene City, Cormasson had tried to present himself in the character of a plain-speaking man, eager to get his business over with and be about his pleasure before returning to space, yet uneasy with the smooth ways of merchants. Now, with Paja, he said heartily, "To speak truly, I've been looking for someone I can trust. Not just to deal fairly—I'm sure most of the other houses are honest— but to know the value of what I have to trade."

"You will find us knowledgeable."

Glancing about shrewdly, Cormasson leaned forward and said, "I haven't told anyone what my chief trade item is. I didn't think most traders would know its real value. But when the subject came up, everyone seemed to think that you were the experts in this particular area." He sat back, looking very pleased with himself, beaming at the old man. Paja said nothing. He refilled their dishes with the sweet infusion and waited.

"I've got books, Paja. Three books from Old Earth, in the time before the great dispersion. One from the nineteenth century, two from the twenty-first. And I may be able to bring you more," Cormasson said triumphantly.

"You are a wise man, Suru Cormasson. There is no one on Roharr with more knowledge of the lost books of Old Earth than the master of this house."

"It took me a few days to learn that, but I'm willing to take the time to learn what I ought to know."

Paja nodded appreciatively. He sipped from his dish, but said nothing. Cormasson, too, drank and was silent for a time, but he soon surrendered to his postured eagerness. Reaching into his shirt, he drew out a small package, carefully wrapped, and held it up for the old man's inspection.

"I've brought one with me. I thought it would be best if I showed you what I've got instead of just talking. The others are safe," he said.

Paja's eyes widened; he was impassive no longer. "To hold such a treasure in my hands and look upon it with my eyes would be a great thing, Suru Cormasson. But I must not deceive you. I know but a little concerning the books of Old Earth. Only Kamparongsang Nine Domorie can judge their value fairly."

"Then he's the one I have to see. But if you'd like to hold it, go ahead, Paja," Cormasson said, smiling benignly and holding out the package.

The old man took it in both hands and laid it on his lap as cautiously as if it were a Quatian crystal-web. For a moment he simply gazed upon it; then, at Cormasson's urging, he began to unfold the soft, clinging wrapping of forlin hide, still as warm and supple as living tissue. At last he drew back the innermost layer and beheld the green leather surface, deeply embossed around the margin, with an intricate design in the center.

"Open it if you like," Cormasson said.

"I dare not."

"It has pictures. You can see what Old Earth looked like a few centuries before everyone left."

The old man looked up timidly. When their eyes met, Cormasson nodded and gestured for him to open the cover. Paja did so with the utmost care. He turned pages slowly, then he caught his breath at the depiction of a man riding on an animal that resembled a haxopod. All around was a dark wood, and in the distance, high and clear against the sky, was a towered and turreted castle. The chiaroscuro of wood and sky, the light falling on the mounted man's stiff garments, the precise limning of leaf and cloud and fluttering distant pennon were unlike anything he had ever seen before.

"Are all books so lovely, Suru Cormasson?" he asked in a hushed voice. "I know now why they are valued so highly."

"Some are very beautiful. They don't all have pictures like this one, though. I saw one that didn't have anything in it but numbers."

"Many people believe that such books contain great knowledge."

Cormasson shrugged. "Maybe they do, if you can make sense out of all the markings. I never learned."

"The master has some skill. It is a very difficult art."

"Would the master of the house wish to see my books? I'm willing to trade."

"I say with assurance that Kamparongsang Nine Domorie will wish to see your books and to trade with you, Suru Cormasson. Is it possible for you to return to the house tomorrow at midday?"

"I'll be here, Paja. I'll leave this book with you, so your master can study it beforehand."

The old man was touched by the offer. He looked at Cormasson with new respect. "Your trust in us shows that you are no ordinary trader, Suru Cormasson. You do us great credit."

"When I trust a man, I trust him completely, Paja. It's one of the things you have to learn if you're going to survive in space."

Paja smiled. "You speak wisely. But I have found that men are more willing to trust others with their lives than with their fortunes."

Cormasson left soon after. He was pleased with his progress so far and looked forward to the following day. His methodical approach was slow, to be sure; he had not yet set foot on Felill or spoken to any of the Christians of Roharr. But that would come. And thanks to his patient planning, when it did come the meeting would appear perfectly natural.

No one would suspect him of anything more than a kindly willingness to bring news from their homeworld.

The next day he came once again to the high, sweet-smelling hedge that surrounded and concealed the house of Kamparongsang. The gnarled stalks were as thick as his forearms, a testament to their great age. They formed an impenetrable barrier at all points save the single narrow entrance.

Cormasson was lavishly entertained in the true Roharran manner. Only when the sun had set and he was sipping wine with Nine Domorie did his host permit his gaze to linger on the package wrapped in forlin hide that lay at Cormasson's side. No word was spoken, but Cormasson understood that it was now permissible to broach the subject that had brought him to Roharr and the house of Kamparongsang.

Later that night, after the trade agreement had been completed, Nine Domorie summoned Paja to join them. The old man arrived bearing a crystal decanter of the rare cordial, amendir, called "Nectar of Ease." It was unique to this world, and was never exported. The host filled three delicate long-stemmed goblets with pale green Stepmann wine, then added three drops of amendir to each goblet. The precious cordial burst into coils of glittering color as it swirled lazily within the lighter wine. Domorie, in a Roharran salutation, touched his fingertips to the rims of the others' glasses. Paja did the same, and Cormasson followed their example.

"We have three things to celebrate: a new friendship, a new partnership, and the coming of Old Earth books to the house of Kamparongsang for the first time in many generations," said Domorie.

"I'll bring many more when I return. I hope you'll both be here to greet me," Cormasson said.

Paja smiled. "I will be gone to the silence, Suru Cormasson. But my master will still guide this house, and in that day he will be as rich in wisdom and honors as he will be in age."

"I hope the honest Paja speaks prophetic words. It is my belief that on your return you will deal with my children's children," Domorie said.

Cormasson raised his goblet. "I hope that if I do, they will be as wise as their father's father."

They drank slowly, in small measure, allowing the amendir

to work its subtle way through their systems, suffusing them with a physical euphoria that had no dulling effect on mind or senses. No one spoke for a long time, and the gestures of the Roharrans became subdued. They savored their own feeling of well-being and took heightened pleasure in the intricate shiftings of light and temperature and sound and scent that Domorie's servants produced in the chamber to accompany the experience of amendir.

Cormasson allowed himself the full delight of the Nectar of Ease, but kept alert for the proper moment. He was close to what he sought. A little more patience, he was certain, would bring him to his goal.

Domorie broke the silence. He began to speak in a soft, contented voice of the great days that lay ahead for the house of Kamparongsang. Over many tenzas they had grown in wealth and influence while remaining small and always staying under the guidance of the original founding family. With the books that Cormasson would bring, their future was certain to be even better. Paja—who was far older than he appeared—related several anecdotes of earlier members of the house. Some of the stories seemed to Cormasson to have no other point than to establish Paja's long and faithful service to the house and his acquaintance with some of its legendary figures. But he listened carefully to the old man's tales and to the master of the house, and waited for his opening.

At last Domorie sighed and said, "It is well to remember the triumphs, but we must also remember the disappointments. All are part of the great web."

Cormasson smiled. "When you speak like that, Domorie, you sound like one of the monastics. Perhaps I should bring you to Peter's Rock, so you can speak with them."

At the planet's name, Paja looked up with a gesture of surprise. Cormasson had not mentioned it in his presence before, and now he observed the old man's reaction.

"I have heard that name spoken, here in this house. Is it the name of the planet of the books?" Paja asked.

"It is, Paja, but you couldn't have heard it before. That's the name the first settlers gave it, and it's not on any of the charts."

"Yet I am certain."

"It's impossible, Paja. You could only hear it from some-one who's been to the planet."

"Yes! There was a trader—long ago, before I was accepted into the service of this house—before I was born—he brought books to the master!" the old man said eagerly.

"The abbot did speak of a trader," Cormasson conceded, "but he had left long ago, taking some of the priest-voyagers with him so they could bring their belief to other worlds. I can only guess at the time of his visit, and I don't know how many times he made planetfall; but if he ever came to Roharr, it would have been . . . oh, as much as two hundred tenzas ago, Roharran. He could easily—"

"Yes, yes, it is so!" Paja broke in excitedly. Turning to Domorie, he said, "In the time of the seventh of your name, a trader came with Old Earth books. In his ship were holy men, the ones who founded the church on Felill."

"I have no memory of this," said Domorie.

"But why didn't the trader ever return to Peter's Rock? He was welcome there. He could have had all the books he wanted," Cormasson said.

"I do not know. But I know he was here," said Paja firmly. "His visit was mentioned once, when I was young."

"We can easily make certain. I'll go to Felill."

Domorie raised a hand. "Let us think before we act. Perhaps the existence of this world should be concealed."

"The holy men must surely have mentioned it to someone in all this time. It doesn't really matter. Merely knowing the name is useless. It's uncharted. But if I go and speak with them, I'll be able to bring a message back to Peter's Rock— perhaps the first word they've ever heard of their voyagers. I think the monks will pay well for that," Cormasson said.

Domorie reflected for a time, then made a gesture of acceptance. "What you say is wise. While you visit Felill, I will study the records of the house and see what can be learned about this trader."

The first missionaries had found eager hearers for their message among the fisherfolk of the rugged island of Felill. Within a year of their arrival they had erected a small chapel on the headland overlooking the harbor. Now, many Roharran tenzas later, the Church of Saint Peter looked down on the fishing fleet and trading vessels. It was the largest building on the island. The cross atop its spire towered higher than any other man-made object on Roharr.

Cormasson arrived on the island late in the day. He found a comfortable stayhouse, and that evening he visited the church on the headland. Compared to the Monastery of the Holy Sepulcher, it was a modest building; but compared to the buildings of Roharr, it was a place of splendor.

The church was nearly empty when he entered. He looked around with an odd sense of recognition: it resembled the founder's chapel on Peter's Rock. The long benches set in rows all faced the plain table where the ritual was performed, just as in the monastery, and the same gaunt and bloodied figure hung on the cross on the far wall. All sound was hushed, and a sweet scent pervaded the still air.

Cormasson singled out a young man who stood in an archway talking to another man and a woman. He wore a coarse dark robe similar to those worn on Peter's Rock. Cormasson assumed that he was one of the churchmen. When the couple left, Cormasson approached him.

"I would speak with the abbot," he said.

"Abbot?" the young man repeated, perplexed. "I do not understand."

"I mean the one in charge here, whatever you call him."

"Ah, yes. Of course, friend. Come, and I'll take you to him."

They went through a door beyond the archway, down a narrow passage, to a small chamber with an open door. Inside, at a cluttered table, sat a slender man, pallid, with a stubble of close-cropped white hair around his pink scalp. He introduced himself as Rever Jossolyn, pastor of the church, and placed himself at his visitor's service.

With just the trace of a smile, Cormasson said, "I bring you greetings from Peter's Rock."

The pastor gaped at him, gave a short laugh of utter astonishment, shook his head and murmured, "Peter's Rock . . ." and then laughed again, a loud free laugh of sheer joy.

"I've just come from Peter's Rock. The abbot told me that they'd sent priest-voyagers to other worlds, but he didn't know to which worlds. When I heard in Ermaccne City of your church—and when I saw the church itself—"

"Does it resemble the monastery chapel?" Jossolyn broke in.

"In everything but size. The monastery is enormous. It would cover half of Felill."

"You have walked on Peter's Rock . . . seen the Monastery of the Holy Sepulcher," Jossolyn said wonderingly, blinking his eyes against tears of overpowering emotion. "In all these years, no one has come. The planet itself is never mentioned. We wondered sometimes if the monastery still existed. And now . . . will you stay as our guest? We have so much to ask you!"

"I've taken a place at the stayhouse by the long pier."

"The stayhouse keeper is an active member of the church. He'll not object if you come here. Surely you will dine with us this night, and tell us of Peter's Rock."

"I will, Pastor. And you must tell me what you've done on Roharr. I'll be returning to Peter's Rock, and the finest gift I can bring the abbot is news of the voyagers."

Dinner in the refectory was long and merry that evening, as Cormasson gave a detailed account of the history of the monastery since the priest-voyagers' departure. His story was accurate in what it contained, but he omitted recent events. Of the coming of the *Garrashaw*, the attack of the *Sthaga-Renga* and Gossard's death, the growing influence of the Sternverein, he said nothing.

When he had finished his account and answered the questions that rose eagerly from the twenty priests at the table with him, the hour was late. Pastor Jossolyn rose and gestured for silence.

"Suru Cormasson, we bless you and thank you for bringing us news of the homeworld. In our excitement, we have surely forgotten half the things we wished to ask you. Will you remain with us for one more day and dine with us tomorrow night?" he asked the starfarer.

"I will stay and speak of Peter's Rock if you will tell me of your work on this planet," Cormasson said, smiling at his little audience.

"We will. And we will give you a copy of our annals to take back to Peter's Rock. Rever Dagris, our soundscriber, assures me that he will have everything ready for you on the day after tomorrow."

"Then, I must stay. But I can talk no more tonight," Cormasson said good-humoredly, clearing his throat. "It's your turn now. Tell me of the early days here."

The priests were each reluctant to be the first to speak, but once Dagris told him of the drowning of priest-voyager Torris in Blackwater Bay, and Quarrier's promise to build a church overlooking his grave, the rest relaxed and talked freely. They jumped from incident to incident, following no time sequence, but Cormasson was not troubled. The annals would give the chronology and tell him all he needed to know. He listened carefully, alert for any reference to the trader Enskeline and the other priest-voyagers who had gone on with him, but none was made. The priests of Saint Peter's were fully occupied with their own mission; they had no leisure to speculate about the fortunes of men who had passed this way more than a century earlier.

Pastor Jossolyn spoke last, to tell of the entrance of the church into political matters on Felill. "So, when the Grand Selector died and no one could agree on a successor, the people came to the pastor and asked him to guide the affairs of the island. He was reluctant, but he felt that he could not refuse them without risking hardship on everyone. Decisions had to be made, and no one was making them. Since then, we've been trying to return more and more responsibility to the people, through their fleet-councils and ship-councils. It is our hope that within another score of tenzas, they will be running their affairs with no help from us," he concluded.

"You've done much good on Roharr," Cormasson said

"God has been generous to us," said Jossolyn, nodding. The others gestured in agreement.

The mood was relaxed and trusting. Cormasson ventured a question. "How did it go with the others? There were others on that trader's ship, weren't there?"

"There were six priest-voyagers in all. Two stayed on Sassacheele, among aliens, and the other two went on with the trader Enskeline."

"Where did the last two go?" Cormasson asked.

"No one knows."

Cormasson cocked his head incredulously. "Do you really mean that, Rever? They just went out with no destination?"

"The priest-voyagers traveled on a free trader's ship. He

had promised the abbot that he would bring them safely to inhabited worlds, but only he himself had the knowledge to choose the worlds. Our priest-voyagers placed themselves in his hands, trusting God to guide him right.''

''He was a good man,'' Dagris interjected. ''His name was Jod Enskeline, his ship the *Rimjack*. Do you know of him, Suru Cormasson?''

''No, but I would like to meet him,'' Cormasson said.

''Perhaps you will. He has been gone from here for more than a century, but time runs differently for you who cross the stars.''

Cormasson shook his head. ''I think it unlikely that we'll ever meet. The galaxy is too big. I wouldn't know where to begin looking.''

Cormasson returned to Ermacene City having learned very little of use; but he had the soundscriber tapes and he was hopeful that a close analysis of them, added to whatever Domorie had gleaned from his own records, would help to narrow the scope of his search.

Roharr was an ideal starting point. In the direction of the galactic core, where Peter's Rock lay, habitable worlds were few and civilized races almost unknown. But in the direction of the rim, civilized worlds by the hundreds spread in a broad cone from Roharr until they stopped abruptly at the Dead Belt, where barren planets circled burnt-out stars in a dim celestial ribbon that—it was said—took seven thousand watches for the fastest ship to cross. Enskeline was somewhere within the cone, on one of the settled worlds; Cormasson had no doubt of this. If the schismatics' ship had ventured into the Dead Belt, it and its precious cargo were lost forever. No experienced starfarer would follow on the mere chance of finding it.

Enskeline, though he was a free trader, was apparently a conscientious man. Cormasson was too honest a man himself to deny an enemy his virtues. Enskeline had chosen for the priest-voyagers worlds where unaided humans could survive and had seen them safely established planetside before leaving them. He might have taken such pains merely to secure his trading relationship with the monastery, but Cormasson did not think so. If that were the case, Enskeline would have returned to Peter's Rock.

There was always the possibility of his death. It was easy for a small ship to vanish in that great emptiness. But Cormasson was certain that Enskeline had lived and pursued the shroud. And since the number of settled worlds in the cone was finite, if he had landed on any of them, he could be traced. Cormasson believed that he would find the trader. His belief had no rational basis; there was no evidence either to support or disprove it. It was an inner certainty, as sure and uncalculated as setting one foot ahead of another and walking on. For Cormasson, who trusted only reason and logic, this was an uncomfortable sensation; but he could not shake it off.

Domorie saw him immediately upon his return to the house of Kamparongsang, but his smooth, soft features were troubled. He received Cormasson with a complicated Roharran gesture of mixed apology, anger, and frustration.

"I have found nothing, Suru Cormasson. Even the name of the trader has been concealed," he said when they were seated.

"The priests told me his name. He was Enskeline, of the *Rimjack*. But why do you say 'concealed'? How can information be concealed from the master of the house?" Cormasson asked in genuine perplexity.

"It is the custom of this house to keep all permanent records in written form. Naturally, they are transcribed in a cipher to which only the master and one trusted assistant hold the key. I found reference, in the records of the seventh master of my name, to the acquisition of many books in a single trade. The books were described in minute detail. But all other information about this transaction—the source, the trader, prices, terms of trade—everything else was in a secondary cipher that neither Paja nor I had ever seen before." Domorie rose and began to pace the circular chamber. "The cipher was unbreakable by any means we know. It appears nowhere else in the records." He turned and faced Cormasson. "This mystery troubles me greatly. What kind of agreement can my predecessor have made that he would conceal so deeply?"

"Apparently, someone after him knew of it. Paja recognized the name of the planet," Cormasson pointed out.

Domorie made a gesture of dismissal. "That means nothing.

A later hand than Seven Domorie's may have concealed the information. Perhaps one of the priests mentioned the name of his world, and it was noted in this house. It does not change the situation."

After a thoughtful pause, Cormasson said, "Is it possible, Domorie, that this secrecy has nothing to do with the books? The trader might have come to Roharr intending only to deliver the books, and stumbled across something else— something potentially more valuable than even the books of Peter's Rock."

"The same thought occurred to me. There are legendary treasures that attract adventurous men—the lost Leddendorf ransom, or the mines of Xhildas . . . the Ninestones. . . . If this trader found the way to one of them, he could become rich enough to buy every book in existence."

"It makes sense, Domorie. Why else would a man pass up a certain fortune? If we can learn where this trader headed when he left Roharr . . ."

Domorie's emphatic negative gesture silenced Cormasson. "Point of origin and destination are not required of visitors to Roharr. I will check, now that I know ship and master. But I expect to learn nothing."

Domorie's gloomy expectation was only partially fulfilled. No record existed of the arrival or departure of a ship called *Rimjack,* nor was there any mention of a free trader named Enskeline. But Domorie was a painstaking man. His connections in the female line of the family gave him access to all port documents, and he and Paja examined them thoroughly. It was Paja who came upon the solitary suggestion of the *Rimjack*'s existence in the terse report of an incident involving an unfortunate alien starfarer.

In the time of Seven Domorie, a Quespodon had arrived at the ring complex seeking a free trader's driveship out of Sassacheele. No one at the port had any knowledge of such a ship. The Quespodon was offered service in the house of Kamparongsang until he could find a berth, and there his story ended.

It was enough to satisfy Cormasson. He knew that Enskeline had left Peter's Rock with a Quespodon crewman and had come to Roharr by way of Sassacheele. He kept this information to himself.

Nine Domorie was quite convinced. After telling Cormasson of the discovery, he said, "There can be no doubt that the arrival and departure of the *Rimjack* were deliberately concealed by Seven Domorie. That the Quespodon was sent to our house is proof of the connection."

"Why wasn't the incident of the Quespodon deleted from port records?"

"Whoever made the entry did not realize his significance. My honored forebear confided in few people, even within the family." Domorie sighed and made a gesture of defeat. "I think our search is at an end. Whatever agreement my ancestor and this trader may have had, we will not learn of it on Roharr."

"We would learn of it if I could find Enskeline."

"This trader might have landed on any world between Roharr and the Dead Belt. No, Cormasson. Go to Peter's Rock with the message of the priests, and return to my children with your ship full of their books. There is great wealth to be had in this trade, and we would be fools to turn aside and chase phantoms. Seven Domorie and Enskeline gambled and lost. That is the only explanation of these mysteries. You and I will learn from their example."

Cormasson agreed with his host. During the remaining days of Cormasson's stay on Roharr, neither man mentioned Enskeline or the *Rimjack*. Their talk was of Peter's Rock and the riches it would bring them.

But when the *Urixi* lifted off, its destination was not the planet of the monastery. It headed into the cone of settled worlds, in search of the *Rimjack*.

X.

Huttoi: The Search

The odds against finding Enskeline were enormous. Outbound from Roharr, Cormasson set about reducing them.

Nearly four hundred inhabited worlds were known to lie within the area between Roharr and the Dead Belt. Assuming that Enskeline had kept his word to the abbot, he had taken the missionaries to one of these worlds. And if he had been honest to that extent, then he would have brought them to some world where they had a chance of surviving and spreading their message.

Fully a third of the worlds were either primitive or at such a low level of culture that their message could not have been understood. Those worlds could safely be ruled out. Nearly threescore of the remainder were known for indigenous diseases that required elaborate precautions of all visitors; Enskeline was not equipped to protect the priest-voyagers against them and would have avoided these planets. Other worlds were known to harbor cultures violently hostile to all offworlders, while some were geologically unstable and dangerous. A few were inhabited by creatures so totally alien that nothing had been learned of them beyond the fact of their existence.

Eliminating all these worlds left Cormasson with one hundred sixty-three possibilities—still far too many to visit one by one in a lifetime. But distance was also a factor, and in this case a significant one. It was reasonable to assume that Enskeline would free himself of the burden of passengers at the first opportunity; this single consideration reduced the immediate possibilities to fourteen worlds.

With a quiet smile of satisfaction, Cormasson extinguished

the charts and switched on the miniature vision tank. He was
ready to lay in a course.

His first stop was D'borri, a warm and pleasant world
whose inhabitants took little interest in trading but were hungry for news. Unlike Roharr, this world had few unexpected
visitors. Its only product worth exporting was moonwood, a
softly glowing substance found in buried nodules in the north
ern reaches of the planet. Moonwood was not wood at all, but
it was suited for fine carving, and so was given its name by
the early settlers. All trade in moonwood was controlled by a
branch of the Sternverein, and this fact made the visit of a
free trader a rare event on D'borri.

The D'borrians were open and talkative, entirely free of
suspicion. When Cormasson told them he was hoping to learn
the whereabouts of an old friend, he was given free access to
the port records. There was no trace of the *Rimjack*.

His next landing was on Yellow January, where he traded
with great success, but learned nothing. On Three Endernells
he spent nearly two planetary years unraveling the story of a
free trader who had visited at a time that fit the voyaging of
Enskeline. At last, satisfied that the tale had nothing to do
with his quarry, he went on to Boneyard, and Zero, and No
More Problems, all of which brought him no word of Enskeline,
the *Rimjack*, or the schismatics. At last he came to Huttoi.

All he knew of this world was that it was an old colony, far
older than any of the others he had visited, settled by refugees
from Old Earth who desired no contact with offworlders. The
only news from Huttoi over the past three centuries was that it
had been peacefully occupied by some alien race. The last
Sternverein observation had taken place over a century ago,
Galactic Standard. By that time, the humans had dispersed
over the face of Huttoi. They and the aliens appeared to have
settled into separate, noncompetitive life patterns, though
a few humans voluntarily served the aliens. Since there was
nothing of value known to exist on Huttoi, the Sternverein
had ignored it ever since.

Cormasson was not long off the *Urixi* when he saw that the
situation on Huttoi was very different from the last reports.
As he left the ring area and headed for a complex of low,
angular buildings nearby, he was greeted by a human woman
and a tall, gaunt alien with narrow, down-slanted eyes that

gave it a permanent appearance of melancholy. Its skin was tinged with blue, and its high columnar forehead was scarified with colored markings. Cormasson recognized the creature as a Nandra. He had heard that they were disdainful of humans, but this one was behaving in what appeared to him to be a friendly manner.

"Welcome to Pilgrimage, starfarer!" the human called with a wave of her hand.

"I thought this world was called Huttoi," Cormasson replied.

At that the woman laughed good-naturedly and the alien made a high droning noise that seemed to express amusement. "So it was at one time. Then our brothers and sisters from the stars came to us, and they called it Tenorrask, for their homeworld," said the woman, laying a friendly hand on the bony forearm of the alien and looking at the Nandra as if to invite it to speak.

"Since the Accord, we have a new name for our world. We honor God and the one He sent to enlighten us," the Nandra said.

"I know nothing of the Accord. There is no word of it among the worlds I've visited."

"It happened seventy years ago by our reckoning, and few ships have come here since that time. Before the Accord we were inhospitable to any but our own kind," said the Nandra.

"But now all are welcome on Pilgrimage," the woman quickly added. "Soon we celebrate the feast of Accord. . . . Will you stay and share it with us, stranger?"

"I will do that gladly," said Cormasson, falling into step with them as they turned toward one of the sharp-edged buildings beyond the ring area. He thought to take advantage of their friendliness and in a casual manner said, "If few ships have landed, you might recall the arrival of a friend of mine, a free trader like me. His name was Enskeline, of the *Rimjack*."

"I recall hearing no such name," the woman said hesitantly.

The Nandra was quite certain. "Only four driveships have come to Pilgrimage, and none was called *Rimjack* or bore a starfarer named Enskeline. Your friend must not have come here."

"Perhaps he landed before the Accord."

"If he did, there is no record of his arrival or departure," the Nandra droned.

Cormasson had felt that he was closing in on his quarry; the Nandra's categorical statement now ended that possibility. There was still a chance that Enskeline had arrived before the Accord, in which case some trace of his passing might yet survive on this world. Cormasson dropped the subject for the time being and contented himself with listening and learning whatever information chanced to come his way.

The day of Accord was a celebration of great significance; that much was clear from the exuberance and buoyant spirits of everyone Cormasson met, human and Nandra alike. But while they communicated their zeal and quickened his own anticipation, they did not make clear to him exactly what great event the day marked. They all knew so well why Accord was a great day that they could not imagine anyone not knowing.

Cormasson gleaned bits of information from the people he encountered, pressing no one, listening to all, and so slowly formed a sketchy idea. Humans and Nandra, after a long period in which they had coexisted in peace but remained far apart, had suddenly turned against one another. It was impossible to tell which race had initiated hostilities, since each took all the blame upon itself. A third race, the Altenorei, were somehow involved, but their role in the planet's affairs was not clear to Cormasson. From what he could gather, the Altenorei dwelt on the planet but were unseen by the others.

The war of humans and Nandra was bitter but brief. Then a human known only as the Pilgrim had come from nowhere and imposed peace. He had communicated directly with the mysterious Altenorei, something no human had ever done before, and the message he brought was the word of God.

When he heard this from an old man, late on the day after planetfall, Cormasson's interest reawakened. "The word of God" impressed him as the sort of phrase a priest-voyager might speak; and if a priest-voyager had come to this world, there was hope of finding out where the trader had gone.

The old man offered to serve as Cormasson's guide on the planet. He introduced him to several inhabitants and showed him the important places. Now they were seated outdoors, eating a light meal under the evening sky.

"What is the word of God?" Cormasson asked him. "Is it what you call the Accord?"

"No, the Accord is an agreement between the three races of Pilgrimage. That was the work of the Pilgrim—to bring us peace—for only in peace can we dedicate ourselves to the word. It is a simple command, starfarer: we must love one another and seek the sight of the face of God."

Cormasson took a deep breath and let it out slowly. He did not look at the man as he asked, "Where do we find the face of God?"

"In showing love for all that lives. . . . In forgiving those who do us wrong. . . . Helping those in need. . . . Sharing the things that God has bestowed on us," said the old man in a voice full of feeling. "If we do these things, we will pass from this life into the presence of God, and the glory of His countenance will shine upon us forever."

Cormasson's heart sank. Here was another childish myth of a happy afterlife, conceived to make palatable the miseries of this one. He had heard many like it. He looked at the old man's benign face. "I understand. When you speak of the face of God, you don't refer to a face that one can really see and touch, as I can see yours. You speak of a . . . of an intangible thing."

"For us, yes, starfarer. For us and all men of this age it will be a spiritual thing to be known only after death. But when the Pilgrim and the Seekers have found the holy cloth and restored it to its home in the mountain, then all who believe will be able to look upon it. The face of God will be returned to His children," said the old man fervently.

Cormasson looked wildly at his companion, half-fearing that the old man was taunting him. But the eyes were closed, and the aged features were transfigured with happiness. There was no malice in this man, only truth. Cormasson had found the trail of the shroud at last.

"Forgive my ignorance," Cormasson said. "I'm still learning about your world and its ways. What is this cloth, and who seeks it? Does a true image of God really exist somewhere?"

"It does, starfarer. God once lived as a man on the homeworld of all humans. As a man He died a cruel death, but to show His forgiveness He left the image of His face on the cloth that wrapped His body." The old man leaned closer, speaking with great intensity, gripping Cormasson's forearm as he spoke. "The cloth was taken from Old Earth in a chest made of all things precious and pure. It has traveled on, to the world Desshe, where it awaits the coming of the Pilgrim."

"Desshe. . . . I've spent my life among the stars, but I've never heard of a world named Desshe. Where is it?"

The old man raised his eyes, which were blazing brightly, and flung his open hand up, pointing to the night sky bejeweled with stars. "Out there!" he said exultantly.

Cormasson spoke with others. They welcomed his questions and answered them fully and eagerly, volunteering any information they thought might be helpful. Everyone wanted to enlighten their rare offworld visitor. He talked with humans and Nandra, with men and women, the old and the young, believers and scoffers. Always their accounts ended the same way—in a closed circle that seemed to be drawing him in like a whirlpool. Where is the face of God? *It is on the world called Desshe.* And where is Desshe? *It is where the face of God awaits the Pilgrim.*

Two days before the feast of Accord, Cormasson slipped aboard the *Urixi.* He had learned all he could from the people of this world. Now he was ready to check their information against the resources of his ship.

He went over every chart, but found no world named Desshe, or any world with a name close to it. He sat at the eyepiece of the tank until his vision blurred and his eyes watered from the strain, but he saw no candidate for the world known as Desshe.

He dimmed the light panels and sprawled across his berth to gather his thoughts. Up to this point he had been chasing a tenuous thread of assumption, supposition, and hypothesis; but now at last he had found an unmistakable reference to the relic. Now, at last, he had a name and a destination.

But where was this unknown, uncharted world? "Out there!" the old man had cried. Poor groundling fool; as if one need only rush out blindly into that great emptiness and find what one sought. These people knew nothing of interstellar navigation, of spaceflight, of the awesome distances that surrounded them. They did not know whether Desshe lay inward, toward Roharr, or outward in the sprawling, ever-

widening cone of settled worlds between here and the Dead
Belt. It might even lie in the Dead Belt itself, an anomaly in
that cosmic river of burnt-out stars and ice-covered cinders
that once were worlds. Perhaps it even lay beyond. There
were said to be inhabited worlds on the far side of the Dead
Belt, though Cormasson had never spoken with anyone who
had set foot on one of them.

The idea of plunging into that void with nothing but a name
to guide him was as close to madness as Cormasson ever
expected to come. Yet he could see no alternative. The
shroud had to be found.

He believed the stories he had heard. There was nothing
strikingly original about them; indeed, they were full of matter fairly commonplace among civilized races; but the legends
surrounding the Pilgrim had the ring of truth. Other worlds
had stories of messengers appearing suddenly to bring peace
or momentous news, to be sure; but the coming of the Pilgrim
was not so very mysterious. On a world scattered and divided,
disrupted by war, men's origins were easily lost. As for his
message of peace, he simply said what Nandra and human
were ready to hear. His words offered a way out of a dilemma
that saved face for everyone, and his quest gave them a
unifying purpose and an outlet for their energies. The Pilgrim
may have been a fanatic, Cormasson thought, but he was a
shrewd one, and a good judge of people—and aliens.

Even the story of the Pilgrim's departure, though it had
analogues in nearly every myth system Cormasson knew, was
more than simply the hoary tale of the holy man taken up by
his god. Cormasson had soundscribed the accounts of three
who claimed to have witnessed the liftoff of his ship—two
old women and a Nandra whose skin was almost purple with
age. He had listened and correlated and checked point against
point. He was firmly convinced that these were indeed eyewit-
ness accounts. The younger people he had spoken with might
have merely been reciting something learned; but these three
elders told what they had seen personally, a sight that had
changed their lives.

The identity of the Pilgrim remained a puzzle. At first,
Cormasson assumed that he was one of the priest-voyagers
who had somehow made his way to this world, but his
competence at driveship navigation made that unlikely. He

could not be the trader Enskeline. Free traders did not become holy men. Perhaps he was a follower of one of the missionaries, converted by their teaching and become a missionary himself. It was impossible to say, and not really worth considering. What mattered was not the Pilgrim's identity, but his mission.

The Pilgrim had accomplished in a very short time, without force, what the Sternverein, with all its weapons, all its troopers, the resources of its white fleet and the hundred worlds that nourished it, had not yet been able to achieve. The races of Pilgrimage had been at peace for seventy of their years, united in a single belief. Humans, Nandra, and the unseen sequestered Altenorei were of one mind. The mutual love they spoke of they displayed in every action.

The Sternverein could command obedience. It could impose its will on recalcitrant races and slowly weed out those who opposed it. But it could not work a change like the one the Pilgrim had brought about.

Cormasson lay for a long time in the semidarkness, sifting his thoughts, weighing and choosing courses of action. At last he swung his feet to the deck and sat up, rubbing his weary eyes.

The shroud existed and was on a world called Desshe: these were firm beliefs. A group of humans, Nandra, and Altenorei had left this world to seek it: this was fact. The shroud was potentially the most powerful object in the galaxy. If it existed, it must be possessed by the Sternverein: these were inescapable conclusions.

A hundred fifty worlds lay between Pilgrimage and the Dead Belt. He might have to search every one of them. If he found no trace of the Pilgrim or the shroud, he would have to seek them in the Dead Belt, and even beyond. He had to find the shroud, or find certain proof that it no longer existed; nothing else would do.

Though he was past his youth, Cormasson was in excellent health and physical condition. He had a long lifespan ahead, but even that might not suffice for this mission. While he followed his quarry from world to world and lay in a sleep near death as he crossed the vacant spaces, centuries would pass for those he left behind. He would return to an unfamiliar galaxy and to a Sternverein that might long ago have forgotten his existence, or worse still, have condemned him as a deserter.

With a sigh, he rose and stretched. There was no point to further delay. Seating himself before the vision tank, he began to lay in a course.

On the first world he reached he found only desolation. The settlers were gone, and their settlement was a jumble of rusting metal and dry, brittle wood. There was no other sign of human life on the planet. Beside the landing ring was an erratic row of long mounds—the graves of those who had succumbed. Slabs of metal, rusted and scored by the unceasing wind and rain, leaned at weary angles over several of the graves. A few symbols remained on one of the slabs, but no message could be distinguished.

Cormasson traded on the next world he reached and restocked the *Urixi* for a long voyage, but he learned nothing there or on his next planetfall. Then, on Iolland, he was told of a sect that called themselves Christians and worshipped in a place they called the Chapel of the Face of God. He sought them out at once.

They were a mixed lot, mostly human, but with a few Thorumbians and a pair of Quespodons among them when he visited their chapel. He was made welcome. When he mentioned the Pilgrim, he was brought at once to the pastor of the chapel, a man well into middle age, completely bald, and of a very anxious disposition. The pastor introduced himself as Pastor Lenteel and bade Cormasson make himself comfortable. Cormasson settled on one of the slabs of bright orange wood jutting out from the rough-surfaced gray wall. Lenteel perched on the edge of the slab next to him.

"Have you word of the Pilgrim? Has the shroud been found?" Lenteel asked eagerly, twisting his bony hands together.

"I hoped to ask you the same question, Pastor. I've come from Pilgrimage. Your knowledge of the Pilgrim is more recent than mine," Cormasson replied.

Lenteel's face fell, but he quickly recovered. Nodding, he said, "I can only tell you that they remained here for a time before going on to Desshe. One of the Altenorei was near death. They stopped here to build a tower where it might recover, but they were too late."

"Unfortunate. Now there are fewer to continue the search."

"No, there are more, trader. The other Altenorei remained behind in the tower with its companion, but six new seekers joined the quest." Lenteel smiled at the trader's surprised expression and added, "The Pilgrim brought the word of God to many on Iolland. This chapel was begun even before he left us."

"I'm surprised they made it this far. It's a dangerous undertaking, Pastor. They're looking for a world that no one knows. Desshe isn't on any chart I've ever seen."

"Even in that, God was bounteous. We know that one of the new seekers had heard of Desshe. He said it was far from here—out where the stars end and the heavens are darkened. He had a name for the place. . . ." Lenteel paused, frowning and knotting his fingers with the effort to recall.

"Was it the Dead Belt?"

"Yes, the Dead Belt! I heard it so long ago, from my father; I grow forgetful. But those were his words."

Cormasson looked up sharply. "Was all this before your lifetime?"

"Oh, yes. The Pilgrim came here one hundred thirty octals ago. He stayed among us for three. I was born ninety-seven octals ago."

Cormasson made a quick mental calculation and realized that his quarry was gaining time on him. Once parted from Lenteel, the Sternverein commander remained on Iolland only long enough to divest himself of all his trade goods. There would be no further use for them, no need to pose as a trader, and the cargo space could be put to better use. He had the *Urixi* minutely inspected while he procured protective gear, replacement drivecoils, medications, water, and weapons. The worlds bordering the Dead Belt were places of extremes; he meant to be ready for whatever he might find.

On the first outer world he reached Cormasson nearly found his death. He was on the verge of leaving when he suddenly collapsed and lay helpless within sight of his ship, alone and far from any hope of aid. For twelve long planetary days he lay in the grip of curaksh fever, howling in delirium and in the throes of a hypersensitivity that made the lightest puff of air against his flesh burn like a jet of corrosive. When he was not torn by pain, he lay paralyzed, his joints locked and muscles stiffened, barely able to draw in enough air to keep alive.

At last the pain subsided and his mind cleared. He came to his senses in the middle of the long moonless night, but found himself at first too weak to rise. As soon as he could walk, Cormasson dragged himself aboard the *Urixi*. At his first clear sight of himself he groaned in despair and revulsion: he was emaciated. His face looked like a skull covered with dry clay; his eyes were red-rimmed and looked unnaturally large. His ribs stood out as distinctly as the exoskeleton of a Rikku, and his arms and legs were like sticks. It would take time, a long time, to rebuild his strength; while he recovered, the Pilgrim would outdistance him still further.

He adjusted the stasis tank for maximum curative function, filled the feeders with nutrients and medication, and after setting a course for Ruxiloma, collapsed in the stasis tank and entrusted his healing to the machine.

He awoke six watches out from Ruxiloma and took stock of himself. His body had recovered. His flesh was firm, his color was good; his eyes were clear, and his breathing was unimpaired; he had escaped the worst effects of curaksh fever. With care, he might even avoid a relapse serious enough to disable him. But his condition was still delicate. His muscles ached after the slightest strain, and his strength was only half what it had been.

Long service in the Sternverein had taught Cormasson the need of remaining in peak condition. He stayed on Ruxiloma, a rugged but hospitable world, until his strength came back. He ate good food; he walked and ran and climbed and followed an ever more strenuous program of exercise. He slept soundly, keeping to a regular schedule of every third watch period instead of attempting to follow the complicated Ruxiloman time reckoning. He had a disciplined mind and an inflexible will; knowing that it was necessary for the time being, he put the search out of his thoughts and concentrated every effort on full recovery. Once he felt his old self again, he boarded the *Urixi* once more to devote himself to the pursuit of the Pilgrim.

For a long time he learned nothing. On world after settled

world, his was the first driveship to make planetfall within living memory. The only other spacecraft known was the ship that had brought the forebears, and in many instances those early ships had been dismantled to provide shelter and tools for the settlers. The ships that survived landing had gone on a generation or two later to take the restless young to new worlds of their own. No one had ever returned from those outward voyages.

He came to Clendorin's Exile, a big low-gravity planet of climatic extremes. The polar regions were uninhabitable wastes of eternal ice, and the land of the equatorial belt was dead baked rock. But the temperate zones, where much of the land mass was concentrated, were blessed with a moderate temperature range, rich soil, and gentle, regular rains. Traders did not visit Clendorin's Exile; it was too remote and had nothing worth trading for. The settlers did not care. They were an independent breed who preferred to leave the comforts of the inner worlds behind rather than be reminded of the society they had fled in disgust. This world was a good home to those who worked hard and respected its dangers. There was enough empty land to assure privacy, and a handful of small communities for those who preferred the company of others.

Clendorin's Exile had no facilities for visitors and no system of exchange other than barter. Cormasson found a homestead one day's walk from the dilapidated landing ring where he had worked out an agreement: three days' work for five days' food and lodging.

He presented himself as a former trader searching for an old friend who had gone in search of a world called Desshe. Mention of the planet inspired no reaction in his host's household; Cormasson wondered if he had been fully understood. The speech of Clendorin's Exile had degenerated into a mumbling, guttural dialect full of unfamiliar terms and confusing contractions, with dropped syllables and missing connectives. With close attention, he could make himself clear and decipher the responses to his words, but communication was uneven at best.

When he returned from the grain mows on his final day of work, Cormasson still had no clear response to his questions about Desshe. Later, as he sat under a tubtree in the long twilight, cleaning his boots, Umath, the master of the household, settled beside him.

"Work no morra, no day gone, you. How go, how stay?" Umath asked.

"I'll stay here and rest until my time is up. Then I'll go and see the settlement."

Umath scowled. "Sellamen bashoo place. Go no you. Go upside, you," he said, pointing to the sky. "Go find Desshe-world, find friend."

"I'll leave here soon enough, Umath. I want to see if anyone on this world knows anything about Desshe."

"Tella Desshe-world, no them. Go cross by sellamen, bashoo."

"If it's so bashoo, I won't stay," Cormasson told him.

Umath sat for a time, thinking, then he left. Soon after, one of the workers who had been at the grain mows with Cormasson moved furtively out of the shadows. He stayed on the far side of the tubtree, deliberately keeping out of sight of the house.

"You say you mean look-find Desshe-world? You come here so?" he whispered.

"I want to find Desshe. Can you help me?"

"Help you me, no. Old Chimma help. Old Chimma go upside, long yestertime, go allwhere. Chimma know all upside worlds."

"Take me to him. I'll pay you."

A hand extended from the shadows and picked up one of Cormasson's shiny boots. "You give these Jebbat?" the voice asked.

"They wouldn't fit. They're too small for your feet."

After a pause, Jebbat said, "You give these, we go see Chimma."

"You take me to Chimma, I give you the boots. When do we go?"

"Come morraday gone sunlow, we go," said Jebbat, and slipped away.

Cormasson rested until late the next day. In the afternoon he returned to the *Urixi* to study the sketchy maps of Clendorin's Exile and make up a traveling pack. Besides food concentrate, he took a packet of stims—small blue pills that were activated by the body's own adrenalin; they could keep a man awake and alert, in top fighting form, for as long as six standard days without long-term damage. He put a spare ripgun in his pack, and extra ammunition. Slinging a pair of low climbing boots over his shoulder and smiling at the thought of Jebbat trying to get his huge splayed feet into those dress boots, he started for the rendezvous.

Jebbat was not talkative. He was a physically big man, very strong, but he gave no indication of any more intelligence than a child. As a guide, he was satisfactory. He seemed to know the way well and was alert. Cormasson was tempted to ask him about Old Chimma, of whom he knew no more than a name, but he decided not to distract Jebbat and possibly confuse him. Answers would come soon enough.

They entered a thick wood of low, bushlike trees interspersed with towering giants whose thick trunks soared up to tufted crowns. The path narrowed. Jebbat began to exhibit signs of nervousness, darting quick glances everywhere and starting at every small sound.

"Is there danger here, Jebbat?" Cormasson asked.

"No danger, no here. Hachee-cat never come here, no him. No bashoo thing here, never no," the guide replied with some agitation.

He was not convincing. Cormasson sensed trouble ahead. He reached into his pocket and closed his fingers on the ripgun.

They went on a short way and came to a place where one of the giant trees had fallen and lay like a head-high wall by the side of their path. Jebbat was quite anxious now. Cormasson readied himself.

Two men sprang over the log; another came at him from the opposite side. All three were armed with cudgels, but they were slow and clumsy. Cormasson brought the ripgun flat across the temple of the first to reach him, staggering the man, then slipped behind the second. The three attackers and Jebbat now stood with their backs to the fallen tree, facing him.

The one who had been hit was shaking his bloodied head. He looked unsteady. The rest, Jebbat included, were undecided what to do. They had lost the initiative, and no one was in command. They knew the thing in Cormasson's hand was a weapon, but they did not know its power. They were bigger than the gray-haired offworlder and outnumbered him. As they glanced at one another, waiting for one to give the command, Cormasson spoke sharply.

"If you attack me, I'll kill you. Look," he said.

He fired a single shot from the ripgun into the fallen trunk at Jebbat's side. The effect on the half-rotted wood was spectacular. The trunk was slammed back a full meter and there was a shower of splinters and torn wood. When the air cleared, the trunk lay in two sections around a gap that the four attackers could have passed through abreast.

Jebbat and the others fell to their knees in abject terror and prostrated themselves before Cormasson. He let them blubber in fear and wail for mercy for a time, then he ordered them to stand.

"Now you know what I can do. Answer my questions. No lies," he said.

He ordered three of them to sit facing the blasted trunk, under strict prohibition not to speak to one another while he took them aside one by one, beginning with Jebbat, for questioning. The men were thoroughly cowed and poured out answers. Their terror increased their incoherence; it was some time before Cormasson was able to piece together the reason behind their attack. When all was clear to him at last, he threw back his head and laughed, long and hard, while the four looked on utterly uncomprehending.

There was no Old Chimma. He had died long ago. No one on this world had ever seen Desshe, none knew its whereabouts. The only time they had heard of it before was when the Pilgrim and his crew of seekers had landed. At first the starfarers had been welcomed, their message heard with sympathy and embraced by some of the people of Clendorin's Exile. But there had been a falling out. The cause was unknown, but the result was clear.

"Show me," Cormasson ordered.

Reluctantly, fearfully, they took him to a high plateau on the shaded side of a steep mountain. Here the sun never shone, and the ice had not melted in the memory of living men. Laid out on raised slabs of smooth, green-veined stone were nine corpses in three rows, preserved by the unbroken cold. In the first row, two Nandra flanked a single human. Three giant headless things lay in the middle row. Disks of opalescent horn gleamed dully in the center of their broad chests. Cormasson recognized them as Wishbones, the creatures of Sassacheele, a simple primitive race—and yet they had somehow become a part of this quest. In the third row lay a second human, with a Thorumbian gleaming like an effigy of polished onyx on either side of her.

"Where is the other human?" Cormasson asked.

His four prisoners glanced at one another fearfully. One of them began to protest his innocence, blaming the deaths on their fathers. Cormasson silenced him.

"One of the humans is not here. Where is the body of the third human?"

Jebbat fell to his knees and cried, "Pillerin no dic, he! Other Desshe-world seeker all die, all they, but Pillerin no die, ever!"

"Where is the Pilgrim?" Cormasson asked coldly.

"Upside! Go find Desshe-world, he!"

Cormasson bared his teeth and raised the ripgun, wanting to annihilate these stupid brutes and then destroy this monument to their fear and ignorance. But his rage passed in an instant. Controlled again, he lowered the weapon and gestured for Jebbat to rise.

"Take me back to my ship," he ordered.

XI. ⎯⎯⎯⎯⎯⎯⎯⎯⎯⎯⎯⎯⎯

Desshe: The Finding

Cormasson voyaged on, to world after world where none had ever heard of the Pilgrim. The long mission began to take its toll. His strength and stamina were tested beyond endurance, and even his iron will yielded now and then to the succession of disappointments. But he forced himself on.

Alone on a sparsely populated waterworld, he suffered a relapse into curaksh fever. The attack was not so severe, nor the pain so great as the first attack, but his recovery was slower. He knew now that the sickness had rooted within him and would be with him all his life, slowly draining his strength and eventually killing him. With the help of the ship's medications and the stasis tank, he could keep damage to a minimum; but there was no hope of a cure until he returned to Occuch.

He had long ago abandoned his efforts to keep track of the Galactic Calendar; he knew only that each time he climbed from the stasis tank to ready himself for planetfall, decades, or a whole lifetime, had passed in the galaxy he once knew. But until now he had kept a careful log of his own subjective time. Here, on a speck of green land rising out of a world of rolling waters, he abandoned that as well. Time no longer mattered. Only the search mattered.

On the high crags of Kallmakester, in a thawtime rockslide, his left arm was shattered so badly that his rescuers were prepared to amputate. At the point of Cormasson's ripgun, they set the arm instead and bound it securely. It healed badly and he never regained full use of it, but he went on.

He no longer spoke of the Pilgrim to the humans and humanoids he encountered. The words were meaningless to them, and to Cormasson himself the Pilgrim and his ship had lost all significance as things in themselves. His mind was fixed on the shroud and its power. He presented himself to the people of these remote worlds as a seeker of the face of God.

They had never seen such a man, or heard such words as he spoke, and they listened and hung on every word. He told them what he could recall of the beliefs of Peter's Rock, and left them marveling at his story of a God who lived and died as a man and then lived again, a God whose image drew believers after Him to the farthest settled worlds in the galaxy and then beyond, into the unknown. On some of the worlds he was asked to stay and teach them how to worship this God. On one world he was offered godhood himself and only escaped his followers by stealth. But he went on.

At last he found what he had been seeking.

The world had no name. It was a speck on the charts, identified by a number and a terse notation: "Settlement unverified." The date of the notation was meaningless. It might have been made a millennium ago.

Cormasson entered a scanning orbit. If there had ever been a settlement here, the planet could not be ignored. He found no trace of life. There was no landing ring, and the surface showed signs of instability. It would be a hard landing and a dangerous visit.

As he studied the data from the surface, one of the scanners began flashing: there was a human artifact below. Cormasson closed in as tightly as the scanner could focus and saw the outline of a ship lying on its side at the foot of a range of low hills. A ship that size was very old. It could have been the original settlers' ship. Cormasson felt a sudden surge of hope. It might be the ship of the schismatics.

He located a solid rock shelf about a half-watch walking distance from the wreck, and set down. The atmosphere tested out breathable, but thin and dry; the gravity was slightly below standard. In cold-climate gear, with supplementary breathing apparatus ready by his side, he found himself comfortable. Anchoring the *Urixi* against ground tremors, he set out for the remains of the other ship.

He walked through a harsh, silent region of naked rock and jagged outcropping. The wind had fallen; everything was still. The only life he saw was the stunted, twisted trees bristling with long tufts of red needles that grew on the sunward faces of the cliffs. At the foot of the cliffs were slopes of scree and small boulders and sometimes one of the stunted trees, thrown down in a rockslide.

Travel was easy over the bare stony ground. In less than half a watch from his departure, Cormasson topped a low rise and found the ship lying before him. His heart leapt with excitement. He dropped to one knee, forcing himself to study the situation calmly instead of running headlong down the slope as he so much wanted to do.

The ship was huge and very old. It had been here a long time: more than a dozen of the stunted trees had taken root in rips and hollows on the surface, and the trees were of a size that bespoke venerable age. It was a first-stage driveship, one of the earliest ships to leave Old Earth in the time of the great dispersion of the human race. How long ago that was by the reckoning of the worlds he had once known, Cormasson could not even guess.

It was not difficult to reconstruct what had happened: The bridgeman had brought the ship down in free landing, and probably succeeded; but a surface tremor had toppled her. On a frontier planet, there was no chance of such a ship's ever being righted again and made spaceworthy. The upper hull was sound, but the underside was deeply gashed; plates were sprung and dented by the force of the fall.

Cormasson made his way slowly down to the wreck, cautious out of long habit. He knew that nothing here threatened him; the gnarled needle trees were the only other living things on this world.

The ship had been methodically gutted. Anything that could be removed had been, and everything too big to move had been stripped. So. . . . There had been survivors—many of them, to judge from the amount of work done—and they had been organized and methodical. No panic showed here, only disciplined work. These people had meant to survive.

But there was no settlement on this planet now. The scanners were clear on that, and scanners could be trusted. Cormasson left the ship and sat down on the slope, his back against a boulder, his face to the faint sunlight, and evaluated the situation.

This could be the schismatics' ship, the very ship the Pilgrim had been seeking. It was the right model, the right size, the right age. But hundreds of similar ships had risen from Old Earth in the first hungry rush to the stars, and many had vanished without a trace. More than likely, this was just one of that lost multitude.

Cormasson had to be positive. The first step was a thorough search of the wreck. If that yielded nothing, he would have to search the planet until he found the remains of the survivors. The chance that they had been rescued was so remote that he did not even consider it.

He sighed and drew himself to his feet. A formidable task lay before him, but it was inescapable. He had to know. If this ancient hulk was indeed the ship from Peter's Rock, then the shroud was certain to be on this world and his long pursuit was near its end.

As he stood gazing at the wreck, the implications of this moment swelled within him. He felt dizzy with hope and excitement. The great work of his life might be soon consummated; a mission that would change the future of all the civilized worlds, shape the galaxy for ages to come, was close to realization. He looked about wildly, forgetting for a moment his utter solitude in the impulse to shout his feelings aloud and share his jubilation with another.

But there was no other. He was alone on a barren world, by a dead ship whose occupants had long become one with the dust of this nameless planet. He shuddered and stepped back a pace. For the first time, he felt the full weight of the isolation he had imposed on himself. Great gulfs of space separated him from the nearest human beings; centuries of time lay between him and the worlds he had left behind; his mission had made him unique in the universe. Whenever he had thought of these things before, he had taken pride in being a man set apart from all others by his own will and determination. Now he felt only an awful loneliness, and the thought of wandering across this wasteland in search of the dead filled him with horror and revulsion.

He rubbed his eyes and shook his head. He fumbled with his breathing mask. A bit more oxygen was what he needed. He knew that his physical condition was deteriorating under the long strain, but now he realized the even greater strain that had been placed on his mind. The solitude, the hallucinations of curaksh fever, the long deep dreams as he lay watch after watch in the stasis tank with his body on the borderline of death and his mind tracing the depths of his unconscious being—these had broken him at last.

Then he heard a noise.

He spun around, but there was nothing to see. The wind was rising. The needle trees on the heights were swaying, but nothing had changed. He feared that his mind was indeed destroyed.

The sound came again, faint and faraway, but unmistakably the thin clanking of a bell. Cormasson felt a rush of relief. This was no hallucination. He was not deluded. A bell was tolling on this dead world.

He remembered the deep-voiced bells he had heard on Peter's Rock, ringing to mark the times of celebration and mourning and worship. He laughed loudly, triumphantly. The schismatics *had* been here. The shroud must be here too. He had only to find that bell and his search was over.

He held himself still, listening, scarcely breathing, until the sound came again from somewhere beyond the hilltop. He set off at once. After the first gentle rise, the climb became steeper and he became grateful for the breathing mask. He made his way slowly up the bare rock slope. As he neared the top he heard the bell again.

From the crest of the hill he saw a steep-roofed building with a cross mounted on the peak. It stood far off on the upland plain. No other building rose in that barrenness. As he drew nearer, Cormasson saw why the building had escaped the scanners. It was small and was in ruins. The walls were of native stone; the steep roof was made of trunks of needle trees and was thatched with their branches, now dried and scattered by the wind. Cormasson could see through the bare rafters from a distance; closer, he saw the fallen rocks that had left the walls breached in a dozen places, open to the wind.

Beside the building stood a framework of tree trunks supporting a bell. A crude funnel hung from the clapper to catch the wind and use it to set the bell ringing when no human hand was left to do the task, and no human ear to hear it.

Cormasson entered the ruined building and stopped, stunned. Before him, at the very center, on a table of smooth stone, under a faded sagging canopy, stood something that flashed and glittered in the light that streamed through the skeletal roof. He came forward slowly, like a man entranced, aware of nothing but the gleaming object on the stone table. It was unmistakable: He had found the reliquary from Peter's Rock—the resting place of the cloth that bore the face of God.

The treasures of Old Earth were clustered on its surface, thick as the grains of dust beneath his feet, set in precious metals finely wrought. All these he recognized; but his wonder grew, and his mind strained, at the sight of other jewels that he had never seen before and metals unlike those on any world he had known. Some were attached to the reliquary; most of them were heaped on the table around it.

A three-lobed stone of milky white pulsed with rainbow colors from deep within. A tiny yellow globe—metal or stone, he could not tell—blazed like a scoop of starlight set in a ribbon of shimmering blue that dizzied the eye. A lump of pale green stone the size of his fist appeared at first glance to be broken off, exposing a jagged surface; looking closer, Cormasson saw that the surface was covered with tiny carved figures, humans and humanoids of every kind, all of them converging on a replica of this chapel that was not half the size of his smallest fingernail. He stared at the scene until his eyes watered, then he fell to his knees before the table, clutching the edge, resting his forehead on his hand. He felt emptied of all strength and will. The search was over. He could rest at last.

After a time he rose and looked around him. On the uneven floor, covered with the blown and drifted dust of ages, lay mounds that suggested the shapes of humans and humanoids. Their posture was serene, as if they had come here to sleep, or to worship. They had not struggled with death, but had accepted it peacefully.

In one corner, under a pile of fallen stone, Cormasson found the remains of something totally unfamiliar. A tough, leathery pouch, dried and sunken, reposed on a score of long, finger-thin, many-jointed appendages which were folded sedately beneath it. Four vertical slits that might have been its eyes—or perhaps its mouths—were turned toward the reliquary. Little else about its desiccated body was distinguishable.

Against the far wall of the chapel he found another such creature in an identical posture.

These were beings from no known world, unlike anything Cormasson had seen or heard of in all his long voyaging among the stars. As he searched the chapel more carefully, he found other unknown beings, all of them long-dead, all settled in what appeared to be a position of quietude and resignation. Nowhere in the chapel, or near it, was there a sign of disturbance. This simple structure of wood and stone, standing alone in an empty waste on an empty planet, was an oasis of peace.

The sky was darkening when Cormasson left the chapel. He had no idea how long the night would last, but he decided to spend it aboard the *Urixi*. He was utterly without superstition, and he knew that there was no living thing on this world to fear, but the thought of spending the night alone in this ancient place, surrounded by alien dead, horrified him. There was a time when he would have laughed at such a reaction, but he did not laugh now.

He returned to the chapel each day. Slowly he came to the conclusion that all of these creatures had journeyed here specifically to die. There was no sign of violence on any of the bodies; they had all died naturally, at peace. But for some reason, they had come immense distances to meet death on this world. Cormasson could think of no other explanation for what he saw, but this explanation itself raised a host of unanswerable questions. He could not imagine why an intelligent being would cross the stars to find a place to die, nor could he see a reason why these beings would bring such treasure with them, only to leave it lying useless on a slab of stone.

Clearly the dead had not come here alone. Others must have believed as they did—believed strongly enough to dare a free landing on this remote and unstable world and run the risk of being marooned here. Yet none had failed in their attempts to land; and all were gone.

Still, the mystery remained of the original settlers. They had reacted with courage and resourcefulness to their misfortune. With what they had salvaged from their ship they might have built a secure settlement. But there was no trace of a settlement on this world. And if they had somehow miraculously been rescued, it was inconceivable to Cormasson that they would have left their most precious possession behind unguarded.

He turned these problems over and over, and at last put them out of his mind. Every line of reasoning seemed to lead to a paradox. This was a planet of mystery, and a planet of mystery it would remain. He had the reliquary; explanations could be left to others.

He had only to get his prize aboard the *Urixi,* and his work was done. For a moment, he was tempted simply to blow the bejeweled chest open and take the cloth that was his true objective; but he abandoned that thought at once. The authenticity of the shroud had to be unimpeachable, and that could only be assured by delivering it to the Sternverein sealed within the reliquary, the chest itself intact. Cormasson was not a lover of beauty, nor was the material value of the reliquary of great importance to him; but he felt a genuine relief at the necessity of bringing it back undamaged: a thing that had survived so long in such an uncertain universe should be allowed to survive a little longer.

The reliquary was very heavy. There was no possibility of his lifting and carrying it. He managed to rig a hoist that enabled him to remove the chest safely from the stone table and set it on a sled made from a section of sheathing cut from the wreck. Then began the slow, circuitous approach to the *Urixi,* seeking a steady, gentle downward track that often left him farther away at the end of an exhausting day's hauling than he had been at first light.

But he reached his ship at last. He worked his precious burden up the cargo ramp. He stowed it carefully, concealing it behind his stock of provisions and planetside gear and securing it against mishap. Once the reliquary was aboard, he immediately prepared for departure. He had no desire to spend another minute on this planet of silence and mystery and death.

Before the end of his third watch starside, his course was set for Sternverein headquarters on Occuch. He dropped into the stasis tank, welcoming the long oblivion, savoring the thought of the triumph that awaited at his next planetfall.

* * *

He was roused four watches out from Occuch. After he had fully awakened and gathered his wits after the long sleep, he climbed eagerly to the deck. The stasis tank had toned and conditioned him throughout the voyage. He felt better physically than he had at any time since his first attack of curaksh fever. It was good to know that the Sternverein's healers would soon be able to cleanse his system of that slow-killing disease forever.

He removed the long white beard that had grown during stasis and cropped his white hair as neatly as he could. His dress uniform, long hidden away, hung loosely on him, but he wore it as proudly as someone else might have worn the robes of a king. On his breast was the gold-and-white Order of Leddendorf, with three bars. He wore no other decoration.

Two watches from his estimated planetfall he began to signal his arrival. He spent some time at the soundscribers, making up his initial report. When he had a satisfactory draft, he checked for response from Occuch. None had yet arrived. He rested, returned to his report, and checked again. By this time he was less than a single watch from arrival, and still no acknowledgment of his signal had come from the Sternverein base. He began to grow concerned.

He had been away for a long time; precisely how long he did not know. It was conceivable that a new system of identification and clearance had been put in use and his signals had not been received, or not understood. If this were the case, then he would surely be under surveillance by other means.

He activated his emergency signal, then began a passive scan of the surrounding space for approaching craft. All scanners were negative. Still Occuch was silent.

Then every alarm on the *Urixi* went off at once. Cormasson staggered and nearly fell as the ship heeled over abruptly, switching from a low approach path to a high holding orbit. One after another, indicators flashed warning lights. Cormasson stared at them, stunned by their message: Occuch was unsafe for landing.

He took manual control as soon as he was able and brought the *Urixi* to the lowest possible orbit for a close scan. As he traced orbit after orbit, the truth became ever more painfully clear: Occuch was dead.

The land had been burned lifeless. It was burning still, and would burn for a hundred millennia to come. The seas bubbled with poison. The atmosphere glowed with death for a hundred kilometers from the surface. Occuch had been destroyed with a thoroughness Cormasson had never imagined possible—not merely destroyed, but rendered forever hostile to life. The whole planet radiated death.

Cormasson scanned every meter of Occuch's surface, hoping to find what he knew could not exist: a single pocket of life. When the fate of Occuch was unmistakably clear, he brought the *Urixi* to a high orbit, and there he held.

He sat at the controls in shock, staring blankly at the instruments. Watch after watch passed, and still he circled Occuch. He could think of nowhere else to go. He was like a man who had looked on the mutilated corpse of his god. He had seen the death of immortality and the end of all hope. To him, the Sternverein had represented order and peace and justice, the only promise of a future in a harsh and hostile universe. Now it was gone. With Occuch, the heart and home of the Sternverein, so utterly obliterated, there was no chance of its survival elsewhere. And if a power existed great enough to destroy the Sternverein, no world, no civilization, could ever be safe.

Cormasson saw no reason to live on. He had broken his health and his mind in a long search that had ultimately proven fruitless. He thought of overriding all the *Urixi*'s safety devices and landing on Occuch. It was a fitting place to die.

But as he reflected on his mission, he realized that it had not been fruitless. He had the reliquary. He had once feared it as a banner to rally those who opposed the Sternverein. Now he saw that it might equally serve to rally a new force to avenge the Sternverein on those who had destroyed it.

Here was a purpose to live for. He rose and went to the forward port, where he stood for a time taking his last look at Occuch. Then he set a new course.

Roharr had changed greatly. The city was sprawled over most of Ermacene. The port was ten times the size Cormasson remembered it, but now it held only two landing rings; everywhere else he saw tall cylindrical structures in which driveships were cradled. There were at least twoscore of them, and they appeared to be interconnected. The ships themselves had the familiar configuration, but he noticed some distinct differences in design.

He had had great difficulty in making himself understood by the crew of the landing area. Now, as he walked toward a soaring dome, half-transparent and half-opaque in a pattern that varied with the motion of the clouds overhead, he felt a pang of apprehension. He was seeing for the first time some of the changes that had taken place during his long absence, and he wondered what other, less visible changes, might have come to Roharr.

As a precaution, he had announced himself as a free trader and dressed in the nondescript outfit he had worn on his last visit here. When he entered the dome he was instructed, by gestures and a torrent of monosyllables, to wait. He was offered, with friendly smiles, a conical vessel of cold, tart liquid to drink while he waited.

He settled on a soft, body-molding bench, assuming that a translator had been summoned. Before he finished his drink, a young woman came up to him. She was copper-skinned and brown-haired, thin and nearly as tall as he was. Plain of feature and plainly dressed, she had a friendly manner.

"Free trader Cormasson, you he? Come outdown starside in ringship call *Urixi?*" she asked.

"I'm Cormasson," he said, rising.

"Anuri, I be. I study lingo, starside speech from oldtime. You understand?"

"You don't speak it exactly as I remember it, Anuri, but I can understand you."

"Good. We sit, talk now, Cormasson," she said, taking a seat opposite him. "Starside, you be longsome, yes? You speak lingo, nobody speak so since far oldtime."

"I've been out long. I don't even know how long. I was trading on worlds out by the Dead Belt." When she looked puzzled by his reference, he said, "I went as far out as anyone has ever gone and come back. I've heard of people going farther, but I've never met anyone who did."

"You say Dead Belt—this be Stars' End, outgone D'borri, outgone exile worlds?" she asked.

"I've been to those worlds. The Dead Belt is far beyond

them. It's beyond Ruxiloma, and other worlds that have no names. I think it must be the place you call Stars' End.''

Anuri was impressed, and she did not conceal it. "You be longsome outgone, Cormasson. Nobody come here from Stars' End, not even in oldtime.''

"How long ago was oldtime, Anuri?"

"Oldtime, we call all before Sosto come save Ermacene.''

"How long ago was that?"

"Soon be two hundred tenza."

The Roharran tenza was shorter than a standard year, but nevertheless a long time had passed. A thought occurred to Cormasson. He asked, "Do you still reckon Galactic Standard Calendar time here, Anuri? Do you know that term?"

She frowned and shook her head. "Words from oldtime. No sense now.''

"When I left Roharr, back in oldtime, I was working under an agreement with the Industrious House of Kamparongsang. Are they still trading?"

"Trade-house no more, Cormasson. Under Sosto, all trade belong to Grand Council. Still so.''

Cormasson thought of those patient traders, investing in the hopes of distant generations. Their system had seemed eternal, and now it was gone, wiped out by one man's will.

"How did Sosto come to rule, Anuri?" he asked.

"Come like you, outdown starside in white ringship. Come protect us from farworld invader.''

"A white ship?" Cormasson asked sharply.

"White ship, yes. Sosto come, then others come. Crews all in black, carry long weapons.''

"What did they call themselves, Anuri? Did they ever speak of themselves as Sternverein?''

She looked perplexed. He repeated the word, and she said, "Never speak so. Never hear such word, Cormasson. All blackjackets say they be Sosto's troopers, no other. Never use word you say.''

Cormasson was silent. The Sternverein was dead indeed if the blackjackets themselves had abandoned the name.

"Do Sosto's descendants rule in Ermacene now?" he asked.

"No more, no. Sosto, all daughters and sons, all dead now. All Sosto's troopers gone.''

"Gone from Roharr?"

"Gone starside, all. Never say where, just go one day in white ship. Seven Masters rule Ermacene now, Grand Council. More than ninety tenza, be so."

"Where can I learn more, Anuri? I want to learn about everything that's happened since I last saw Roharr."

"We see Council, you settle trade, then we go find all you want. Trade first, must."

Cormasson shook his head. "I have nothing to trade, Anuri. I took a chance going that far out. I hoped I'd find things no one ever found before. But there's nothing out there. Barbaric people, barren worlds, emptiness . . . there's nothing, Anuri. That's all I can tell your Council."

She rose and held out her hand to him. "You tell, so."

Cormasson's case, though it had its interesting features, was not considered important enough to take up the time of the Seven Masters who comprised the Grand Council of Roharr. Anuri ushered him before a trio of junior councilors who heard his account politely but quickly lost interest when they learned that he had brought no trade goods back from the remote worlds. They cared little for a ghost out of Roharr's past. Hurrying through the routine hearing, they granted Cormasson a twenty-day stay, subject to medical clearance.

The medical examination was almost as perfunctory as the hearing. The examiners furnished a brace for Cormasson's arm, now nearly useless, and did nothing more. Curaksh fever, in its dormant phase, was difficult to detect, but the examiners did not attempt a close examination, and Cormasson remained silent. The disease was not contagious; even so, one could never be certain how downside healers would react. He might be isolated, or put aboard the *Urixi* at gunpoint and sent from Roharr. He did not want to leave this world without learning the fate of the Sternverein.

With Anuri's assistance, he was admitted to the central soundscriber banks. She obtained all the available material on Sosto—a surprisingly small amount, Cormasson thought—and translated it for him. The word *Sternverein* was never mentioned, nor was there a hint of the origin of Sosto and his blackjackets. They were warriors from other worlds who had come to protect Roharr against the threat of invasion; no further identification was given.

Digging further into the history of the period, Cormasson

found frequent references to reports of distant battles and refugees. The fear of invasion had been real and pervasive, making possible Sosto's rise to power. But after days of hearing and rehearing all the available information, and questioning Anuri closely about the interpretation of every vague phrase, Cormasson knew little more than he had learned from the remarks she made at their first meeting.

The actions of Sosto and his supporters on Roharr had violated a basic Sternverein policy of planetary intervention: no trooper was to set himself up as a ruler and establish a dynasty. There had been a fundamental breakdown of loyalty and discipline. Cormasson remembered the dead world of Occuch. Perhaps that was the source of those rumors of battles and the tales of frightened refugees; the Sternverein itself had collapsed, or been destroyed, and Sosto and his troopers were only saving themselves. The information was so scanty and so superficial that it was virtually useless. It seemed that no one had cared to properly chronicle the events of those days.

Cormasson thought then of another source of history that might well be more complete than these carefully censored official records. The annals of the Church of Saint Peter had been kept with scrupulous accuracy; and though their primary interest was not in history, the monks would be sure to record the significant facts of their society.

"When I came to Roharr last, there was a church on Felill. I'd like to go there before I leave," he said to Anuri.

"No church on Felill now, Cormasson. No church since far oldtime."

"What happened?" he asked, not looking at her.

"Long ago, Cormasson, and small thing. Not sure, I be. Priests take power, then people say no more church, no more priests, all I know."

"Doesn't anyone know what became of them?"

"Church come down, priests go. Nobody know where," said Anuri carelessly.

Once again Cormasson felt the cold clutch of despair. He had done the impossible, and it did not matter. The Sternverein was gone. The Christians of Felill were gone. The relic rested secure on the *Urixi,* brought back from halfway across the galaxy, but no one cared.

Then he thought of Peter's Rock, isolated from the turmoil of the rest of the worlds. His own troopers and their descendants were standing guard over that world. Whatever the rest of the Sternverein might do, they would remain loyal to their duty, and the monastics would follow their faith.

There was one last hope.

XII. ————————————

Peter's Rock: *The Return of the Pilgrim*

On the third Spiritsday of Lent Minor, near sundown, a very old driveship made planetfall on Peter's Rock. A gaunt man emerged from the main port and made his way unsteadily down the ramp. Halfway to the ground he stumbled, collapsed, and lay unmoving on the ramp.

Rever Darmase was the first to reach him. He waved the others back. "Come no nearer!" he cried. "This man is sick. Who will help me care for him?"

"I will!" a young novice replied.

"Then bring me a shelter and two mats, and bring the emergency medical kit from the infirmary—and food and drink for two days. The rest of you, keep away and tell others to keep away from us until we know what sickness the starfarer suffers from," Darmase called.

He looked anxiously at the open port of the small ship, fearful of possible infection escaping but unable to close the port himself. Turning his attention to the starfarer, who had stirred and groaned, he helped him to the ground.

"We're bringing medicine and a shelter for you. Do you understand me?" Darmase asked.

"Peter's Rock? Here . . . Peter's Rock?" the man rasped.

"You do understand! Yes, this is Peter's Rock, and we will care for you. Relax now until the medicine comes."

"Sternverein? Base . . . here?"

"No, this is Peter's Rock," Darmase repeated, speaking slowly and distinctly. "We can help you, but you must relax. We'll talk when you're stronger."

The starfarer shook his head slowly. "Curaksh fever. Ninth

attack. No help. Only on Occuch. Occuch . . . gone now,'' he said dully, and then was still.

Darmase felt the man's forehead. It was burning. His pale cheeks were mottled with red. His breathing was deep and slow. Waves of trembling intermittently shook him. The symptoms were common to hundreds of diseases that awaited travelers on distant worlds. Some were deadly and highly contagious; others were no more than a brief discomfort. "Curaksh fever," the man had said. An unfamiliar term, but the same sickness might be known by scores of names. That confusion had cost many lives in the terrible times when refugees from the faraway wars were arriving.

When Lindren, the novice, arrived, he and Darmase erected a shelter and carried the sick starfarer inside. They laid him gently on a soft mat. While Lindren undressed and washed their patient, Darmase began his tests. He had, for a time, assisted the infirmarer and was skilled in the use of medical equipment.

It was soon clear that what the stranger called curaksh fever was a sickness known under several names, all of which referred to the extreme sensitivity of the skin during the initial attack and resultant pain: "flaying sickness," "devil's touch," and most commonly, "fleshfire fever." No one on Peter's Rock had ever been cured, and no one had been known to survive more than three attacks. Darmase marveled that the starfarer had spoken of this as his ninth attack of the sickness.

Looking down on the wasted body, seamed and scored with red ribbons of subcutaneous hemorrhaging, Darmase knew that there was no medicine that could help this man. He was far gone in the terminal stage of the fever. All that he and Lindren could do now was ease the pain and pray for the sufferer.

As the days passed, the man's seizures diminished and his hallucinations stopped. Even though his sickness was not contagious, Darmase decided to keep him out in the shelter near the landing ring. The weather was fine, and the long trip to the infirmary seemed best avoided since nothing could be done for the dying man anyway.

Sometimes the starfarer gained consciousness for a few moments, but his speech was baffling. Much of it was intelligible, but there were many unfamiliar terms. He spoke the

Church English of Peter's Rock as if he had learned it long ago and had half forgotten it, as if time and sickness had stolen bits of it from his memory.

One night Darmase awoke from a doze to find the man staring at him. His eyes were clear, and the color in his face was subdued.

"I am on Peter's Rock," he said.

"Yes, you are. You've been very sick. Do you want something to eat? Are you thirsty?"

"Thirsty."

Darmase brought him cool water and helped him sit up to drink. The man then lay back, his eyes closed, and was silent for a time.

"Sternverein. They were here once," he said without moving or opening his eyes.

"I've heard that name. But I can't recall where, or what it meant. You said it before, when you arrived."

"Sternverein troopers. Men and women in black. Came in the time of Abbot Gossard . . . and Ollenbrook," the man said weakly.

"That was very long ago. I'll speak to our recorder. He'll be able to find the references in the annals. Now I think it's best that you try to sleep."

The man did not reply. When he appeared to be sleeping soundly, Darmase left the shelter and sat down beside Lindren.

"I heard our patient speaking. Has he recovered?" the novice asked.

"He's regained his senses, but I don't see how he can ever recover. If this is his ninth attack, he shouldn't even be alive," Darmase said in a hushed voice.

"He might have been wrong about that. He was pretty confused when he said it."

"That's true. But he's very weak, and his heartbeat is erratic. And you can see the hemorrhaging. I think he's dying. He keeps asking about the Sternverein. 'Men and women in black,' he said. Do you know that word?" Lindren concentrated, frowned, then shook his head. Darmase said, "I've heard the word myself, I'm sure, but I can't remember what it refers to. I'm going to ask the recorder. If it's in the annals anywhere, he'll find it."

"Wasn't that the organization all the wars were about, long time back?" Lindren asked suddenly. "Rever Onston spoke of it once, I think. People came here fleeing from it, he said."

"I don't think so," Darmase replied cautiously. "This man speaks of Abbots Gossard and Ollenbrook, and they were dead for centuries before the fugitives began arriving."

"That's right. I must be mistaken."

"We're not historians, either of us," Darmase said with a smile. "We'd best leave this to the recorder."

But it was not the monastery's recorder who came to the shelter three days later; it was the abbot himself, Abbot Venn. He had served as recorder for a time and still retained interest in the annals of Peter's Rock. He was familiar with the old forms of Church English, though he had never heard it from the lips of an offworlder. When Darmase reported the dying starfarer's questions to him, the abbot's interest and sympathy were aroused.

He went to the monastery library and heard the soundscriber accounts, going back to the very earliest. References to the Sternverein were few but significant. After those early times, there was no mention of the Sternverein until the time of the fugitives, more than a century past, and by then the name was spoken in fear. From that time to the present, there was nothing.

Venn and Darmase walked to the ring area together in the light of early morning. The patient had passed a bad night, with another period of delirium and a rise in temperature. Darmase was worried.

"You did right to keep him in the shelter," Venn said reassuringly. "We have no cure for fleshfire fever. The long trip to the infirmary would only have caused him discomfort to no purpose."

"Those were my own thoughts, Abbot."

"I have met few starfarers, but from all I know they prefer to die aboard their ship, or at least within sight of it. Since we cannot cure this man, we should at least make his passing easier."

"I fear it's soon to come, Abbot."

Venn entered the shelter and found the sick man sleeping.

His breathing was shallow. He lay absolutely motionless on his back, his arms by his side. His gaunt hands seemed enlarged, and the red seams on his skin were beginning to darken and merge. His forehead was burning.

The abbot sat quietly in prayer until the man opened his eyes. For a long time he showed no sign of awareness, but then he turned his head slightly and fixed his gaze on Venn. Still he did not speak.

"I've come to tell you what I know about the Sternverein," the abbot said. The sick man's eyes grew alert. Venn leaned closer and said, "Would you like water, or something to eat?"

"Water," said the dying man in a voice barely more than a breath.

Venn poured a dish of water and supported the man's head while he drank. Wetting a cloth, he laid it on the fevered forehead; then, seating himself close by the starfarer's side in easy view, he began his account.

"Many centuries ago, a giant white ship came to Peter's Rock. It was sent by an organization called the Sternverein, which sought to trade with us. The ship brought new members to our community and new tools to aid us in our daily work and our mission. In exchange for books from the monastery library, the Sternverein agreed to carry our priest-voyagers to other worlds and to protect our homeworld against attack.

"The white ship returned once and took our priest-voyagers as had been agreed. The ship-settlers who remained among us taught us to defend our world, and four times when marauders landed on our planet we withstood them. But the white ships never returned. No driveship came to Peter's Rock for a long time. Then they suddenly began to arrive one after another. There were years when two ships arrived.

"These ships bore frightened people fleeing from a great war that involved the Sternverein. We never learned the full story of what had happened, only fragments. No one seemed to know the whole truth. It appears that a struggle for power broke out in the highest echelons of the Sternverein, dividing the organization and leading at last to open warfare. The refugees spoke of terrible destruction—of entire planets devastated and whole races destroyed. We offered them shelter on our world, but few accepted. They were so fearful that they wanted only to flee to the farthest reaches of the galaxy.''

Venn reached down and took the starfarer's skeletal hand in both of his, a gesture of consolation and comfort as he said finally, "The last fugitive came here more than a century ago. Since then, we have not heard the name of the Sternverein spoken until your arrival.''

The dying man gripped Venn's hand with surprising strength. "Gone?'' he said in a harsh croaking voice.

"I think the Sternverein is indeed gone.''

"What happened . . . settlers . . . here?''

"Those early settlers from the white ship helped to save the monastery. They brought vitality—new ideas, new methods. They taught us to defend our world against savage attack. Without them, the monastery might have been devastated and plundered, all our work destroyed.''

The starfarer stared at Venn. Then he began to laugh weakly, until coughing silenced him. Venn helped him to a sip of water.

"I hope my news comforts you,'' Venn said.

The man did not reply. He stared at Venn for a time, silent, then closed his eyes and lay still. When he opened them again, he tried to raise himself, but he could not.

Venn propped him up and asked, "Can we do anything for you? Did you come here for a special reason?''

"To die,'' the man said faintly.

"A man can die anywhere. Why here? Are you of our faith?'' Venn asked. When the man did not reply, he went on, "Do you seek something? Tell me, and I'll try to help you. Why did you come to Peter's Rock?''

"Sought . . . face of God,'' the man said, his voice barely audible. "Relic . . . shroud of God.''

Venn was stunned. "Where did you hear of the Holy Shroud?'' he asked.

The starfarer looked up at him and laughed again, a soft rustling sound barely more than a breath. "Found it . . . on Desshe. Found it,'' he repeated, and he laughed again until coughs shook him and he slumped back, gasping.

Venn sat by the dying man, his mind whirling. He had

heard the words clearly. There could be no mistake. This man had found the Holy Shroud, the lost relic, the most precious object in all creation; and his life was slipping away, moment by moment, and he might never speak again.

Venn prayed. He had always been a man of strong faith. Ever since his childhood he had prayed each day for the return of the lost relic. Now, at last, it seemed that his prayers had been heard and answered. He prayed for the dying man cradled in his arms to speak just once more.

The starfarer did speak at last, but now his words were wild and all but incoherent. His mind was gone; the end was very near. In his ravings, he spoke of a pilgrim, a seeker of the face of God. He babbled of far worlds, long lonely voyages, terrible suffering. As he went on in his hoarse, cracking voice, Venn was filled with wonder, for he was hearing first hand of things he had once believed to be no more than idle space legends.

Venn knew the annals well. He had heard of the mysterious figure called the Pilgrim, a human who roamed the stars in search of a great lost treasure. Visitors had told of a strange alien race, headless beings with voices of brilliant light, who had learned of God from a human castaway and devoted the future of their race to finding Him. He had heard tales of a remote and barren planet where God dwelt in a temple made of the most precious offerings from every race and world, and gave healing—and sometimes blissful death—to those who sought Him faithfully. And once he had heard that far world called Desshe. He understood now that all the tales were true.

The man fell silent once again. Then, suddenly, in a terrifying gesture, he reached up and seized Venn by the throat in a powerful grip. "On my ship—take it! Take it!" he cried, and then fell back. His breathing became deep and slow. Then it stopped.

The port had stood open for sixteen days. When Venn stepped aboard the driveship, a thin coating of dust already lay on the level surfaces. Insects had begun to build their homes in sheltered places.

Venn had thought at first of boarding the ship alone, but he decided to bring with him Rever Onstan, the monastery's recorder. He was not sure what he could expect to find, but he had a strong suspicion. If it were true, he feared that he would be quite overcome and wanted someone with him for support.

They searched the ship methodically, finding nothing unusual. Finally, they came to the cargo hold. It was dark in there and stuffy. They turned their handlights to full strength. Venn found the controls to open the cargo door. As the light streamed in, he and Onstan cried out simultaneously at the glint of precious metal.

They tore away the padding, and Venn stepped back. He was trembling now. His voice shook as he whispered, "The reliquary. It's the reliquary. He brought it back!"

Onstan kept working until all the padding was removed. He walked around the reliquary, examining it closely. Venn joined him. As they beheld the gleaming metal, the glowing jewels, the exquisite workings of precious materials into something far more precious, an awe came over them.

"These stones . . . these pulsing stones . . . and that bright one . . ." said Onstan.

"And that metal that seems to flow . . . they are not of Earth," Venn said.

"I studied the faxes before we left, Abbot. This is the reliquary, but it's . . . it's different. It's changed," Onstan said fearfully.

Venn laid his hands on the cool metal. "Think what must have happened in all those centuries, Rever Onstan! Other worlds. . . ."

"Other races, Abbot. That's what the schismatics said we must do, and they did it. They brought God to the alien races. And the aliens believed!"

"Yes. Those tales . . . the stories of the healing God on a far world. We dismissed them as mere fancies, but they must have been true."

"It's a miracle. We're in the presence of a miracle, Abbot," said Onstan, falling to his knees.

That very day, the reliquary was removed from the ship and brought to the monastery, where it was subjected to a meticulous examination. It had been much embellished. The back, once plain, had been covered with a malleable metal and set in an intricate geometric design with small twinkling gems of a kind unknown on Peter's Rock. All the other surfaces had been enriched with unfamiliar stones and metals of great beauty, worked into the original design and made part of it. The reliquary rested on a new base, with six legs of shimmering white metal worked in a dazzling gold-and-red filigree that the human eye could not trace. Yet, despite all the additions, there was no sign that the reliquary had ever been opened, or even of an attempt to open it.

The abbot pondered and prayed for guidance. At last he gave the order that the reliquary be replaced in its long-vacant niche in the founder's chapel. Nothing was to be removed from it, nor was it to be opened. They had prayed for centuries for its return, he said; now that God had returned it, let them accept it as He had sent it, with faith.

After a great ceremony and feast, Abbot Venn knelt alone before the reliquary. For the first time in many days, he could reflect in peace upon recent events. Onstan had spoken of a miracle, but Venn saw nothing of the miraculous in the return of their relic. It was the working out of a plan beyond human capacity to understand, but it was not a miracle. When the Christians of Peter's Rock had been weak and divided by pride, the shroud had been taken from them and hidden on a far world. There other races had learned of it, and sought it out, and believed. After the passing of centuries had purified the Christians of Peter's Rock and they were again in accord, the shroud was given into their care again.

Venn had no doubt of what the future required. Unknown races, creatures unimagined, would come to this world, and they would be welcomed as children of God. The work was to begin at last.

Before rising to join the others, the Abbot said a final prayer for the nameless starfarer who had brought the relic home. His clothing had been unmarked, his ship lacked all identification. If it had not been for the soundscriber tapes from Roharr, they would never have known anything about him. His long search ended, he lay at rest in the crypt beneath the chapel, in the company of Abbot Gossard and the others who had given their lives for the faith. He wore the plain black uniform they had found carefully stored aboard his ship. On the stone above his body were the simple words: ''A pilgrim who found the face of God.''